"Frank Leslie kicks [a] story into a gallop right out of the gate."
— Mark Henry, Author of
The Hell Riders

THE
DANGEROUS
DAWN

FRANK LESLIE

Author of *The Savage Breed*

SIGNET

SIGNET

$5.99 U.S.
$7.50 CAN.

ISBN: 978-0-451-22888-8

50599

S EAN

Praise for F~~~~
and His Yakima ~~~~

"Frank ~~~~ ~~~~
a buffal~~~~
rod wh~~~~
of a W~~~~
irresist~~~~

"Frank ~~~~
gate. . . . Raw and gritty as the West itself."
                    —Mark Henry, author of *The Hell Riders*

"Explodes off the page in an enormously entertaining burst
of stay-up-late, read-into-the-night, fast-moving flurry of page-
turning action. Leslie spins a yarn that rivals the very best
on Western shelves today."
                    —J. Lee Butts, author of *Written in Blood*

"Hooks you instantly with sympathetic characters and sin-
soaked villains. Yakima has a heart of gold and an Arkansas
toothpick. If you prefer Peckinpah to Ang Lee, this one's
for you."
                    —Mike Baron, creator of *Nexus* and *The Badger*
                                                comic book series

"Big, burly, brawling, and action-packed, *The Lonely Breed*
is a testosterone-laced winner from the word 'go,' and Frank
Leslie is an author to watch!"
                    —Ellen Recknor, author of *The Legendary Kid Donovan*

Also by Frank Leslie

The Guns of Sapinero
The Savage Breed
The Killing Breed
The Wild Breed
The Lonely Breed
The Thunder Riders

THE DANGEROUS DAWN

Frank Leslie

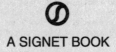

A SIGNET BOOK

SIGNET

Published by New American Library, a division of
Penguin Group (USA) Inc., 375 Hudson Street,
New York, New York 10014, USA
Penguin Group (Canada), 90 Eglinton Avenue East, Suite 700, Toronto,
Ontario M4P 2Y3, Canada (a division of Pearson Penguin Canada Inc.)
Penguin Books Ltd., 80 Strand, London WC2R 0RL, England
Penguin Ireland, 25 St. Stephen's Green, Dublin 2,
Ireland (a division of Penguin Books Ltd.)
Penguin Group (Australia), 250 Camberwell Road, Camberwell, Victoria 3124,
Australia (a division of Pearson Australia Group Pty. Ltd.)
Penguin Books India Pvt. Ltd., 11 Community Centre, Panchsheel Park,
New Delhi - 110 017, India
Penguin Group (NZ), 67 Apollo Drive, Rosedale, North Shore 0632,
New Zealand (a division of Pearson New Zealand Ltd.)
Penguin Books (South Africa) (Pty.) Ltd., 24 Sturdee Avenue,
Rosebank, Johannesburg 2196, South Africa

Penguin Books Ltd., Registered Offices:
80 Strand, London WC2R 0RL, England

First published by Signet, an imprint of New American Library,
a division of Penguin Group (USA) Inc.

First Printing, February 2010
10 9 8 7 6 5 4 3 2

To George and Sandy Loner,
for keeping this stray dog and his three curs
off the grubline,
Taylor Park, Colorado,
Summer of '09

Chapter 1

Yakima Henry sat up slowly and reached for the horn-gripped .44 hanging from a bedpost.

He slid his other hand across the naked whore sleeping curled beneath the quilts to his left, as though to shield her from a bullet, and gentled the .44 from its holster with a soft snick of iron against leather.

Raising the gun, he stared at the figure silhouetted in the window, against the glowing snowy night. The man, clad in a bulky blanket coat and broad-brimmed hat, slid one long leg over the window ledge, into the room.

There was a faint spur ching. His breath smoked in the room's darkness. The twinkling starlight glistened on the long barrel of the revolver in the man's gloved right fist.

Yakima's low growl sounded loud in the room's brittle, wintery silence. "That's far enough, Cisco."

The intruder grunted with a start, and swung his gun toward Yakima. Before the man could trigger a shot, possibly pinking the whore beside Yakima, Yakima squeezed the trigger of his Colt .44. The gun roared like a cannon, causing the whore to lift her head, screaming, and for the man called

Cisco to give another, shriller grunt, and fall straight back out the window behind him.

"Easy, senorita," Yakima said in the dense silence following the pistol's roar. "That was just Cisco."

The girl sat up, holding the several layers of quilts up to her neck, her own breath frosting in the air between her and Yakima. Her chest rose and fell quickly as she breathed. "Damn you, gringo! You nearly gave me a heart stroke! Who's Cisco?"

"Feller I fleeced at stud earlier. I just had a strange crawlin' feelin' he was gonna come lookin' for his money. And I had a feelin' he wasn't gonna ask polite for it, neither. . . ."

Yakima cursed and threw the quilts back from his long, brawny frame that, after his and the Mexican whore's prolonged frolic several hours ago, he'd covered with his wool winter balbriggans and socks. It got damn cold of a night this high in the December Rockies. What he was doing here when he should have been in Arizona or New Mexico or southern Texas, he had no idea. Just an especially bad episode of saddle fever had struck him too late in the year, and here he was, caught between storms on his way to Wyoming for a rumored job guarding gold shipments.

Yakima got up, sucking his breath sharply against the brittle night air, and stomped over to the window. Cisco was bent backwards over the sill, hanging by his knees, his head and shoulders outside, his spurred boots raking the inside wall as he spasmed.

Yakima peered over the man's bent knees clad in coarse checked trousers. His head hung nearly to the drifted snow that was dark with the blood that was gushing out the hole in the center of his chest. His high-crowned hat lay nearby, near the gun-shaped hole marking the spot his gun had fallen into the drift and which likely wouldn't be seen again until spring.

Cisco's teeth clattered. He groaned, panted, and fell suddenly silent. His body slacked down the outside wall, and his spurs ceased their raucous chatter inside the room. All Yakima could see in the shadowy, snowy night was the man's black hair capping the pale oval of his mustached face.

"Damn fool."

Yakima heard the patter of bare feet and strained breaths. He turned to see the whore—whose name he couldn't remember though he'd found himself liking the girl for vague reasons beyond her man-pleasing talents—run up behind him, holding a quilt around her shoulders. Her long hair fell in thick cascades down her arms.

"Is he dead?"

"Deader'n last year's Christmas goose. Cisco's got no one but himself to thank." Yakima narrowed a wary eye at the girl. "Is there a lawman in town?" A half-breed whom trouble followed like a hungry mutt, Yakima tried to steer as wide as possible from lawmen. Even when he didn't start trouble, he seemed to always be the one paying for it.

"Not till spring. He gets the chilblains." The whore continued to peer over the windowsill at the dead man's face. "I haven't seen that hombre."

"You weren't about to, neither," Yakima said with a humorous chuff. "Not the way I turned his pockets inside out. Never seen a worse poker player. I could read the number on each card in his eyeballs, and he couldn't bluff any better than a Baptist preacher caught with his pants down in a Nevada whorehouse."

The whore snorted and rubbed her cheek against Yakima's shoulder. "You're a funny gringo-Indio. I'm going back to bed—it's cold!"

"Yeah." Yakima looked around outside, seeing nothing but the dark cabins huddled in the snowdrifts, smoke rising darkly from stone hearths and tin chimney pipes. Beyond the mountain-ensconced village, steep, black ridges shouldered against the vast sky dusted with twinkling starlight. "What's a nice Mexican girl doin' in a cold place like this?"

"It's a long story, and it's too cold to talk," the girl said, crawling shivering back into the bed. "Suffice it to say, I fell in love with the wrong gringo who took me north and left me here to fend for myself."

She watched in horror as Yakima lifted the dead man's boots above the windowsill, and shoved the man's legs outside where the body hit the ground with a rustle of packed snow. Sucking a shocked breath, she said, "You have no respect for the *dead*?"

"Not the dead that tried to kill me."

Yakima looked out at the carcass lying piled up and half-buried in the deep, dry snow. There was only one set of purple boot tracks in the glittering snow leading to the window. Satisfied that Cisco had been working alone, Yakima drew both shutters closed with a raspy, wooden bark, then made sure the locking nail was in place.

"Besides, he ain't goin' anywhere. I'll haul him over to the undertaker first thing in the morning."

Yakima wheeled, shivering, his long hair flying out from his shoulders, and ran back to the bed and dove under the covers, drawing them up over his head and snuggling up tight against the warm, supple girl who smelled faintly of smoke, pine, and, inexplicably, fresh lemons.

Damn, he wished he could remember her name. He thought it started with a K. Maybe a C. Carlotta?

"There is another undertaker in town, isn't there?" His

voice was muffled by the girl's naked breasts which, compared with the cold air beyond the quilts, fairly burned his lips and cheeks as he nuzzled them.

"Si." A sadness pitched her voice. "He came for Rosie Dawn last week. She sleeps there in his shed."

Yakima kissed the girl's left nipple. "Rosie Dawn?"

"Si. One of Ma's girls. A bastard named Larsen shot her in the cabin by the creek." The girl's voice hardened with anger. "He thought she knew where some stolen money was stashed, but she wouldn't tell him, so he shot her. He was crazy drunk. When he isn't drunk, which is seldom, he's a sniveling coward. A luckless bandito—a robber of banks thinking Rosie Dawn was his route to easy money."

"Did she know about the loot?"

The whore hiked a slender shoulder. "If she did, she didn't tell me. I think it is a lie. The banditos around here are a suspicious lot, killing on whims. Especially Larsen. Rosie was the girl of Pedro Camargo, and everyone believed Pedro told her where he stashed the loot from the bank holdup in Juniper Bend before the marshals marched him off to prison.

"He died there. Someone stuck him in the back. Good riddance, Pedro Camargo. The world is better off without you, as Rosie was. . . . Now she lies in a coffin. My God, how cold she must be!"

Yakima lifted his head up above the quilts and looked into the girl's dark-brown eyes, her black hair fanned across the pillow beneath her head. She had a doll-like face, delicately featured, with a small nose and smooth, flawless cheeks. Her upper lip was slightly upturned. "I bet she doesn't feel a thing."

"How do you know?"

"I'd place good money on it. She's probably not as cold as we are."

"Dios, how could she not feel it—out there all alone." She raised a small, fragile hand to Yakima's heavy jaw, caressed his scarred chin with her thumb. "Without a man to warm her."

She bunched her lips as though she were about to cry, and then she lifted her head and kissed him gently, running her hands through his hair. Suddenly, she smiled and pushed him onto his back. "Warm me up, gringo-Indio!" she laughed, straddling him and wrapping her arms around his neck. "I don't want to feel the cold anymore tonight!"

"We could put some more coal on the brazier," Yakima suggested, wrapping his big arms around the girl's back and feeling himself come alive as she wriggled around on him.

"This is cheaper!"

She rose on her knees, reached down, and caressed him.

"Cheaper for who?" he laughed.

"This one's on the house!"

Afterwards, she gave little girlish grunts and groans of contentment as she snuggled against his chest. "My name is Glendina . . . if you're wondering."

Yakima jerked a surprised, chagrined look at her face. Her eyes were closed, but her lips lifted a faintly mocking smile.

He kissed her forehead, touched her nose, and drew her tighter against him. "Good night, Glendina. In the morning, I'm gonna buy you a big breakfast."

"Because you forgot my name?"

That was partly why. Also, because he just plain liked her, and there weren't many folks Yakima Henry liked anymore. At least, not living ones.

But he didn't try to explain all that.

"Because after cleaning out Cisco's pockets, I'm about as flush as I've ever been, and I got no one else to spend it on. Now shut up and go to sleep."

He felt her moist lips spread against his chest.

Chapter 2

Yakima had never slept so well after shooting a man.

He attributed his deep slumber to the thin, cold air, the inky winter darkness, and the talents of the sexy sporting girl, Glendina. When he finally managed to swim up to full consciousness, he was amazed to find himself sweating. He pulled his head out from under the quilts and squinted into the room lit by the red gas lamp smoking atop the crude dresser and thin slivers of blue dawn light pushing through the cracks in the closed shutters.

The girl stood in front of the low, sheet-iron stove, on top of which a pan of water hissed and steamed. The stove was stoked to glowing. Rubbing a sponge around under her upraised left arm, Glendina turned toward the bed.

"Good morning, sleepyhead," she said in her thick Spanish accent.

Yakima raked a thick paw down his face, and smacked his lips. "What time is it?"

"Six."

Yakima threw the covers back and dropped his legs to the floor. The warm, moist air felt good. The floor was still cold—probably not much above ten degrees outside. He hated the thought of going out into it, but he had to saddle his black stallion, Wolf, and head out. The storm that had trapped him here had passed, and if he didn't want to get caught in this snowbound village till May, he'd better leave pronto. Just climbing down out of the mountains would be a three-day journey, and then he had another week's ride to his destination—Crow Feather, Wyoming.

He watched Glendina as she dipped her sponge in the steaming water then lifted the sponge to her ample breasts, jostling the nicely shaped orbs as she lightly scrubbed herself. Her damp hair clung to the sides of her face and her shoulders. Her tan skin glistened in the red lantern light.

He snorted softly. There were worse places to get trapped in the winter.

She turned to him, frowning.

"Why you laugh? You think I'm funny?" She feigned a hurt look, pooching that upturned lip.

Yakima chuckled. "No, I think you're pretty as a picture, and if I don't get out of here soon, I'm liable to be here till the crocuses bloom." He looked at the pan. "Got anymore of that?"

She ran the sponge across her belly then dropped it into the smoking water with a plop. "You can have this. I'm finished."

She pulled her wrapper up from around her waist, and closed it about her shoulders. She gave Yakima a quick peck in passing, lightly raking her hands across his washboard belly, then dropped onto the bed, drawing her bare legs up to her belly and propping her head on her elbow. He fished the sponge out of the water and began to wash himself, starting on his broad, muscular chest and working down.

"You have not forgot your promise?"

"What promise?"

"You promised to buy me breakfast, bastardo!"

Yakima laughed again as he ran a soap sliver across the sponge then began scrubbing his haunches. "Oh, that? Well, what the hell? I guess I have a few coins to spare." He glanced at his saddlebags sitting in a near corner, where the late Cisco had been trying to get at them. "How 'bout if we both have breakfast on Cisco?"

She stretched her legs out like a cat, frowning with gentle castigation. "You must not make fun of the dead. You killed him and he's dead—a bad man—but you must not speak of him now. He's with the saints. One shouldn't speak ill of those who've gone to the saints."

"Well, shit," Yakima said, glancing at her over his shoulder, "you just did yourself!"

"Did what?"

"Speak ill of the dead. You said . . . ah, never mind." He laughed and continued to scrub, crouching low. He likely wouldn't get another bath until spring, so he'd better make the most of this one.

Finished washing, he dressed. Kissing Glendina on the cheek and leaving her brushing her hair in front of her small, cracked mirror, he donned his mackinaw and flat-brimmed black hat, and with his prized Winchester Yellowboy rifle in his gloved right hand, his saddlebags on his left shoulder, he headed out into the brutal cold.

His fur-lined moccasin boots crunched in the deep snow banked against Glendina's cabin, as he made his way around to the back, where the lousy gambler and sore loser, Cisco, lay frozen stiff as a marble slab.

"Shit." Yakima looked down at the dead man, whose open, ice blue eyes were frost-rimed and snow-glazed.

He should have hauled Cisco to the undertaker last night,

when his body had still been pliable. Now he was going to have one hell of a job, wrestling the man across town.

As Yakima stood cursing himself while staring down at his handiwork, he heard a woman cough behind him. He turned to the cabin west of Glendina's, where a tall, stout figure ambled into the snow from an open back door, wrapped in several thick blankets, a night sock on her head. A brown paper cigarette smoldered between her thin lips. She turned to the wood stacked against the cabin's rear wall, and glanced at Yakima.

Ma Dillard was the only madame in the village. She ran and operated several cabins here and there about the canyon. Stopping suddenly before the woodpile, she removed the cigarette from her teeth, spewed smoke into the cold, still air, narrowed her tiny, deep-set eyes at Yakima, and planted her left fist on a hip stout as a beer cask.

"Was that you shootin' your gun off last night, half-breed . . . wakin' me from a goddamn deep sleep?"

Yakima hiked a shoulder. "This sonofabitch would have shot me if I hadn't shot him, and stolen my poker winnings."

Ma stared at Yakima hard. Her face and neck were like ten pounds of rolled suet. She shook her head with disgust and took a deep drag from her quirley, letting smoke dribble out her little, dimpled nostrils as she said, "My whore all right?"

"Fine as frog hair."

"You didn't bruise her none, didja, you big half-breed son of a bitch?"

"Not a mark on her."

Ma wagged her head again then poked her quirley between her teeth and grabbed a stick of split cordwood from the top of the pile. Yakima had spied a child's toboggan leaning up against the single-hole privy twenty feet from Ma's back door.

"Say, Ma?"

The woman turned toward him as she continued stacking wood in her arms, the quirley sagging from her lips.

"Mind if I borrow your sleigh over yonder? Make it a helluva lot easier to drag this sonofabitch over to the undertaker's."

She turned half-around toward the privy then scowled again at Yakima. "You bring it back? I use it to haul groceries around to my girls."

"I'll have it back within the hour."

The old woman snorted and, hefting about six chunks of wood in her arms, waddled back inside her cabin, hooking a foot to drag the door closed behind her.

Yakima hauled the sled over to Glendina's shack, rolled Cisco on top, and pulled the stiff carcass around the shack and into Crystal Creek's main drag—a narrow, winding street between unpainted board shacks and log cabins, all mostly silent but spewing blue pine smoke into the frosty, lightening air. The high, jagged peaks around the village were all charcoal-colored in the dawn's pearl wash.

Between buildings on the south side of the street, Yakima caught occasional glimpses of the creek that was panned every summer for the gold that washed out of the higher reaches but that was now buried under three feet of snow and half again that much ice.

Most folks left here in the fall, to winter a couple thousand feet lower. Those that had no other homes remained here, whoring and drinking mainly, or supporting those who whored and drank. It wasn't a bad town as far as mining camps went—in spite of a few crooked gamblers—but damn, it was cold!

The undertaker's shop was where Glendina had told Yakima it would be—beside the drug emporium and directly across the street from the town's only livery barn. Yakima was surprised to find the double doors on the shop portion of the undertaker's house open this early in the morning. A faded sign over the door read ELKHART'S UNDERTAKING AND FURNITURE.

He stopped the sleigh in front of the doors, and immediately a yellow cur that had been digging in the snow near a tall pine from which a gutted red elk carcass hung, came over to give the bone-cold gambler several wary, tentative sniffs, growling uncertainly. Yakima didn't shoo the dog away.

"Go ahead and piss on him, dawg," he grumbled as he tramped up to the dark opening, shifting his saddlebags on his shoulder and squinting his eyes to see into the shed's even darker bowels.

"Ain't open yet," sounded a raspy man's voice from inside. There was a scraping of wood against wood, and then a boot clomp.

"I don't care if you're not open," Yakima said. "I got a man that needs buryin'. If you're not open, I'll just leave him here, and you or the dog or whoever can do with him what you want when you are open. It's too cold for me to argue, and I sure as hell ain't haulin' him back to where I shot the sonofabitch."

Yakima turned to kick Cisco off the toboggan but stopped when the blurred figure in the bowels of the shed growled, "Hold on! Hold on!" The figure, whom Yakima took to be Elkhart, shuffled across the hard-packed earthen floor, his tall, stooped frame clarifying as he approached the open doors. "Who ya got there?"

"A privy snake known as Cisco. I didn't catch his last name."

Elkhart stepped out from between the doors clad in a long, ratty buffalo coat, a deerskin cap with earflaps covering his head. He had close-set eyes and a big, red nose. He toed the carcass with a furred boot. "This the gunshot I heard last night?"

Sound carried well around the canyon, Yakima reckoned. He said, "Tried to take me to the dance for the fleecing I gave him at poker."

Elkhart nodded and sniffed. "I was over to the Ace in the Hole when you was playin' him. Cisco Dervitch. Heard he got run outta Hawk's Bend for riggin' games with a whore."

"How'd they do it?"

"She'd work the table, sittin' on the players' laps and lookin' over their cards. She'd flash her eyes like this"—the ugly, bulbous-nosed undertaker gave a bizarre demonstration of a pretty sporting girl blinking her eyes coquettishly—"at Dervitch, signalin' the cards they was holdin'."

"That's kinda worn out, ain't it?"

"Yeah, well . . . who's gonna pay to bury him?"

"I don't know. I shot him. I sure ain't payin' for his funeral."

"Mister, do you work for free?"

"Doesn't the town have a fund or somethin'?"

"No, the town don't have a fund or somethin'."

Yakima kicked the frozen cadaver's black, undershot boots. "Those must be worth somethin'. And he left his gun in the snow outside Miss Glendina's shack."

"I suppose you want me to go dig it up."

Yakima had given the toboggan's rope a tug as he turned away. Now he turned back to Elkhart, scowling. "Mister, maybe you should consider another line of business. I think you're bored with this one."

"Ah, shit—at least help me get him in a box."

"No need for a box. Just throw him in a hole."

"That's the law here. No one gets buried without 'em bein' in a box. The ground buckles under all this snow and frost, and when spring comes the dogs and the coyotes start draggin' bodies around. Shit, a few years ago, before the law, old Milford Mulligan's big collie, Shep, dragged one carcass back to Mulligan's yard, so the girl who delivers Mulligan's eggs in the mornin', Mary Fitzpatrick, stumbled on the carcass of the druggist's dearly departed, half-devoured ma, Mrs. DeSoto!"

The undertaker wagged his head sadly. "You could hear that poor girl's scream all the way to Snow Point twenty miles down canyon!" He stooped to grab Cisco's ankles. "Let's get him inside. I got a fresh box on sawhorses over by the stove."

Yakima set his saddlebags down, lay his rifle across them, and snaked his arms under Cisco's shoulders. The dead man had such little give to him that Yakima half-expected his arms to break clean off. As he straightened with the dead man sort of twisted in his own arms, Yakima backed into the shed, looking behind him so he wouldn't stumble over the scrap lumber littering the floor.

Coffin lids and half-finished furniture pieces of several shapes and sizes leaned against the walls, and four coffins in various phases of completion were stacked together in a corner. Odds and ends of lumber lay everywhere, and tools and sawdust littered shelves on every wall. The heady smell of pine hung thick in the cool air, as did smoke from the heating stove.

A sealed coffin stretched across sawhorses against the long, low building's right wall, under a snowy, frosty window. Another was just beyond it. Probably dead folks in both.

Strange profession. To be so close to death every day. To have your life depend on it, in fact.

"That one back there," Elkhart said, jerking his chin toward the coffin leaning up against the rear wall, near the bullet-shaped black stove that ticked and breathed like a napping dragon. "I was savin' it for Ed Sorenson, as he's expected to go any day now, but I got four more ready to go. This time of year, with the cold bein' so hard on the old folks and the babies, they go fast."

Yakima was halfway across the deep room when hooves clomped dully in the snowy street. He looked beyond the undertaker to see a wagon drawn by a stout, shaggy dun mule pull up in front of the open doors. A blocky man in a dark-blue wool coat and cloth-billed watch cap sat in the driver's box, his breath steaming in front of him, freezing in his thick, dark-red mustache.

"Ah, hell," Elkhart grumbled, glancing over his shoulder and grunting under the weight of Cisco's legs. He turned toward Yakima, his horsey face red from exertion. "Let's set him down for a moment. This gent's come for the whore."

Chapter 3

Yakima hadn't seen the lidded coffin to his right. Now as the undertaker lowered Cisco's legs, swinging them toward the coffin, Yakima had no choice but to do likewise with the man's shoulders. When they had the frozen body on the coffin, Elkhart ambled back toward the front of the shop, hiking a shoulder and canting his head to one side, as though to stretch kinks from strained muscles.

The man in the wagon was wrapping his reins around the brake handle.

"Mr. Barstow," the undertaker called. "I was expecting you yesterday."

The man in the wagon turned toward the shop. His face was ruddy and thick-mustached—from what Yakima could see of it from far back in the smoky shack, and below the bill of the man's watch cap.

He did not respond to the undertaker's admonition.

"You were in such a hurry to fetch your daughter," the undertaker said in his falsely affable, mildly castigating tone, "that I rushed to get her ready for you yesterday. And then you didn't show up!"

The newcomer climbed stiffly down the far side of the wagon and came shambling around the rear of the box, his high-topped, lace-up boots crunching in the packed, dog-yellowed snow fronting the shop.

"I had business." Barstow stopped to reach over the wagon's tailgate, unlatching it with a wooden bark.

"Yeah, I heard about your business," Elkhart said, chuckling. "Heard you had a couple buckets of beer over to The Blue Spruce, sang a couple songs with Rosicky's woman, and took a long nap above their cabin. Night-long nap."

Barstow lowered the tailgate, letting it drop with a slam that rattled the whole wagon then shuffled toward the undertaker. He had the heavy, shambling gait of a Midwestern sodbuster. Dakota, maybe. Or Nebraska. "She's ready to go? I gotta get started. Got a long pull ahead."

"She's *been* ready, Mr. Barstow."

As Yakima stood warming his back at the chuffing stove at the rear of the shop, he watched the undertaker lead the honyonker, Barstow, into the shop and over to the coffin stretched across sawhorses under the shack's sole window.

The undertaker set his hand atop the lid. "Here she is. Dressed just like you wanted."

Barstow stood facing the coffin, his broad shoulders sloping, his arms hanging straight down his sides, deerskin-mitted hands resting against his thighs clad in coarse wool trousers. He didn't say anything, and neither did the undertaker, their frosty breaths mingling in the twilight of the shop as it faded above their heads.

The undertaker glanced several times at Barstow, curiously, impatiently, until Barstow set a fist on the lid and said in a voice that sounded slightly thicker than before: "Okay, let's see her."

The undertaker turned his head toward Barstow, who

was several inches shorter but wider. "You sure you wanna do that? Look, I'll be straight-up with you—I couldn't get her eyes to close all the way. Now, that's a little unsettling to some folks, so what I did was—"

"Open the lid, Elkhart," Barstow growled. "I wanna see my daughter, make sure you put her in the dress I gave you."

"I put her in the damn dress."

"I wanna see."

"All right, all right," the undertaker said. "Have it your way, Barstow. Not exactly the trusting sort, are ya?"

Elkhart reached across the coffin and lifted the lid that was not nailed down. He leaned the lid against a half-finished dresser behind him then turned back to the coffin, and he and Barstow stared into the box.

There was a three-foot gap between the men, and through this Yakima could see the lower face of a young girl—a waxy, fine-featured face frozen in death's repose. As the undertaker shifted his weight around nervously, Yakima saw the blue polka-dotted bandanna that had been wrapped around the girl's head, holding a penny over each eyeball.

"See," Elkhart said. "I couldn't keep her eyes closed. You said your trip'll take a few days? You're hauling her down to Rolette? You keep those pennies tied down on her eyes. By the time you get to Rolette, they should stay closed on their own, and your wife can see her before you put her in the ground."

Barstow shambled a little closer to the casket. Elkhart backed up some, as though to give the man a little privacy. Barstow rested his hands on the sides of the freshly planed box from which slivers of wood curled, and Yakima could see the man's lips slide back away from his teeth as he made a face. Barstow sucked a sharp breath and shook his head—whether in sadness or disapproval, it was hard to tell.

"Sorry, Barstow," Elkhart said. "She was a good girl. Everybody liked her around here."

Barstow turned his head toward the undertaker, and Yakima saw the hard brown orbs darken a little as the skin above the man's nose wrinkled. "Did you lay with her, Elkhart?"

"No!" Elkhart scowled in revulsion. "I'm a married man, and my wife won't put up with me cavortin' with whor—I mean, with workin' girls. Of course I haven't laid with her, and I'm insulted that you asked me such a question."

Barstow studied the undertaker for a time, and then the muscles in his rugged face softened, and he turned back to his daughter in the casket, nodding. "Okay, then. I'll take her home. I'll get some food for the trail an' such, and I'll take her home. That's where she belongs. That was where she always belonged anyways. Not here . . . cavortin', like you say."

Barstow turned to stare out between the open timber doors, where the winter light was gradually intensifying, as though a dirty shade were slowly being lifted from a lamp. A light snow was falling now, and the yellow mutt was sitting in the middle of the street, scratching an ear with a hind leg. It was so quiet that Yakima could hear the dog grunt with satisfaction as it scratched.

When Elkhart had set the lid on the coffin, he hammered the six nails that had been only half-driven through the wood, sealing it. While he did this, Barstow stared outside, but Yakima couldn't see what the man was looking at. Maybe the dog, or maybe he was trying to judge how much snow would fall and possibly block his trail home. Yakima didn't know what he was thinking, but he could feel the man's sadness—a heavy weight in his knees and a ringing in the ears—as if the sadness were his own, until it *was* his own and he was wishing he'd left Cisco Dervitch in the snow outside Glendina's shack.

"Hey, breed," Elkhart said when he'd pounded the last nail in the coffin lid. "Help Mr. Barstow with his daughter, will ya? If I do any more heavy lifting this morning, I'm gonna be down all afternoon. Won't get a damn thing done."

Yakima glared at the man pressing a fist against the small of his back and stretching from side to side, softly groaning. Not that this was the first time Yakima had been addressed as "breed." He'd had a lifetime of it. The casual way in which the undertaker was trying to order him around layered the gloominess he'd felt at Barstow's plight with a keen edge of anger.

Drilling Elkhart with one more steely glare, resisting the urge to backhand the man, Yakima took one end of the coffin. Barstow tossed some coins on a coffin lid, and as Elkhart thanked him and swept the coins into a palm, jingling them with satisfaction, Barstow took the other end of his daughter's coffin, and backed toward the door, cursing under his breath as he stumbled over wood scraps and tools and knocked a square off a stool.

When they were outside, the yellow dog came up to sniff around the coffin. Barstow set his end of the box on the wagon, and then Yakima shoved it up against the front panel and the driver's boot.

Barstow raised the tailgate and latched it, grunting softly, his breath frosting in the air around his head, freezing in his mustache. Without so much as a glance at Yakima, or another word to Elkhart now standing between the shed's open doors, he tramped around to the front of the wagon, climbed aboard, and released the brake. He swung the shaggy dun mule around and clomped off the way he'd come, the falling snow obscuring the coffin-laden buckboard like a beaded white curtain.

Yakima and the dog stared after him.

"Have a safe trip home, Barstow!" Elkhart yelled.

The dog moaned and trotted off.

"That son of a bitch," Elkhart said when Barstow pulled his wagon up to the narrow street's right side, and stopped in front of a log shack with a high porch and a sign announcing simply FIVE SENT BEER. "Look at him. Gonna get him another bucket of beer."

"I reckon I'd have a couple buckets of beer if I'd come to town to retrieve my dead daughter," Yakima said.

"Shit, a man like that don't throw money around unless he has it."

Yakima frowned at the hawk-nosed undertaker. "Huh?"

"She told him where that money was hid. The loot Pedro Camargo stole from the bank in Juniper Bend."

"How could she tell him?"

Elkhart swiveled his bulbous nose toward Yakima, and furrowed his bushy silver-brown brows with incredulity. "She didn't die until after the old man got here. He was with her for two hours at Ma's before the poor girl expired. The doctor tried to get the bullet out but it was too close to her heart. Probably shouldn't have tried. She'd probably be on her back and spreadin' her legs again by now if the doc had left her alone."

Elkhart cursed and turned back toward where Barstow was tramping up the cantina's steps, heavy-footed, kicking snow from his boots. "Sure enough. She told him where she hid it when ole Pedro got hauled off to the hoosegow."

"If the girl had got rich off her boyfriend's stolen loot," Yakima said with a caustic chuckle, "why in the hell would she be spending the winter in Crystal Creek?"

Elkhart leaned over, closed one nostril with the index finger of his right hand, and blew a wad of snot into the snow. "Pedro just got himself greased last month," he said, straightening and running a sleeve of his buffalo coat across his nose. "I imagine she was waiting for spring to light out with the stash." Elkhart chuckled. "I'll guaran-damn-tee ya, breed, she didn't *dare* go dig it up before Pedro was snuggling with snakes. Pedro weren't the sorta fella you double-crossed, even if he was locked up. Hell, we all figured he'd have busted out by now and come back for the loot himself."

The undertaker laughed darkly as he stared toward the tavern into which Barstow had disappeared. "Sure, she told her old man. Who the hell else would she tell?" He turned to Yakima. "Come on. Help me get ole Cisco in a box, will ya?"

"I don't think so, Elkhart." Yakima scooped the toboggan's rope out of the snow and began tramping back through the snowy village, the toboggan singing along behind him. "I've had all I can take of you on an empty stomach."

"Hey, where you goin'?" the undertaker called indignantly.

Yakima kept walking, his head pointed forward, hearing the snow tick against his hat and squeak under his moccasin boots, feeling hollowed out and in dire need of breakfast.

"Of all the uppity damned Injuns," came Elkhart's voice behind him, pitched low with bitter disgust. "Don't you ever come around here lookin' for a handout then, neither!"

Yakima threw an arm up and kept walking.

Chapter 4

Yakima turned down the unplowed side street where Glendina's shack sat huddled in the snow beside Ma's. The young whore was outside, shoveling a path through the snow to her front door. Her hair was down, and she wore an old blanket coat on her shoulders. White pantaloons were stuffed inside her ragged rabbit fur boots. She wore nothing on her head or on her hands, and her hair tumbled across her shoulders, swinging this way and that as she shoveled.

She threw a load of snow into the growing pile beside the door, and turned suddenly toward Yakima, her brown eyes betraying a touch of surprise. When he'd stood the sled up against Ma's privy, he returned to Glendina's cabin. She stood leaning on her shovel, regarding him skeptically, one fist on her hip.

"You found your way back," she sniffed.

"You thought I'd get lost?"

"Men have little sense of direct.... *Ah, Yakima, what are you doing?*" she laughed as he ducked down suddenly, wrapped an arm around the girl's waist, and threw her over his shoulder.

She dropped the shovel and pummeled his back with her fists.

"Holy Christ, girl—I've never known anyone so suspicious," Yakima said as he walked back into the street, holding the girl like a feed sack on his right shoulder.

Glendina laughed and squealed and kicked halfheartedly, demanding to be let down until he finally set her on a frozen rain barrel. She squealed again as he ducked down between her legs, and jostled her up behind his neck for a shoulder ride.

Doing a childlike imitation of a galloping bronco complete with whinnies and knickers as he nipped at the chuckling girl's pantaloon-clad legs, he mounted the steps of one of the only two cafés in town—The Crystal Creek Inn. It served the best grub in the village, though the woman who ran the place with her two beefy daughters had been left holding her hand out when personalities had been awarded.

He set the girl on the top step and ushered her, breathless and laughing, through the eatery's front door on which the day's menu, chalked on a scrap of black slate, dangled from a nail. Yakima closed the door and looked around the dark, smoky room in which the smell of lard and smoked sausage hung heavy.

A stool-fronted counter ran along the left wall, with the kitchen behind it. A couple of burly villagers sat atop the stools, and a few more sat at the half-dozen tables arranged willy-nilly about the rest of the cabin. All heads turned toward Yakima and Glendina, as did that of the woman who ran the place—Mrs. Landers, who peered through the long, rectangular hole in the kitchen's plank wall with a look of disgust.

Yakima waved to her. The woman wrinkled her nose and

turned away, and Yakima ushered Glendina to the lone table at the front of the room, by the only window in the front wall. With a gentlemanly flourish, he held the girl's chair for her, for which she thanked him with a society lady's charm, then sank into the chair across from her.

The swing door to the kitchen opened, and one of Mrs. Landers' chubby, dumb-eyed daughters waddled out with two plates in her pale, puffy hands. When she'd delivered the plates to a pair of villagers at the back of the room, she made a swing past Yakima and Glendina's table, but rather than stop, she continued on into the kitchen.

Yakima and Glendina looked at each other. Glendina quirked her lips.

The chubby daughter of Mrs. Landers waddled out of the kitchen again, this time with the coffeepot. When she'd refilled the half-dozen stone mugs around the room, she again headed back toward the kitchen. Before she could make the door, Yakima grabbed her apron and tugged. The big girl stopped abruptly, scowling.

"Momma says she done already tolt you we don't serve half-breeds. She made an exception yesterday, since you were caught in the storm and all, but she said it was your last time. And she said that if she did serve you again, she couldn't. . . ." The dullard let her voice trail off as her eyes darted disapprovingly toward Glendina then flicked quickly back to Yakima. ". . . she couldn't serve her."

"You gotta serve us," Yakima said levelly.

"Momma reserves the right to serve who she wants."

"Tell your momma that if she doesn't serve us," Yakima said, turning his head toward the woman looking in from the long kitchen window, and raising his voice, "I'm gonna shoot the place up, and then I'm gonna haul her out back and pound her fat ass with a chunk of split stove wood."

The other breakfasters had fallen silent. Yakima felt their eyes on him.

The dull-eyed Landers girl, lower jaw dropping and pasty cheeks coloring up like a Colorado sunset, turned her head slowly toward her mother. Mrs. Landers bunched her lips and barked angrily, "Serve 'em and get 'em outta here, Rena!"

The girl turned back to Yakima, scrunching her lips.

"The lady will have the huevos rancheros," the half-breed said. "I'll have the same. And we'll both have coffee. Lots of coffee."

The girl scrunched her lips again and yelled, "Two huevos, Ma!"

Glendina leaned toward Yakima. "Do you think she'll poison us?"

"Mrs. Landers? Nah. Bad for business."

When the food came, Yakima had to admit to a little apprehensiveness at first, but after the first few bites and he didn't feel like flopping down on the floor and barking like a rabid dog, the delightful succulence of Mrs. Landers' cooking overtook him. Hungry after a long night of frolic and shooting, he couldn't shovel it in fast enough.

Glendina must have been hungry, too, because she nearly matched him bite for bite, hunkered down over her plate with her fork in one hand, a corn tortilla in the other, pausing only to swill the bitter, black coffee smoking in its chipped stone mug.

She'd just taken a loud snorting sip of the belly wash when, swallowing hard, she said, "Look."

Yakima followed her gaze out the window. He used the knuckles of his left hand to rub a clear spot in the glass then squinted into the snowy street to see the bereaved Mr. Barstow pull the wagon hauling his daughter's snow-dusted coffin up to the mercantile on the other side of the street.

"Senor Barstow," Glendina said in a thin, vaguely curious voice.

The blocky man in the heavy, thigh-length, blue wool coat, deerskin mittens, and billed watch cap, wrapped his reins around the brake handle. Moving with the slow precision of a man who'd put a bucket of beer under his belt, and maybe chased it with a shot or two, Barstow climbed down from the driver's box, slipped a little in the snow, then moved around the rear of the wagon to mount the broad steps to the mercantile's loading dock.

He climbed heavily, one plodding step at a time, steadying himself with a hand on the step's right rail.

Yakima felt a stone drop in his well-filled belly as he stared after the bitter man.

"She's in there."

Yakima looked across the table at Glendina. The girl stared through the window, holding a yolky forkful of food halfway to her mouth, a sad, lonely look in her brown eyes that reflected the soft, gray light from the frosty glass.

"In there all alone."

"Told you," Yakima grunted, inexplicable annoyance poking him as he continued eating, "she don't know nothin' anymore. Eat your food."

She gave him a defiant flare from under her dark-brown brows. "It gives me a chill, is all. Besides, you didn't know her, Indio."

Yakima greased his last chunk of fried potato with green chili and egg yolk. "You two friends?"

"No. Not really. She was too pretty for me to like her much, but she brought me my wash from the Chinaman's once."

"Pretty, huh?"

"And she sang good." Glendina glanced out the window once more then turned back to Yakima. "But she was quick to anger and I heard she called me a greaser behind my back."

Yakima laughed.

Movement out the window caught his eye, and he turned to see Mr. Barstow walk with slow precision down the mercantile's broad loading dock steps. He carried several burlap sacks of different sizes. Three men who'd appeared as though from nowhere stood at the bottom of the steps, one on the street, one with a boot cocked on the bottom step, facing the loading dock.

The men were fur-clad against the cold. Holsters showed beneath the hems of their coats. The one with his foot on the bottom step held a rifle negligently in his folded arms.

"What is it?" Glendina said.

"Mr. Barstow must have made some friends over at the beer hall."

Just then, as Barstow gained the bottom of the loading dock steps, the man with the rifle moved in front of him and shoved him hard with a hand to his chest. The unsteady Barstow tripped over the step behind him, sort of half-twisted around, dropping a couple of his sacks, and fell on his rear.

"Or maybe not," Yakima mumbled.

Glendina sucked a sharp breath. "*Mierda!* What do they want?"

"More than the time of day, I have a feelin'."

"*Bastardos*."

Across the street, Barstow tried to get up, but the man with the rifle levered a cartridge into the rifle's breech—Yakima could hear the metallic rasp—and jammed the barrel against Barstow's chest, about four inches below the man's thick neck.

His yell penetrated the front wall of Mrs. Landers's eatery, but Yakima couldn't make out the man's words above the low hum of conversations around him and the sizzling sounds emanating from the kitchen.

"Stay here." Yakima took another deep slug of his coffee, and rose.

"Don't shoot any more hombres, Indio," Glendina anxiously urged, "or they'll bring the law here!"

Yakima went out, setting his hat on his head. Across the street, the three bullies were still forming a half-circle around Barstow, the one still pressing his rifle against Barstow's chest. Leaving his coat open and flipping the right flap back behind the staghorn grips of his Colt, Yakima moved down the eatery's steps and into the street.

The man with the rifle was leaning low toward Barstow, who glared up at his assailant stubbornly. The rifle-wielder was saying something in too low a voice for Yakima to make out, but the man's voice was pinched with anger.

"I tell you," Barstow said, holding up his mittened hands in supplication, "I know nothing about that. She told me nothing!"

"Well, see now, we just find that a little hard to believe," said one of the men standing in front of Barstow, spaced about three feet left of the other, partly blocking Yakima's view of the trio's quarry.

The man with the rifle grated out, "Now, like I done told you, old man—"

He stopped and jerked his head around when Yakima said, "Mr. Barstow, I thought you'd have left by now. If you don't leave soon, you're gonna get stuck here another day." He made his slow, sauntering way toward the mercantile, hooking his thumbs behind his cartridge belt. "I got a feelin' another storm's on the way. You never know around here."

"Butt out, breed," advised the man with the rifle, keeping the maw of his Winchester pressed taut against Barstow's chest. "This ain't none of your affair. Now, scoot."

The other two men had half-turned toward the street, narrowing their eyes at Yakima continuing to saunter toward them, idly kicking snow chunks with his fur-lined moccasin boots.

"Looks like Mr. Barstow took a tumble," Yakima said. "I appreciate you fellas helpin' him up. He must have stopped over to the beer hall after he loaded his daughter up, and them steps are a mite icy."

"What the hell is Barstow to you, mister?" asked the man who stood on the street. His long, sandy hair tumbled straight down from a blue knit cap, and one of his front teeth was chipped.

"We became acquainted over to the undertaker's."

"You did, didja?" asked the man with the rifle. "You become so acquainted you're suddenly his guardian angel?"

"Seein' how he's a mite tipsy and there ain't no one else to help him, except you fellas, of course, I reckon you could say that. But you sure are takin' your time, and, mister"— Yakima narrowed his eyes at the man with the rifle—"if you think you're gonna swing that Winchester toward me, you better think about it one more time. I don't mind you removing it from Mr. Barstow, but if it starts toward me, I'll blow your right eye out the back of your head before you can get it even half aimed in my direction."

Chapter 5

The three men stared at Yakima.

The man with the rifle had removed the barrel from Mr. Barstow's chest and slid it two inches toward the half-breed, and had frozen. He was still crouched toward Barstow, his head turned toward Yakima, and his pale, gaunt cheeks were mottled red. He had a thin patch beard, a scar on his chin, and his eyes were as yellow as a tabby cat's beneath the brim of the shabby, cream Stetson tied to his head with a red knitted scarf.

The man flanking the man with the rifle said dully as his eyes flicked between Yakima's horn-gripped Colt and Yakima's face, "You're pretty fast, huh?"

The half-breed shrugged. "A little rusty, maybe—it's been a long winter. If that rifle doesn't drop straight down to the boardwalk, though, and if that hammer isn't eased down against the firing pin nice and slow, I'm gonna have some practice right quick."

The three men stared at him. So did Barstow, his eyes wary, speculative.

Finally, the man with the red scarf lowered the rifle barrel and depressed the hammer with a faint click.

Yakima continued walking forward, until he was two feet ahead of and between two of the three men drilling him with sharp, enraged stares.

He turned to the man with the chipped tooth. "Hightail it."

Chip Tooth's nostrils flared. "Why, you're a damn half-breed. I don't reckon I take orders from you."

"Hightail it."

Chip Tooth's nostrils flared wider. He turned to the man to his left, and the corners of his long mouth rose in a snide grin. Suddenly, his left hand flew up and back toward his right shoulder, and as the back of that hand started whipping toward Yakima, Yakima ducked.

The hand whipped through the air where his head had been, and he buried his right first in Chip Tooth's belly. Chip Tooth stumbled back, loosing a great *whoosh!* of expelled air as he folded. The man to his right went for his gun. He'd started to bring it up, when Yakima smashed the edge of his right hand against the man's wrist. There was a dull crack under the sleeve of the man's heavy coat.

He screamed, and his .45 hit the boardwalk with a thump.

In the periphery of Yakima's vision, he saw the man with the rifle face around and raise his Winchester. Yakima pulled the man with the broken wrist in front of him.

The rifle roared.

The man with the broken wrist jerked as though someone had touched him with a cold hand. His eyes snapped wide. Then they dulled, and their lids grew heavy.

Yakima looked down to see blood oozing from the man's right side and his upper right arm. The bullet had torn into his back and, after apparently ricocheting off his sternum or ribs, exited out his side, shattering his arm. As he stumbled forward, face muscles slackening, Yakima shoved him out of his way to see the rifle aimed at him, smoke curling from its maw.

The shooter's face stared over the barrel, eyes glazed with shock.

Yakima swung his right moccasin boot back and forward, connecting solidly with the underside of the rifle's receiver. The Winchester flew straight up, and, pinwheeling, arced backward to hit the loading dock with a clattering thud. The shooter screamed, kicked the steps behind him, and piled up against them, his eyes riveted on Yakima as though on a rabid bobcat moving in for the kill.

Yakima stepped back, sliding his .44 from its holster and rocking back the hammer. The man he'd belly-punched was on his knees, veins popping out in his crimson face as he stared wide-eyed at the back-shot man lying belly down in the snowy street. The snow to the right of the man was turning as red as a patch of summer rose. The man who'd shot him lay back against the steps, to Barstow's left, propped on one elbow, his chest rising and falling sharply.

"*Shit!*" He shifted his exasperated gaze from the dead man to Yakima. "You made me shoot my cousin, you son of a bitch!"

"Get up," Yakima said, waving his cocked .44 and gritting his teeth. "Both of you—get up and haul Cousin over to the undertaker. Elkhart'll be glad to see you. Heard he's havin' a fire sale on caskets. Don't let me see your faces again, or you'll be joining ole Cuz six feet under."

The two men looked at each other. Finally, the one with the long red scarf gained his feet, grunting. He ignored Barstow who was sitting on the steps amidst his dropped sacks as before, looking dazed. Wincing dreadfully, the shooter walked over to the dead man.

"Harley?" He prodded the carcass with a boot toe. He

sobbed, tears dribbling down his cheeks, and said in a pinched, sorrow-racked voice, "Harley—you got any life in ya, Cuz?"

Yakima stepped back, keeping his gun aimed at the dead man's cousin and the other man holding his arm across his belly as he climbed awkwardly to his feet.

"Shit," he said, looking down at the dead man. "He ain't movin' one damn bit."

"That's cause he's dead!" sobbed the shooter, glaring at Yakima, tears dribbling down his craggy cheeks and into the snow at his boots. "Goddamn half-breed sonofabitch made me shoot my own cousin. My own blood!"

Crouching, he took Harley's arms while the other man took Harley's ankles. Continuing to glare at Yakima, they half-carried, half-dragged Harley down the street toward the undertaker's.

When they'd drifted into the screen of gently falling snow, the crunching of their boots dwindling into silence, Yakima turned to Barstow, who had started to gather his packages. When he'd gathered the one marked COFFEE, he straightened and looked at Yakima with that utterly expressionless mask that spoke nothing of his emotions, if there were any emotions. He glanced at the scuffed bloody snow where Harley had lain with sullen interest, and then he reached over his wagon's tailgate and carefully set his packages into the box beside his daughter's casket.

Without a word or even another glance at Yakima, he climbed into the wagon, unwrapped the reins from around the brake handle, released the brake, and shook the ribbons out over the horse's back. The wagon rattled ahead and out into the street.

Yakima watched it recede into the pines at the far end of town, dwindling fast.

He turned toward the undertaker's shack at the other end

of town, and saw Elkhart ushering the two men and the dead man into his shed and out of sight, the yellow cur eagerly sniffing the ground behind them.

Yakima holstered his six-shooter and tramped back toward the café. Glendina stood just outside the front door, hunched as if chilled, a dark, skeptical look in her eyes. Several faces shone in the window flanking her, including that of Ma Landers.

"You're bad, Indio," Glendina hissed, shaking her head. "Very, very bad."

"Because I provide the local undertaker with a little business?" Yakima opened the door. "Come on." He beckoned to her. "Let's go in and slug another cup of belly wash before I hit the trail."

"Bad," Glendina repeated, shaking her head as she walked through the door, shoulders hunched against the cold. "Soooo baaad."

Two hours after Yakima had left town, he trotted his black, blaze-faced stallion Wolf along the shore of a frozen, high-altitude lake.

The snow was no longer falling, but it was cold up here, maybe just above zero, and the sky had closed like giant tufts of gauze over the high ridges around him. He heard the muffled shrieks of a hawk, but he couldn't see the bird hunting above the clouds.

He made his way around the lake, Wolf starting at the riflelike cracks of the shifting layers of frozen lake ice, and, at the lake's far end, he drew the stallion to a halt. He stared straight over the black's head with sullen green eyes—the eyes of his German father—and set his lips in a straight line.

Ahead, the trail had been buried by an avalanche. Chunks of snow littered with pine branches, cones, and needles lay in a heavy, jumbled mass over the trail Yakima had taken through these mountains several times before—a trail that was usually swept clear of snow by the high-altitude winds.

But no amount of wind was going to sweep the mess before him away. The trail would be closed until late May or early June. There was another route down the northern side of the range, one that was more sheltered and thus likely clear, but it was also longer and slower, cutting through several canyons and mining villages on its circuitous drop to the Arkansas River valley below.

Yakima cursed. The avalanche looked recent, probably occurring yesterday or last night. He'd missed the open trail by less than twenty-four hours.

Not one to stew over something as relatively insignificant as a blocked pass, however—he'd been served up so much shit in the past few years that a blocked pass was nothing more than a minor annoyance, even if it made him late for his prospective job—he swung Wolf around and booted the black back the way they'd come.

He'd ridden around the far side of the lake and started into a canyon, following a path that had been hard-packed in the snow by the heavy, iron-shod wheels of log dreys, when he checked Wolf down suddenly. He'd heard something. There it was again—the clomp of a horse's hoof. A man's voice rose through the silent pine forest on both sides of the trail that angled down through the snow-laden trees.

Another voice sounded from the trail below. The speakers were too far away for Yakima to make out the words, but he recognized the second voice. Or thought he did. He'd have bet silver cartwheels against stew bones that it belonged to the red-scarfed cousin of the recently deceased Cousin Harley.

He reined the black around and swung him off the trail

and into a snag of rocks and dwarf pines. Shucking his
Winchester Yellowboy from the saddleboot, he ground-reined
the stallion then jogged through patchy snow, most of it
cleared by the wind, and across the trail he'd been following. He dropped down the shoulder of the slope and into the
pine forest, meandering around snowdrifts and silently leaping deadfalls.

Chickadees piped in the branches around him, and somewhere a jay gave a raucous cry.

He continued across the slope, angling gradually down
toward the hooves he could hear clomping on the snowy
trail. He had to work his way around a giant pine that
had toppled last summer, pulling up its entire ball of roots
that was as large as a small cabin, and then dropped behind
a fir tree just beyond. Edging a glance around the tree, he
stared down the slope toward a snowy clearing about sixty
yards below.

The hoof clomps had died. No sounds except for the
chickadees, the scratch of branches in a vagrant breeze.

A cricket of apprehension hopscotched along Yakima's
spine. He looked around. A man ran through the snow to his
right, about seventy yards away, moving toward the forest.
Yakima bolted out from behind the fir and ran along the
slope, weaving around trees, heading toward another clearing.

Something screeched over his head and hammered a tree
to his left. The whipcrack of the rifle sounded like an eagle's
death cry. Yakima flung himself forward, hitting the ground
on his belly just as another bullet screamed before plunking
into a deadfall log behind him.

Again, the whipcrack of the rifle flatted out across the
canyon, echoing.

Yakima scurried up to a broad fir, staying low, squeezing his Yellowboy in his gloved hands. From out in the clearing ahead and right came the sound of labored, raspy breaths and the snicking of displaced snow.

He glanced around the tree.

The man with the red scarf was running up the slope through a clearing, trees behind him and to both sides but open ground between him and Yakima. Open except for a large boulder, that was. The dead man's cousin appeared heading for the boulder, holding his rifle up high across his chest, kicking snow up around his thighs.

His scarf blew out behind him in the wind.

Yakima stepped out from around the fir and fired three quick rounds from the hip, levering and firing, the brass cartridge casings flying back over his shoulder. When the smoke cleared from in front of the half-breed's face, he saw the man lying on his back about ten yards from the boulder. He'd thrown his rifle away from him. His arms and legs were spread, and he looked as though he'd dropped out of the sky.

In the left periphery of his vision, he saw something move and stepped back behind the tree as two slugs plowed into it, spraying bark. The rifle cracks echoed shrilly. Another slug hammered the tree, making the entire trunk quiver, and the crack of that report joined the echoes of the other two, dwindling as though sucked straight up into the steel gray clouds.

There followed a silence like that at the bottom of a deep cave.

Thunder rumbled.

Thunder?

Yakima, pressing his back to the tree, looked up at the

dirty sky through the fir's spidery limbs. He'd heard winter thunder in the mountains before, but, shit, it was too cold for some mountain-bred hybrid of rain and snow.

Thunder rumbled again. It continued rumbling.

Yakima felt the ground shudder beneath his boots.

A worm of dread flipped in his gut. He'd heard that particular grade of rumbling before—about two years ago, when he'd been guiding the beautiful Faith into the mountains of Colorado, on the run from Bill Thornton's bounty hunters.

It had been an avalanche then.

Casting a dreadful glance over his right shoulder, he saw that it was an avalanche now, too—a tongue-shaped sheet of snow ripping away from the sheer stone ridge behind him and falling straight down the mountain with ponderous but what he knew to be deadly sureness.

It was a narrow mass, but he was right under it—in the dead center of its path.

The gunfire had jarred it loose.

Son of a bitch!

Chapter 6

The snow hit the bottom of the ridge like a massive water-fall, splashing up snow at the ridge's base and resounding like giant train cars coupling.

Heart hammering, Yakima jerked his head around. The only near cover was the boulder to which dead Harley's now-dead cousin had been running. Yakima bolted off his heels and ran, lifting his knees and scissoring his arms, holding the Henry in his right hand.

A bullet whistled past his head. A rifle roared. Yakima gritted his teeth.

Dead Harley's fool cousin's fool friend hadn't yet realized he was in the path of an avalanche. Yakima stopped suddenly as the rifle crashed again, and racked a shell into his Yellowboy's breech. The man whom Yakima had punched in the belly stood about thirty yards away, holding a rifle to his shoulder. Powder smoke wafted around his head.

Yakima fired. The avalanche's loudening roar had distracted him, and his slug chewed bark from the tree just behind his target. Quickly racking another round, Yakima fired again.

His target jerked back as the front of his coat buffeted with the force of Yakima's shot. As the man stumbled against a tree behind him, Yakima lowered his Yellowboy and glanced to his left.

The snow was rolling toward him like a giant, white, froth-rimmed wave. It rumbled and shuddered and belched. The roiling cloud grew larger and larger as it barreled down the mountain.

Yakima's heart lurched into his throat. He wheeled and ran for the boulder, breathing hard and gritting his teeth as the rumbling grew louder and louder behind him and the earth fairly leaped beneath his moccasins.

There was a deep drift twenty feet in front of the boulder. The snow slowed him down as he high-stepped through it. Glimpsing the wall of white closing on him, he stopped and snapped his eyes wide as he turned toward the ridge.

The chunks of tumbling snow plowed into him like a locomotive heading downhill without breaks. It hammered him backwards and suddenly he was tumbling end over end, hearing his own groans and grunts as the snow made brusque snicking and thumping sounds all around him. He heard branches snapping and vaguely realized, as the snow pummeled and rolled him, that the avalanche had swept him into the trees.

He was smashed down hard with a great *"GNAW"* of expelled air, his head pounding and his ears ringing, an enormous weight on his chest. He fought for breath but could only get a sip of mostly icy snow through his lips. He felt the snow all around him—a solid, frigid ocean wave holding him in a viselike grip, pressing him down hard, smashing him.

He fought for air, heard his own thin wheeze. He opened

his eyes, saw only blackness, felt only the painfully icy snow pressing against his eyeballs.

Bayonet blades of panic seared him, his heart thudding like a blacksmith's hammer against his ribs. There was a roar inside his skull. He tried to reach for the bowie knife under his coat, but the snow held his right arm down tight against his belly. His other arm was flung up against his head.

He was a goner. In the worst way possible.

Buried alive.

He tried to draw another breath, but the giant weight on his chest wouldn't let anything in. His temples hammered. The roar grew louder.

Everything went dark.

He woke sweating to raging heat and thought he must be in hell. But then he opened his eyes and saw that the heat came from a modest-sized fire burning very close to him, and that a pot of beans bubbled on an iron spit suspended over the flames.

He didn't have a stitch on. He was swaddled in blankets. He lay upon a springy bed built of pine branches. Beneath his head was his own saddle. His clothes, his shell belt and .44, and his rifle were all piled beside him.

He looked around, wincing against the throbbing in his head, the confusion. The last thing he remembered was the avalanche beating him to what had felt like a fine powder.

"You want some coffee? Beans?"

The voice echoed slightly around what Yakima realized were rock walls. He was in a cave. To the right of the fire was the cave's entrance—an oval-shaped, ragged-edged opening of dull gray light. Snowflakes swirled past the opening, a few flakes careening inside and lying like chicken down on the cave's hard-packed earthen floor.

"Coffee'll do you good," the voice said. It was vaguely familiar. "I'll doctor it for you."

Yakima followed the sound to a figure sitting on the other side of the fire, against the rock wall opposite. The figure shifted around behind the light, and then as a cup rattled and the man reached into the fire for a dented black coffee-pot, an umber glow touched the hard, lined planes of the face of the murdered whore's father—Barstow.

The man's thick mustache was beaded with melting snow and frost. Yakima watched him, perplexed, as the man poured coffee into a cup then set the cup back on a rock near the fire's glowing coals. Barstow flicked ashes from his cheek with the back of a grimy coat sleeve then bit the cork from a brown bottle.

Yakima heard the liquid splash into the coffee, and his mouth watered at the prospect of the toddy. While he was oven-hot on the outside, he felt as though every bone was filled with ice. Barstow pounded the cork back into the bottle's lip then extended the steaming cup around the fire to Yakima.

The firelight danced in his eyes, which owned a liquory sheen. Yakima wondered how long the man had been sitting here drinking toddies while Yakima slept. He felt as though he'd been out a couple of days.

As he got a rubbery hand around the cup and found his voice, he croaked, "How long?"

"Few hours." Barstow gave the beans a stir with a long-handled spoon then sat back against the cave wall. "Your horse is out yonder with mine and the wagon. Grained him good. He's good."

Yakima propped himself on an elbow, leaning as close

to the fire as he could without getting burned, and held the cup to his face, bathing himself in the fragrant steam.

"I went the same way you did," Barstow said in his low, toneless voice. "Found the pass blocked and came back to head down through Louisville. I'd pulled off the trail when I heard the riders comin'. Seen it was them two from town. I decided to sit tight till they come back, but then I heard the shootin'. I climbed the slope to watch, and I seen the avalanche run you down and cover you up. Dug you out with your own Winchester. You weren't down deep, but there were some nice chunks on top of ya."

"I feel like a train hit me."

"I've dug fellas out of avalanches before, when I first came to Colorado and was mappin' for the stage companies." Barstow sipped his coffee and shook his head. "Gotta get 'em out fast. Get 'em warm and dry fast."

Yakima sipped the coffee. Even his lips felt thick and rubbery. "Thanks."

"I reckon you did the same for me, sorta."

Yakima hiked a shoulder and took another sip of the rejuvenating brew. "Just the same. If you hadn't tried that pass, I reckon I'd be a goner."

"Me, too," Barstow said, one corner of his mouth fluting up with a bemused smile. "In town, I mean. I've never been handy with a gun, and I reckon I've outlived my fists. Too stove-up. Boy, I used to get into some fights, though."

Yakima sipped the coffee and racked his dull brain. Then he remembered why the cousins of Harley had been after Barstow. According to Glendina, they thought his daughter had told him the whereabouts of the stolen loot.

Barstow must have read the question in Yakima's eyes.

"They thought Rose knew where her boyfriend hid some money he stole." Barstow's voice was a disapproving growl.

He stared at the toes of his worn boots crossed before him. "They thought she told me before she died. She didn't tell me nothin' about that. I reckon if she knew, it's out there with her now."

He turned to look out the cave's gauzy entrance.

Yakima looked in the same direction. He remembered Glendina's reaction to the dead girl in the cold pine box, and he shivered.

"Found the horses of the two who tried to buck you out," Barstow said. "You can take 'em, sell 'em. Sell their tack. Both got good saddles on 'em."

"You take 'em."

Barstow shrugged. "All right." He threw another pine branch onto the flames. "Hope it don't snow much. I gotta get home. Shouldn't have come in the first place. It was Rose's ma made me. Me, I didn't have nothin' to say to that girl. No, sir. She was finished with me when she took to whorin'. And I was finished with her."

Yakima looked at the man across the fire. The flames flashed in his eyes as he stared dully into the flames, the corners of his thin-lipped mouth turned down. "You got more kids to home?" Yakima asked him.

Barstow shook his head. "Evelyn couldn't have no more after Rose. After Rose, it was all finished. Everything. And here I am out in the damn cold mountains, haulin' her worthless carcass back to her ma. If Evelyn wanted her buried at home so damn bad, Evelyn shoulda come and got her her ownself. Waste o' damn time." He picked up a plate and shoveled smoking beans onto it with a long-handled spoon. "We never even woulda known about the shootin' if the stage driver didn't send word. Damn that man, stickin' his nose in!"

He set a fork on the plate, and handed the plate to Yakima. He filled another plate for himself.

"Kinda hard on the girl, aren't ya, Barstow?" Yakima said, sitting back against the cold cave wall. "She was your daughter. Your own flesh and blood."

Barstow ate hungrily, sitting back against the wall and shoveling the food into his mouth, not caring that he left half of each forkful in his mustache. "I don't know what she was, where she come from. She wasn't my flesh and blood. Oh, when she was little we got along. Didn't last, though. She wasn't twelve before she was lookin' at me crossways, actin' all uppity. Then she started after the boys from the neighboring ranches."

Barstow shook his head as he ate. "Always after the boys. And, of course, since she had a wild look about her, the boys weren't hard to catch. I couldn't keep that girl on a short enough leash, I'll tell you that. Then one mornin' her ma comes out to the barn where I'm shoein' a mule, and she says Rose left a note on her bed. She was lightin' out for the mining camps with her Beau, Billie Lee Squires."

Barstow laughed. "Rose and Billie Lee was gonna make it big in the mining camps."

"What happened to Billie Lee?"

The honyonker shrugged. "Prob'ly got himself shot. He was a saddle tramp who fancied himself a card sharpie and good with a gun. Little scrawny fella. Rose thought he was right handsome. Probably has his bones strewn around some canyon out here. Little piker."

Yakima finished his beans and helped himself to more coffee. He kept the fire built up. When the blue light in the cave entrance had nearly faded to darkness, Barstow went out to check on the horses.

Feeling returned to Yakima's limbs. A little too much feeling. The more he warmed, the more he felt the pummeling he'd taken from the avalanche. He had stiffness and bruising in odd places—both buttocks, the back of his neck, his tailbone, his upper arm. His right knee felt half-sprung.

Barstow came back, stomped snow from his boots, and shivered.

"Colder'n a witch's tit out there." He doffed his watch cap, swiped it across his thighs. "Probably hear trees explodin' before long."

"Snow still fallin'?"

"No."

"Gonna get cold then."

Barstow had grabbed only a couple of snowy pine branches. He swayed drunkenly as he tramped over to the fire and dropped the wood on top of that which he'd already piled beside it. Yakima didn't say anything, but the snow from the new wood would dampen the dry stuff.

When Barstow had settled in with another cup of coffee to which he added a couple shots from his bottle—one of three bottles resting against the toe sack beside his blanket roll—Yakima got up and dressed in his luxuriously warm clothes. Barstow sat scowling into the fire, a hand splayed across his mustache, his thumb stretched over his leathery cheek, as Yakima donned his mackinaw and went out.

He checked on Wolf and the mule, relatively content where Barstow had tied them beneath a sprawling fir, well sheltered by boulders. The wagon sat nearby. There was no tarp over the box. The coffin inside was capped with an inch of downy snow that glittered in the starlight slanting down through the branches. The gear from Yakima's bushwackers' mounts was there, too.

The silence out here was so heavy it rang. Yakima's toes felt as though nails had been driven through them.

His breath puffing visibly before him, the half-breed kicked up enough deadfall for an armload. When he returned to the cave, Barstow sat back against the wall, snoring loudly with his mouth open. Yakima tossed some blankets and quilts over the man, built up the fire, and rolled up in his own soogan, groaning as the cold, hard cave floor made his bruises yelp.

Chapter 7

Sheriff Clayton P. "Duke" Dodge pulled his buckskin gelding up in front of the open doors of Elkhart's Undertaking shed in Crystal Creek, and looked over the rims of his round, steel-framed spectacles at the man sitting just right of the open doors, on a pine log cut into the shape of a chair.

"You the undertaker?"

The man didn't say anything. He was a tall man, maybe fifty years old, with a billed watch cap, a denim jacket coat too light for the climate, and a long, unshaven face. He sat with his head tipped back, lower jaw hanging, mouth forming a broad black oval. His mittened right hand was wrapped around the neck of an uncorked brown bottle propped on his thigh.

Sound asleep.

Duke Dodge glanced at his two deputies flanking him—Boyd Shanley and Calvin Miller. They looked from the undertaker to Dodge, scowling. Calvin Miller, who was twenty-two years old and wore a brown derby hat tied to his head with a purple scarf that his girlfriend back in Juniper Bend had knit for him, hiked a shoulder and grinned. "Likely drunk, Sheriff. Not much else to do up in these parts of a winter."

Dodge looked at the undertaker again. The man hadn't moved.

With a disgusted sigh, Dodge, a big man in a quilted deerskin coat and bearskin hat with the earflaps tied beneath his chin, stepped heavily down from his saddle. Holding his reins in his mittened hands, he tramped over to the undertaker, bent over, and said loudly into the man's left ear, "Kinda early to be taking a nap, ain't it, there, fella?"

Someone chuckled, and a voice said, "Why, he can't hear ya, ya damn fool. That there's Elmer Schaefer, Crystal Creek's illustrious mayor, who was found early this morning in that very position outside his shack—froze up like a month-old side of venison."

Dodge jumped back, scowling at the man whose ear he'd just spoken into then, turning to the one angling toward him from across the street, said, "Dead?"

"Deader'n a post. Had a fallin'-out with his wife—the meanest, ugliest old heifer in town—last evening. He went outside to drink his mind off of it, like he usually done. Ugly Elsie woke up this mornin', went out for firewood to start breakfast, and found old Elmer sittin' on a low part of the pile in the very same position he's in now, with that bottle frozen so tight in his fist that I hauled 'em both over together in my wheelbarrow."

"Shit in a bucket!" Dodge exclaimed.

"What's the matter?" said the tall, horse-faced man striding toward him through the coating of fresh snow in the street, holding a whiskey bottle in the crook of one arm, a sack of coffee beans in the other. "Ain't ya never seen a dead man before?"

A yellow cur dogged his heels, regarding Dodge and the two deputies with pricked ears and a tail raised in cautious curiosity.

"I've seen dead men," Dodge said, scowling down at Elmer Schaefer, noting that his blue jaws did look a tad on the waxy side. "But probably not as many as you have. Don't particularly care to see 'em. Usually when I *do* see 'em, I know they're dead. This fella here—he looked so alive, sittin' there. Only sleepin'."

"Yeah, winter's right handy that way. Makes my job a helluva lot easier, I tell ya. And it don't get so smelly around here like it does in July."

As the man passed Dodge and went on into the shed, heading for the stove at the back, Dodge squinted into the gloom after him. "You're Elkhart, I take it."

"That'd be me." Elkhart slung his coffee onto a shelf and set his bottle on a coffin propped on sawhorses. From the same shelf he took down a black mug and a leather mitt, and used the mitt to lift the steaming coffeepot from the warming rack of the stove.

Dodge followed him a few feet into the shed and shucked out of his mittens. "Where's the girl? The one called Rosie Dawn."

Elkhart glanced at him as he poured, steam rising like smoke in the brittle air. "Rosie Dawn? Hell, her pa, old Barstow, come and got her yesterday mornin'. Haulin' her home to bury her?"

"Where's home?"

Elkhart set the coffeepot back on the stove and sauntered back toward Dodge and the two deputies sitting their horses in glum silence, the youngest one, Miller, staring incredulously, a little horrifically, at the dead mayor.

"Why?"

"Cause I'm sheriff over to Juniper—"

"I know who ya are," Elkhart said, sipping his piping hot brew. "I been over to Juniper Bend. If I recollect, you been over here visiting our prize whores, time or two." He smiled with satisfaction. "But that don't answer my question."

"Look, you smartass sonofabitch." Dodge had been retying his ear flaps down snug beneath his chin, but now he stopped to scowl, red-faced, at Elkhart. "I'm the one answering the questions here."

Elkhart frowned.

Boyd Shanley leaned out from his saddle as though in private conference with his boss. "Uh . . . I believe you mean *askin'*, Duke."

Dodge turned to glare at the man.

"You'll be *askin'* the questions," Shanley said, a cautious expression on his deep-eyed, bony face with its two-day growth of beard stubble. "You said you'd be *answerin'* the questions."

"Goddamnit," the sheriff snarled, his craggy, fifty-five-year-old features turning a deeper shade of red. "So goddamn cold out here, I can't think straight." He turned to the undertaker and thumbed his spectacles up his nose. "You know what I mean, Elkhart. I'll be *askin'* the damn questions. Now, kindly tell me where this Barstow fella took that girl, or so help me, I'll come in there and pistol-whip you, wipe that smartass grin off your face once and for all."

Elkhart held his coffee up close to his chin as he came a few steps closer to Dodge, grinning wolfishly. "You figure she knew where Camargo hid that money, don't you? And she told her old man."

Dodge just stared at him, jaws hard.

"Goddamn, that is it. Shit, I only charged that sonofabitch the goin' rate for that coffin, too. Hell, he's prob'ly out there right now, diggin' up that fifty-six thousand dollars in stolen greenbacks!"

Dodge reached under his coat and pulled out a big horse

pistol. Waving the gun around like a knife, he stomped toward Elkhart.

Jarred from his reverie, the undertaker jerked back, wincing as he slopped coffee on his naked hand. "All right! All right! Christ, I shoulda gone after the son of a bitch myself. I heard the bank was offering a nice reward for that dinero—a full ten percent, if Billie Wild's blather can be believed."

"Christalmighty, man!" Dodge exclaimed, getting right up in front of Elkhart and grabbing the man's ratty buffalo coat. "You're really wantin' to feel some cold steel against your cheeks this mornin', aren't you?"

"Rolette! Rolette!" Elkhart yelled as Dodge pulled his head with its hawk-nose right up in front of his own bulbous beak that was glowing not only from years of drink but exasperation.

Elkhart turned his head to one side and squeezed his eyes closed, cowering from the big pistol in Dodge's fist. "He took her out to his ranch by Rolette! That's all I know! Rolette, damn ya! Rolette! Now, don't hit me. It's too damn cold to get rapped with a goddamned pistol barrel!"

"That's all you needed to say, mister." Dodge lowered the pistol. "He pull out yesterday, you say?"

"That was what I said. Yesterday mornin'. He won't be chewin' up the trail in that old wagon of his. The stage company keeps it plowed out as long as they can, but the way the snow's been fallin' lately, them drifts up the pass beyond Ruby Springs'll be good and high."

Dodge turned and walked back to his horse, none too eager to climb back into the cold saddle. His ass was sore. He wasn't used to long pulls in any weather, but mountain winter weather least of all.

He followed young Miller's gaze to the dead mayor, then

returned it to Miller. "Ain't you seen a dead man before, Calvin?"

Miller turned slowly toward the sheriff, his blue eyes looking pensive, stricken. He shook his head slowly. "I reckon not, Sheriff. It's a sight to behold, ain't it?"

"That one is, anyway. Sorta looks like he could take a drink just any old time and offer you one, don't he?"

Dodge laughed to cover his own squeamishness. Odd how such a sight could turn a man's insides to mush. He thought vaguely of lighting here in Crystal Creek a spell, maybe bedding down with one of the whores. Unfortunately, the best one—the one who looked at a man like he was a human being and not a rat scarfing up the food on her plate, was the dead one: Rosie Dawn. He'd heard the Mex girl was all right, but she was new. He hadn't tried her yet.

Dodge's mind had only half-strayed, and now a peevishness poked him, inspired by the dead man left out in plain sight on such a cold, lonely winter morning. He turned to Elkhart standing back in the shadows looking like a kicked dog: "Why in the hell don't you get this man in the ground where he belongs, Elkhart, you damn fool?"

"Hell, I can't even get him in a coffin, froze up like that. I gotta get him thawed out, and that requires wood, and that mule-headed English boy, Simms, ain't brought me the wagon load I ordered yet. He charges five dollars for a skimpy load, too." He sniffed and rubbed his burned hand on his moth-chewed buffalo coat. "Sure coulda used that loot. Or," he added quickly, eyes widening unctuously, "the reward money for turning it in, I mean."

Dodge snorted and grabbed up his buckskin's reins. "Well, fellas, let's work our way down the trail. We'll get us a cup of coffee at Dawson's Corners."

He turned out a stirrup and was about to poke his fur-lined boot through it, when Elkhart ambled out of the shed, looking pensively westward toward Ruby Springs: "Why do you s'pose the little whore told her pa, anyways? When she wouldn't tell no one else?"

Dodge dropped his boot from the stirrup, scowling at Elkhart. "Who the hell else was she gonna tell? Why not her old man?"

"I don't know," Elkhart drawled. "He was just such a . . . such a dark little man. A stiff shirt. Can't imagine they got along—happylike, anyways. That girl was so bright-eyed and bushy tailed. What I seen of her, anyways. I don't frequent sportin' girls, like some." He gave Dodge a faintly mocking smile. "Me bein' happily married an' all."

Dodge grumbled, grunted as he poked his boot through his stirrup, and heaved himself into his saddle, the leather creaking sharply in the bitter air.

"Well, the point is, she did—at least, according to unsubstantiated rumors that have been burning through these mountains like a wildfire." Dodge quickly tied the earflaps snug beneath his chin and thumbed his glasses up his nose. "Maybe you, Mr. Elkhart, wonder too much and work too little."

"How the hell you figure that?" the undertaker said, scowling indignantly up at the lawman, who reined his horse out into the street.

Dodge nodded at the dead Crystal Creek mayor lounging back against the open shed door, the yellow cur sniffing at his boots. "Leaving a dead man in the street in open view of all the town, and for flea-bitten mutts to sniff. The town *mayor,* no less. If I was the law up here, I'd see you got him in a box and in the ground pronto . . . if you had to burn dry shit mucked out of a barn to do it!"

As Dodge and his deputies rode westward down the snowy

street, the yellow cur turned to stare after them, growling deep in his throat.

"Don't mind him, Louie," Elkhart grunted, casting his own dark gaze after the trio. "Just another bottom-feedin', badge-totin', whore-mongerer. And I'll bet dollars to your venison liver snacks that he'll be collectin' more than just the reward on that Camargo stash."

Elkhart turned to see about dragging the dead mayor into the barn to start getting the man thawed. "I hope Pedro's brother Pablo finds him—shoots his fat law-bringin' ass—and takes all the loot with him to Mexico where I won't hear about it no more."

Chapter 8

Dodge lowered his head and squeezed his eyes shut as a downdraft of thick, blue smoke swept over him and his deputies, redolent with the smell of pine and spicy sausage. Behind him, the youngest of the two deputies, Miller, coughed. "Holy-jeebers—like to blind me!"

"Just a reminder that someone's stayin' warm," said the older man riding beside him, flanking Dodge. "And eatin' a nice breakfast."

"Quit complainin'," Dodge said as his buckskin clomped westward along the street. "You said yourself, Boyd, you was startin' to get cabin fev . . ."

The sheriff of Juniper Bend let his voice trail off. The smoke had cleared, and he heard boots stomping as three men filed out of the mercantile just ahead and on the street's right side. Single file, they started down the loading dock steps, watching their footing, as the steps were rimed with ice and snow.

Dodge angled the buckskin over to the three horses tied to one of the three hitch racks fronting the loading dock, and the man leading the two others down the steps—a lean, blue-coated man with a patchy brown beard and cold, cunning eyes—lifted his gaze to the three horsebackers approaching him.

"Well, well," said Dodge, lifting a flap of his quilted hide coat above the handle of the big horse pistol thronged on his right thigh. "What the hell have we here?" He chuckled as the buckskin stopped in front of the steps, and leaned forward on his saddle horn. "Snakehead Dawson, Phil Little, and Luis Lavoto." Dodge ran his gaze to each man coming down the steps in turn. "How is it that news of easy money always brings the coyotes out of their burros, the snakes out of their holes . . . even in the middle of a friggin' mountain winter?"

The sheriff chuckled dryly as all three hardcases stopped before him, Snakehead Dawson in the street and the other two halfway and a third of the way down the steps, respectively.

"Well, shit," said Snakehead Dawson, grinning out from beneath the dirty brown muffler wrapped over his head in the fashion of an old immigrant woman, a black lock of hair curling over his forehead. "If it ain't the famous sheriff of Juniper Bend! Lookee, boys—this here's Duke Dodge, an old friend of mine. If you ain't met him before, well, this'll be a real treat."

The man behind him on the steps said, "Can't say as I have met Sheriff Dodge, but it sounds as though he's met us." Little's yellow eyes moved slowly across Dodge and his flanking deputies, all of whom sat their saddles with their hands on their pistol grips.

"Oh, I don't 'spect we've had the pleasure in person," Dodge said, voice teeming with sarcasm. "The only one I got to know a little bit when he was gracing one of my jail cells, littering my floor with his toe nails, is Snakehead here. You fellas"—he raised his eyes to Little and the Mexican,

Luis Lavoto—"I know from pretty pictures I got hangin' in my office."

Luis Lavoto, holding a toe sack in the cradle of his left arm, bit off the top of a fresh tobacco braid and, chewing with his mouth open, showing his brown, crooked teeth, said, "You got pictures of us? Shit, I didn't pose for no photograph. There must be some mistake, amigo."

He had the bottom of his gray-black wolf coat raised above the grips of two pearl-gripped Colts, and, while Dodge could see that his hands were occupied at the moment, it wasn't hard to imagine those long, pale fingers dropping to the guns in a blur of quick movement. Printed on the wanted circular, Dodge remembered, were the warnings "fast," "seemingly eager to kill," and "contrary to authority."

"Nah, it ain't no mistake." Dodge was aware of the cold bone-handled grip of his .45 under his gloved palm. Damn, he wished he wasn't wearing that glove. "But I got no time for you three today. I'm just gonna warn you to go on back to where you came from. Obviously, you heard the rumor about Pedro Camargo's stolen loot. I heard the same thing. It may or may not be true, but I figure it ain't. At the same time, I don't want you three on the trail after it. Only thing that can happen with you three around is bad things, and I'm in no mood."

Dawson said, "You don't think it's true? Shit, everybody suspected ole Pedro told someone where he stashed that loot. He had too big a mouth on him not to. Now, it ain't likely he'd have trusted anyone from his own gang, especially since he was the only one put away. But a girl . . . a *purty* girl. Now, that makes sense!"

"Ma said that Rosie Dawn had an hour with her old man before she kicked off," Phil Little said, casually toeing a hunk of ice, one hand on the step rail. The grips of his Smith & Wesson shone through a side slit in his green-striped blanket coat, as did the handle of a huge bowie. "Said she heard the words 'stolen' and 'money' through the dyin' whore's door."

Little looked up, his yellow eyes flashing in the wan light as he grinned. Long, sandy hair tumbled down from his ratty rabbit hat, curling snakelike over his shoulders.

"It was probl'y her big mouth—spreadin' it around that she might or might not know where the loot was—that got her killed." Dodge slitted an eye at Snakehead. "You take your boys on back to where you came from. Or, better yet, head on down to Arizona. I hear the winter's real pleasant down there."

"You can't tell us what me and the boys can do, Sheriff." Snakehead was indignant. "Just cause you got some pitchers on your wall. Now, if you wanna rustle us in on charges, that's one thing. You're free to go ahead and try. Ain't he, Luis?"

The Mexican grinned as he chewed. "*Sí.*"

Little said softly but clearly in the cold, quiet morning, "If it's trouble you're after, Dodge, you're stackin' the makin's up right high."

Dodge felt a worm of apprehension wriggle around on his back.

He glanced at his two deputies, who returned the glance with wary ones of their own. Shanley would be willing to dance if Dodge was. But Cal Miller was fresh off his father's little shotgun ranch. He'd likely never killed anything but rattlesnakes and coyotes at calving time. He tried to wear a tough look, but it was only hide deep.

"No time for you three," Dodge said. "But don't worry, Lavoto, if I did have time, I'd be leadin' you down to the lockup at Juniper Bend. Don't let me catch you fellas on our backtrail, now—hear? Or I'll arrest you for interfering with lawmen in the . . . uh . . . application of their pursuits." Flushing slightly, but keeping his eyes on the three desperadoes and his hand on his gun handle, he reined his horse away from the loading dock. "Or whatever the hell them muckety-mucks call it."

"What's your slice of this, Dodge?" Snakehead called, jutting his chin. "You goin' after the reward . . . or the whole damn pot?"

Dodge gave the man a hard grin as the buckskin continued west along the street, both Shanley and Miller falling in behind him, turning their heads to look back at Snakehead, Little, and Lavoto. The three had been gunrunners down in Arizona for a time, before deciding that rustling up here, away from the Mescaleros, was a safer bet. So far, it had been, and all three were slippery enough to stay three steps ahead of the law. And none was above shooting a man, especially a lawman, in the back.

"That damn Lavoto—I hear he's greased lightning with a six-shooter," Deputy Miller said when they were clear of the mercantile and the last of the village's snowcapped shanties were falling back behind them. "Heard he killed two Arizona Rangers in the streets of Bisbee, and said he'd kill anyone who dragged 'em away and tried to bury 'em as long he was in town."

"Shit," Shanley chuckled dryly. "They musta got awful smelly."

Dodge, relieved to be out the trio's shooting range, laughed as well, throwing his head back on his shoulders. "Did that warning go for the coyotes, too?" He laughed again. "Lavoto—you gotta love that chili-chompin' pebberbelly."

* * *

The three lawman continued over Blankenship Pass and down through the brushy drainage of Wolf Willow Creek. They stopped once to warm themselves over a small coffee fire and to chip holes in the creek to water their horses. Mounting back up, fortified by coffee and jerky, they clomped out over the hilly, snow-dusted sage meadows toward Bear Peak.

It was while traversing a shallow valley with low, fur-clad hogbacks on both sides, that Dodge held up suddenly on the shoulder of a hogback blown clear of snow, and reached into a saddlebag pouch for his field glasses.

"Expectin' someone, Duke?" Shanley said, stopping his blue roan just below Dodge.

Cal Miller dismounted and stretched his legs, rubbing his butt. "I swear, my ass done froze to my saddle."

"I don't know if 'expectin's' the right word." Dodge showed his teeth as he adjusted the field glasses' focus wheel, staring along their backtrail marked by three separate scuffed trails in the snow-dusted fescue and mountain sage. "I got an itch behind my left ear, and it don't go away when I scratch it."

"Yeah, well, I got a froze ass, and it don't go away when I rub it." Miller laughed at his joke.

"Hell, kid, I figured you'd be used to sittin' all day in a saddle, wet-nursin' slow elk," Shanley said. He slid his eyes to Dodge, and his voice dropped an octave. "You think Snakehead's bunch is shadowin' us—don't ya, Duke?"

"I figure that was what's got my ear itchin'. It's usually like someone's shadowin' me. Started back when I was riding with Sherman down in Mexico. I knew when we were gonna get hit by them damn Lipan Apaches because that itch would flare up. I tried to tell Sherman and the non-coms, and they made fun of me at first, said I should put some foot oil on it, or rub some horse shit and kerosene back there, but after the first couple ambushes, they all started crowdin' around me when we rode patrols, watchin' to see if I startin' a scratchin' fit."

"I don't doubt your scratchin' fits a bit, Duke." Shanley chuckled and rubbed his gloved hands on his saddlehorn, warming them. "I've rode with you plenty when you had one comin' on. Prob'ly saved us from that Moon Johnson Bunch last spring." He stared at the sheriff, Shanley's own deep-socketed eyes mantled with straight, frosty, gray-brown brows. "See anything?"

Dodge shook his head. He lowered the glasses, set his wire-rimmed spectacles back on his nose, and turned to Shanley. "Do me a favor, will you, hoss? Ride over to the other side of the valley and follow the timberline back to that hat-shaped hill we passed. Ride up and look around. If it's anything, if it ain't just that this scratch has started playin' foo-fang-foo with me, come on back. Don't try to tussle with those boys alone."

"You got it." Shanley slipped his Spencer repeater from the saddle boot under his wool-clad right thigh. "If they're back there, I'll spot 'em."

Dodge continued glassing their backtrail. "Me and the kid here'll continue on up the valley. We'll wait for you at Holcomb's line shack."

"Good 'nough," Shanley said. "Step it up there, Blue," he told the roan, booting the gelding on around the shoulder of the hill, heading toward the southern timberline, gray-spotted with leafless aspens and from where occasional crows sent their raucous cries into the cold, gray sky hovering low over the valley.

The old deputy loped the roan along a twisting game

path through the sage and occasional, hard-crusted drifts that rose to the horse's hocks. When he gained the timberline on the valley's far side, he found another trail, likely one stomped out by mule deer, cutting across the mountain's shoulder, about thirty yards inside the pine forest.

Here he wouldn't be seen by anyone looking up valley. Anyone, say, shadowing him and old Duke and the kid, Miller.

Shanley's deeply eroded and sun-browned face slackened at the remembered image of the kid rubbing his ass and grousing about the cold. Probably had his mind on that girl, a cook's daughter from the far side of Black Mesa, who he was always buying bolt goods for at the general store in Juniper Bend. Miller was likely having no trouble staying warm on these cold mountain winter nights, like some were . . .

He came to where a canyon cut into the mountain shoulder, and dropped down into it, the blue moving easily in spite of a few slips and slides on the snowy, icy turf. The game trail continued up the ridge on the canyon's other side, and he was about to make for it, when something moved in the corner of his right eye.

"Whoa, Blue."

Shanley shuttled his gaze toward an aspen growing where the horseshoe-shaped canyon ended at a steep, fir-clad wall. Something dangled from a low branch of the aspen.

Fingering his Spencer repeater in his gloved hands, Shanley reined the blue toward the tree. Frowning, feeling a small knot tighten in his belly, the deputy looked around the canyon, seeing nothing but pines, a few aspens, the steep ridges, and the sage and bromegrass spotted with patches of ice-crusted snow.

He turned his head forward, and stopped Blue as he

stared at the rope dangling from the aspen's branch—a rope that had been looped and knotted into a perfect hangman's noose.

A soft thud sounded.

Shanley hipped around with a start to see three horseback riders clomping toward him. They were bulky figures, bundled against the cold. Two wore hats. One wore only a wrapped blanket over his head.

They all had Winchesters aimed at him.

As they drew within ten yards, Shanley saw that Snakehead Dawson was grinning.

Chapter 9

Yakima woke in the predawn shadows.

Barstow was still sawing logs on the other side of the fire, lying flat on his back, head propped on a flour sack. Only his mustached face with its slack jaws showed above his several blankets and torn quilts.

Yakima yawned, scrubbed sleep from his eyes, and, groaning softly against his aches and pains—some sharper, some duller—rose from his blanket roll and dressed quickly in the brittle air. He was still shivering even after he'd pulled his fox fur moccasins on and wrapped a scarf around his neck, pulling it up tight around his ears.

Quickly, he built a fire with trembling hands, first blowing on the tinder then gradually adding kindling, coaxing the flames to life. When he had them leaping, he went outside and scraped snow from a crusty drift into the coffeepot, then set it on the fire.

Barstow hadn't stirred. His deep, regular snores resounded off the cave's rock walls. Yakima had awakened to the logsawing a couple of times during the night, but fatigue and the bone-deep aches and pains had mostly kept him under, and he felt better for the rest.

When he'd warmed himself by the fire, sipping his first cup of coffee, he went out and checked on Wolf and Barstow's mule, both having weathered the night in the sheltered hollow below the cave. Yakima fed the beasts a few handfuls of grain, then went in, fished a pan and his foodstuffs from his saddlebags and war sack, which Barstow had piled on Yakima's side of the fire, and made a breakfast of corn cakes, side pork, and bitter green tea.

He ate with his fingers, dipping chunks of the crumbly cakes in the hot pork fat, while Barstow rolled onto his side away from the fire, smacking his lips and grunting, and continued snoring.

Yakima gave a chuff and shook his head. He glanced at the empty bottles, both lying on their sides. The old honyonker was likely to sleep all day after last night's binge. Yakima considered rousting him, but that wasn't his job. When he'd finished eating, he built up the fire and left a strip of side pork and two corn cakes on the man's plate, and filled his cup with the tea leavings in the pot.

Packing up his gear, Yakima headed out, saddled Wolf, and slapped the rump of Barstow's mule. "Good luck, there, fella. Hope you make it back to the home stable before another storm blows in."

Wolf rippled his withers and snorted, eager to be moving, as Yakima stepped into the saddle. A foot scuff sounded from the cave, and he turned to see Barstow poke his head outside, looking the worse for wear, a torn quilt thrown over his shoulders. The old honyonker looked up at the steely sky then scowled down at Yakima.

"I didn't realize it was mornin'. You shoulda woke me. I got no business sleepin' in like that."

Yakima pinched his hat brim at the man, and reined Wolf away from the cave. "Luck to you, partner."

"Hey," Barstow called. It was more of a rasp. "Why don't we ride together?"

Yakima looked at him.

Barstow hiked a shoulder beneath the quilt. "Since we're headed in the same direction and all. I didn't realize there was this much snow up here—I could use some help with the wagon."

Yakima looked at the wagon with its snow-dusted coffin and jumble of gear including the dead men's tack, a frost-rimed grease bucket, a shovel, and a pick. He looked at the mule who looked back at him over his shoulder.

Yakima's conscience bit him. He had to get to Crow Feather inside of ten days if he was going to apply for the gold guarding job. In spite of the poker money he'd won off Cisco Dervitch, he needed a job. It would be a long winter with nothing to do, and the money wouldn't last forever.

But if Barstow hadn't dug him out of the snow yester-day, he'd be a goner. Of course, the man probably wouldn't have taken any interest in his half-breed ass if Yakima hadn't already saved his own bacon in Crystal Creek, but that was carving the roast a little thin. His candle had been a whole lot closer to being snuffed than Barstow's had.

Truth was, he had no use for the man. But he owed him. And the poor girl in the box had no business out here. Dead she might be—and that was no business of Yakima's—but even a poor, raggedy-heeled whore deserved to be taken home as fast as possible, and buried proper.

Not left out in an old rattletrap wagon by a no-account father who'd have let her be buried on Crystal Creek's boot hill if he hadn't been railroaded by the girl's mother.

Yakima rubbed a gloved hand across his jaw. He thought of the pretty whore he'd loved and married and had in-tended to spend the rest of his life with. Faith had been taken from him too soon, killed by fork-tailed bounty hunters sent by her old pimp, and Yakima would have hated to see her hauled around like a load of seed corn.

"Let's get a move on, then," he grumbled. "We're burnin' daylight here."

Barstow turned and shuffled back into the cave. Yakima waited in brooding silence, watching the light slowly brighten though it looked as though it would be another cloudy day. He didn't have to wait long before Barstow appeared with a toe sack loaded with gear slung over his back. He was nibbling the chunk of side pork as he made his way down the steep shelf from the cave, and tossed his gear into the wagon.

He quickly rigged the mule and hitched it to the tongue then stood near the wagon's left front wheel, scowling at the coffin as he pulled the flaps of his billed cap down over his ears. "Ay, yi, yi—a hell of a place to be, and I wouldn't be here if the girl hadn't left home in the first place. And neither would she."

He clucked, shook his head, and climbed heavily into the driver's box. Yakima reined Wolf out toward the main trail, meandering around snow-dusted rocks, cedars, and junipers. He heard the mule clomping and snorting behind him, giving an occasional obligatory bray as Barstow cursed and spat.

When Yakima made the main trail, dusted with about two inches of fresh feathery down, he glanced back over the fir-covered ridges in the direction of Crystal Creek. He'd left nearly twenty-four hours ago but wasn't more than five miles away, he figured—what with the looping back from the shorter, blocked route followed by his own near demise in the avalanche.

Staring off, he narrowed his eyes slightly. The purple smudges of horse tracks shone in the snow. He dipped his chin and turned his head, following the tracks from far to near as they passed beneath Wolf's belly and continued on up the trail and over the next low, pine-sheathed hill beyond.

Several sets overlaid. Either a single large group or a couple of smaller packs. Could be woodcutters or saddle tramps who'd found themselves in the mountains during a brutally cold December.

Could be gunslicks answering the siren call of rumored loot . . .

Yakima glanced back at Barstow gritting his teeth beneath his brushy mustache and muttering curses at the mule that wasn't any too eager to get moving this cold winter morning, the sunrise still a good half hour away.

Yakima chuffed a curse of his own. He'd be a day or two later than intended getting into Rolette then branching onto the main trail leading north into Wyoming and his destination of Crow Feather. Which meant he'd probably lose out on the gold guarding job and end up swamping hop houses for pennies and pisswater, dragging away the drunks.

He'd done worse. His gold winnings would last him a month or two, anyway.

Hearing the wagon squawk and clatter behind him, the steel-shod wheels, and the mule's hooves crunching snow, he toed Wolf westward along the trail, glancing heavy-browed once more at the tracks of the recent riders.

They weren't a mile from the cave before they ran into trouble.

During the night, a deadfall fir had fallen into the trail. There wasn't room to go around, and with the wagon they couldn't simply pass over it as the riders who'd gone ahead of them had done. Yakima and Barstow had to unhitch the mule and use the beast to pull the fir out of the trail then hitch it back to the wagon.

The maneuver cost them a half hour of grim, silent labor.

They ran into another delay around noon, when the mule couldn't pull the wagon up a low but steep hill that was crusted with ice from a runoff spring. Both men, using a bow saw and an ax from Barstow's wagon, sawed and chopped pine and fir branches from tree trunks and arranged them in two lines, wagon-width apart, along the slope.

After the first cutting and arrangement, they started the wagon up the hill again. It still slipped and slid, fishtailing and kicking the bows out from under the wheels.

The mule loosed several angry brays that were answered by peevish crows flitting about the columnar forest over which the sky hunkered tight as a drumhead.

Yakima and Barstow cut and arranged more bows, and only after they'd tried the hill again and failed and cut some more did the mule finally pull the wagon up and over the crest, the coffin sliding this way and that amongst the gear in the box.

With that obstacle successfully negotiated, Yakima and Barstow built a fire in a little hollow beside the trail, to make coffee and warm themselves. Yakima's toes and fingers were numb, and he couldn't feel his nose.

The end of the day was marked by a gradually darkening of the low clouds, a slow bleeding of tree shadows out from purple trunks, and a drop in temperature marked by a thick coating of ice on Barstow's mustache and a heightened ache inside Yakima's moccasins. His nose now felt as though a giant bee had bit it.

It was time to seek shelter.

The thought had no sooner passed over Yakima's consciousness than Barstow lifted an incoherent grunt behind him and tossed a mittened thumb toward the left side of the trail, toward a gap in the forest.

"Sheepman's shack up thataway," Barstow said after half-rising in his stopped wagon and spatting a thick gob of phlegm over the wagon's left front wheel.

Yakima checked Wolf down and peered into the narrow gap, his breath frosting thickly in the air before his face. The cold was a chill blanket engulfing him. Weathered stone escarpments rose above the treetops beyond the gap, and a slight thinning in the pine forest in that direction indicated a clearing.

If the gap was a trail, no hoofprints marred the crusty snow covering it. He and Barstow had been following the scuffed, uncertain trail of several riders all day—riders who'd been steadily outdistancing them—and the gang or gangs had continued on past the gap.

"Anybody usin' it?" Yakima said, spying no mare's tails of smoke rising from the gap.

Barstow shrugged. "I stopped there a few times, back when I was prospecting these parts. Never did see no one using it. Abandoned most like. Likely cattleman drove the wooly boy out."

Yakima lifted the top of his scarf up above his ears, and tightened the knot. He'd frozen his ears—not to mention all his fingers and toes—enough times over his years of wandering the high country and the northern plains to have developed a keen sensitivity to frostbite.

Old before his time . . .

He grunted at the droll reflection and toed Wolf into the gap. The tree trunks had caught most of the snow, and what had found the trail lay in shallow, icy drifts lightly coated with the dusting that had fallen slowly throughout the day. One good thing about the cold—it held the snow at bay.

As Yakima and Wolf meandered along the narrow gap, Yakima studied the forest to both sides with the habitual caution of a man, a half-breed, who'd grown all too accustomed to danger. No stalkers that he could see, however. The only tracks belonged to rabbits and foraging sparrows and chickadees. A big jackrabbit watched him from atop a deadfall, its heart hammering visibly in its chest and its big ears vibrating, nose twitching. When it had enough study of the unexpected interlopers, it leapt high, wheeled, and bounded off through the snow-crusted slash.

Yakima clomped around a bend in the hidden trail, and the forest opened to both sides. Ahead, at the base of the eroded scarp, the cabin sat under a heavy cloud of churning wood smoke. The smoke sat down close to the shake-shingled roof, under a downdraft.

The wagon rattled up behind him, and he raised a hand. Barstow stopped the mule and stared ahead from beneath his shaggy red brows and the bill of his watch cap.

"Stay here," Yakima told the honyonker. "I'll check it out."

Leaving Barstow and the wagon back near the trees, fifty yards from the cabin, Yakima toed Wolf in a broad arc to the right of the place. A few outbuildings hunkered, sun-silvered, and dilapidated, around the perimeter, as did a lean-to stable and corral to the cabin's right. There were no tracks in the patchy snow of the yard, and Yakima saw no animals in the stable.

The smoke, however, made it plain someone was here. Who? And would they give shelter to strangers?

Only one way to find out.

Lifting the hem of his mackinaw above the butt of his .44, he put Wolf up against the corral's barely attached front pole gate, and dismounted. He gave the reins a toss over an unskinned pine log rail then, looking around carefully once more, tramped through the low, crusty drifts to an icy front stoop propped a foot above the ground by stones.

The cabin, a little larger than a squatter's hut, boasted two windows, one on each side of the door. Both were shuttered, but the one to the door's right wasn't bolted. He pulled it open a few inches and shoved his eye up to the warped, steam-clouded window, squinting into the cabin's murky shadows and quivering pools of fire- and lamplight. He was looking over a roughhewn table, toward a broad, fieldstone hearth in which large flames leaped and danced.

There was something in front of the fire—large and blocky and silhouetted against the orange light. The object moved, and what appeared two large wings sort of flapped and then the pale, cracked moon of a glistening wet rump appeared below a dark mass of what was apparently a blanket.

The person standing in front of the fire—with a round, perfect butt—was bending toward the fire and holding the blanket out away from her body, letting the fire's heat caress her breasts and belly.

"Ah, hell," Yakima said against the tightness in his throat.

Chapter 10

As Yakima's eyes adjusted to the light and shadows within the cabin, as well as the steam-clouded glass, he saw a round, wooden, iron-banded washtub on the floor to the right of the woman's pale right calf. The tub's soapy water glistened in the firelight, as did the backs of the woman's wet legs and rump.

A tightness grew in Yakima's chest to go with the one in his throat. At the same time, chagrin bit him. He was about to pull back away from the window, but then the woman swung around suddenly, facing him, full pale breasts jostling as she scrubbed them with the blanket while tossing her wet, chestnut hair back behind her shoulders.

Self-recrimination flooded Yakima—but not enough to pull his nose away from the warped, steam-clouded window glass when confronted with a nice pair of breasts. As the woman kneaded her own bosoms luxuriously while bathing in the warmth from the massive fire she'd built—Yakima could feel the inviting heat through the window—he felt a primitive tug down deep in his loins.

Suddenly, the woman froze.

A muffled cry sounded and, clumsily drawing the blanket around her shoulders, reached toward a shelf.

Yakima jerked back, shame searing him as hot as any fire. There was the ping of breaking glass, and a sharp thud. Wood slivers from the closed shutter raked Yakima's cheek as a muffled crack sounded inside the cabin.

Yakima pulled back away from the window, automatically raising his hands in supplication. "Sorry," he said not loudly enough to be heard inside the cabin. "I didn't . . . I didn't . . ."

From inside rose the slap of bare feet, and Yakima threw his hands higher as the timbered Z-frame door swung inward and the woman's head appeared through the two-foot opening, her face bunched with exasperation.

"What the *world* are you're doing?" she screamed.

"Ma'am, I'm sorry. I was only—"

Yakima stopped as the woman shoved her bare arm and a brass-plated Colt Navy through the opening. She extended the heavy gun one-handed, squinting as she aimed unsteadily at Yakima.

Yakima shouted, "Don't shoot, lady!" and dove over an empty stock tank standing in front of the porch.

POP!

As Yakima hit the hard snow-crust, the woman's bullet barked into the snow about twenty feet behind Yakima.

"Git!" she screamed. "Git away from here, you damn savage!" She fired again, but this shot was wild, as well, pinging off a rock about ten feet to Yakima's left.

Yakima hunkered low, awaiting the next bullet. When it didn't come, he raised his head slowly, edged an eyeball over the top of the stock tank. The woman remained standing in the door's narrow opening, half-raising the horse pistol that appeared as large a smithy's anvil in her tiny, flour-white hand. Her damp hair hung in a mussed chestnut mass over her right shoulder only partly covered by the gray wool blanket, and fire flashed in her hazel eyes.

"Go on," she ordered, waving the heavy gun toward the wagon at the far edge of the yard, where Barstow stood peering over the back of his mule. "Go on back to where you came from, or I'll shoot both of you lewd miscreants!"

Yakima detected an Eastern accent. A foreigner, this lady. Probably feeling frightened and isolated even before she'd spied his rugged visage ogling her through the window— his broad, Indian-dark face with a nose knobbed from several past breaks, two widely spaced green eyes set deep in weathered socks, and long tangled black hair falling from his flat-brimmed plainsman hat to broad shoulders clad in a smoke-stained mackinaw.

He couldn't blame her for having her neck in a knot, but it wasn't getting any warmer out here and he doubted he and Barstow would find another fire before they both froze up as stiff as the man's dead daughter.

"Just looking to get warm, ma'am. We spied the smoke of your fire, and I just came over to check it out. I didn't mean to spy on you."

"Well, you were spying, weren't you?"

Yakima felt his ear tips warm. He had a feeling he and Barstow were going to be holing up under a pine tonight. "Didn't mean any harm. I see I spooked you pretty good. We'll mosey."

He turned away and started back toward the wagon, keeping his eyes on the woman and the big gun in her hands. There was always a chance she'd get lucky and pink him. She stared after him, shunting her gaze between him and the wagon.

"What's that in the wagon?" she asked. "It looks like a casket."

Yakima stopped. "Barstow's hauling his daughter home from Crystal Creek."

"Daughter?"

"Girl got herself shot."

Yakima started to turn away again, but again the woman's voice stopped him. "Do you men have any food?"

Yakima glanced over his shoulder at the wagon. Barstow was still crouching down behind his mule. Yakima turned back to the woman. "Some cornmeal, beans, and side pork. A little jerky."

"You don't have any tea, do you?"

"Yes, ma'am." Yakima had acquired a taste for green tea after spending a summer laying railroad track with a Shaolin monk from China who'd called himself George because no one in this country could pronounce his actual handle. From George, Yakima had also picked up some useful Eastern fighting techniques.

The woman hesitated, frowning. She let the heavy gun sag lower. "I'll trade you my fire for some food and tea."

Yakima curled his aching toes in his moccasin boots. "Fair enough."

"But you mustn't come in until I've dressed. And you must promise on your honor not to try anything . . . brazen. I have a gun, as you can see, and I'm very good with it."

"I see that, ma'am." Yakima tried to keep a straight face.

"Well, all right, then."

The woman started to close the door. She stopped and looked uncertainly out once more, shifting her troubled gaze from Yakima to Barstow and back again. Pulling the gun in, she closed the door with a click.

* * *

Yakima unsaddled Wolf and turned the horse into the stable, where there were a couple of shocks of relatively fresh hay. Barstow unhitched the mule from the wagon. He left the wagon outside the corral, though a fine snow was beginning to fall from the low, dirty sky, and stabled the mule.

When he and Yakima had finished rubbing down the beasts, graining them, and supplying buckets of water from the well in the yard, they gathered their soogans and possibles, and tramped through the snow to the cabin. Yakima knocked on the front door, stepping back away from it, in case the woman decided to pump a couple rounds through it.

Crisply, she said, "Come in."

Yakima opened the door, stomped snow from his moccasin boots, and stepped inside, Barstow following and pushing the door closed behind them. Yakima looked around the dense, smoky shadows, enjoying the caress of the warm, humid air.

When his eyes had adjusted to the inner dusk, he saw the woman standing on the room's far right side, before a cot and behind her washtub, facing him and Barstow tensely. She wore a long, fur coat with a wide collar—a damned expensive swatch of marten or mink—and her wet hair hung down behind her shoulders. She had her arms crossed inside the coat, but Yakima glimpsed the brass of a gun barrel peeking out from a coat fold.

Yakima leaned his Winchester against the wall by the door. He liked to keep the Yellowboy near to hand, but the rifle wouldn't do much to put the woman at ease. Moving forward, he set his war bag on the table, slung his saddlebags over the back of a slatted chair, and began rummaging around inside.

Barstow stood before the door, studying the woman in hushed silence. The woman looked away from him, and then

Barstow, as though jarred from a doze, set his own bedroll and canvas war bag on the table. He took quick, mincing steps around the table, and turned his back to the fire, shivering.

He removed his mittens, dropped them at his feet, and rubbed his hands together, grunting and sighing and occasionally brushing his frozen mustache with a coat sleeve. He crossed his arms, hunched his shoulders, and shifted his weight from foot to foot, coaxing warmth back into his limbs.

Yakima had fished pots and pans from his saddlebags. Now he took the wooden bucket the woman had apparently used to fill the tarnished copper steamer sitting near the fire, and went outside. He returned a moment later, having filled the bucket with well water, and filled his coffeepot, setting the pot on the fire.

He got busy making a stew of sorts from frozen side pork, frozen beans, and a shriveled frozen potato he found at the bottom of his war bag. As he worked, he couldn't keep his gaze from straying to the woman who stood where she'd stood before, obviously unnerved. She was a beauty with wide, hazel eyes, long lashes, and fine, even facial features, skin smooth as ivory. He remembered how she'd looked naked—heart-twistingly comely, long-legged, full-hipped, with jostling ripe breasts.

She sucked her lower lip as he gaze strayed to Yakima's. He turned away from her suddenly, and she said, "You can add my tomatoes to that, if you'd like."

Yakima followed her gaze to the two tomato tins on the table, near the lamp.

He reached up behind his neck, and slipped his Arkansas toothpick from its sheath—five inches of tempered, razor-edged steel with a brass hilt and leather-wrapped handle.

A sharp gasp sounded.

Yakima looked at the woman. She'd jerked back, her fear-bright eyes on the savage-looking blade.

Yakima raised his free hand, palm out. "Can opener."

The muscles in her face slacked as Yakima jammed the point of the knife into one of the lids, pried it off, and did the same to the other. When he emptied both cans into the stewpot, he placed the pot on the fire in front of which Barstow continued to warm himself. The coffeepot was boiling, so Yakima lifted the pot from the glowing coals, tossed a handful of tea inside, and swirled it.

He filled three cups with the steaming brew, slid one to the far end of the table with a glance at the woman. "Sit down and have a cup of tea. Maybe it'll help you decide we're not here to cut your throat."

The woman studied him, then drew the corners of her mouth down, pulled a chair out from the table, and sat lightly down. She set the gun on the table and slid the steaming cup toward her.

Yakima sat down at the table, leaning forward and wrapping his big, scarred, cherry bronze hands around the cup, facing the fire. "Have some tea, Barstow. Warm your bones."

The honyonker glanced at the tea as though at a diamondback he'd just discovered on the table.

"Go ahead," Yakima said. "Do you good."

As Barstow reluctantly sat down, his bones creaking audibly, keeping his frosty hat pulled low over his brows, Yakima sipped the tea and looked at the woman. "Just you out here? You and two cans of tomatoes?"

Keeping her elbows close to her sides, she lifted her cup in both hands. "Please, no questions."

Yakima snorted, trying to lighten the mood a little. "That wasn't part of the agreement."

The woman sipped her tea.

"Name's Henry," Yakima said. "Yakima Henry. That's Barstow."

She took a dainty sip from the dented, fire-blackened cup, lowered the cup halfway to the table, and said just loudly enough for Yakima to hear above the snapping flames, "Veronica Berryman."

"I didn't see any horse tracks," Yakima said, prodding her further. "You from around here?"

Her cheeks flushed, and she shot a fiery gaze at him. "I told you—no questions!"

She gasped when a loud whinny rose from the stable. Her cup slipped from her fingers. Tea spilled across the table. She grabbed her gun and jerked back in her chair, working desperately to get the hammer cocked.

"Someone's out there!"

Chapter 11

Deputy Sheriff Calvin Miller dropped out of his saddle, stumbled a few feet from his horse, and promptly spewed his breakfast onto a sage shrub. He retched twice more then, raking a handful of crusty snow across his mouth and first-growth mustache and goatee, looked once more at the body of Boyd Shanley hanging from the cottonwood branch.

The front of Shanley's coat was bloody. He'd been shot before he'd been hanged, but he must have been alive when the killers had slapped Shanley's blue roan out from beneath the elder deputy's ass, because he'd kicked out of one of his boots and half out of the other as he'd strangled.

The fallen boot stood upright in a clear patch of ground beneath Shanley, while the other dangled off the dead man's ankle. Miller and Sheriff Duke Dodge had seen Shanley's hat when they'd ridden into the canyon, looking for him when he hadn't showed at the line shack. The weathered Stetson lay atop a small spruce, as though someone had positioned it there. Likely it had just fallen like that when Shanley had been shot out of his saddle, before he'd been dragged—kicking and fighting, judging by the scuffed snow and frozen dirt—over to the aspen, and lynched.

"What the hell'd they do that for?" Young Miller gagged. He thought he was going to vomit again, but there was nothing left in his belly.

"Cause they're kill-crazy sonso'bitches," Duke Dodge said, sitting his horse under the aspen tree, left of Shanley.

The big sheriff held his reins tightly in his left fist; he held his cocked Winchester in his other hand, the butt pressed against his thigh. He showed his teeth as he looked around the small canyon anxiously.

"Calvin, I'm gonna need you to get back on your horse," he growled.

Miller stood slowly, his knees feeling spongy and his stomach aching from the violence of his retch. "Snakehead and Lavoto, you think?"

"Yep."

"Why?"

"Cause they want that loot for themselves." Dodge tore his gaze away from the surrounding, quickly darkening, pine-carpeted ridges to give his young deputy a hard look. "I'm not gonna tell you again, Calvin. Mount up. We're getting out of here. We're sitting ducks in this canyon."

Miller shambled over to his horse and, heart thudding anxiously, still feeling queasy, pulled himself heavily into the leather. "What about Boyd?"

"He's not goin' anywhere. We'll cut him down later."

Calvin squeezed his reins in his mittened right hand as he looked around. He kept thinking he heard bullets screaming toward him, and the pops of rifles. But it was only his own raspy breathing and the hoof thuds of Dodge's horse on the frozen, snow-patchy ground.

"You think they're still around?" he asked the older lawman.

"Don't know." Dodge rode toward the mouth of the canyon through which a darkening flat shone, brushed lightly with the salmon of the setting sun bending through high clouds. "But I aim to find out."

Miller clomped after the sheriff. He glanced back at Shanley—the poor old deputy left hanging there for the crows. Miller felt a tightness in his throat. He wondered what Ginny, Shanley's "old gal," as he'd called her, was going to do now that Shanley was gone. Probably go back to whoring full-time though she'd gotten fat and wrinkly since she and Shanley had thrown in together, cutting wood, drinking ale, and playing poker in Shanley's hut out by Cobre Gulch.

"What the hell, Calvin?" Dodge had stopped his horse suddenly to glare back at Miller. "What are you gonna do if they start cutting down on us—throw snowballs at 'em?"

With a start, Miller reached down below his right thigh and slid his Spencer carbine from his saddle boot. He racked a shell into the chamber and rested the rifle's stock on his thigh, like Dodge was doing with his Winchester. He offered a weak smile at the sheriff still regarding him with disapproval over his right shoulder.

Dodge chuffed, shook his head, and touched spurs to his buckskin, looking around at the scuffed tracks on the ground as he trotted toward the canyon's mouth. Miller, a toxic amalgam of shame and terror setting his heart hammering in his chest like a sledge, gigged his piebald after the sheriff, and prayed that if he and Dodge were to meet up with Snakehead Dawson, Phil Little, and Luis Lavoto, he wouldn't pee his pants or do some other crazy thing to make a complete fool of himself.

He followed Dodge out the canyon mouth and onto the basin beyond, their horses' clomps sounding unusually loud now in the cold dusk. Dodge suddenly brought his buckskin to another halt, and studied the ground, slowly lifting his head to stare westward—the direction he, Shanley, and Miller had been heading before Dodge had ordered Shanley to scout their backtrail.

"Sonso'bitches continued west. Probably followed that streambed yonder, which is why we missed 'em when we were heading back to find Boyd."

Dodge spat and leaned against his rifle. His horse blew. He looked at Miller who rode up abreast of him trying hard to look recovered from his lapse back in the canyon.

"You got yourself shook down, Cal?"

Miller swallowed the sour juice in his throat, and tried to put some steel in his voice. "I'm all right now, Sheriff. Seein' Boyd just hangin' there . . ."

"Shanley was your second dead man, I reckon."

Miller didn't say anything.

"Two in one day," Dodge said, shaking his head. "Let me tell you something." He slitted an eye sagely at the young deputy. "You'll find solace in helping me track his killers and bringing all three to justice."

Miller threw his shoulders back. "Let's get after 'em, Sheriff."

"Tomorrow. Too dark now. Colder'n a witch's tit out here." Dodge spurred his buckskin forward. "We'll hole up for the night at Holcomb's line shack, start tracking those killers again first thing in the morning."

"Suppose Snakehead's holed up at the line shack?"

Dodge chuckled dryly then hardened his jaws. "Wouldn't that be cozy?"

Young Miller trotted his pie up close to Dodge's buckskin as he and the sheriff rode west along the narrow, twisting trace that the stage company tried to keep graded all winter for its coaches.

Miller's back crawled, and the hair under his collar pricked. In his mind, he saw Snakehead's men shadowing him and Dodge through the brittle winter night, planting their rifle sights on their quarry, slowly squeezing their triggers.

No gunshots came as the two lawmen angled off the stage road and into a side canyon then up over a low, rocky pass before drawing rein in a box canyon. Holcomb's line shack was a little dugout with a lean-to stable off its left side. It was fronted by a stack of moldering pine and aspen, mostly unsplit.

There were no horse tracks or sign of any kind that other riders had ridden here ahead of Dodge and Miller. That the place was abandoned was further indicated by a small, low shadow sliding out the shack's open front door to disappear into the sage and rocks right of the place. A coyote or a fox, probably, using the shack as a burrow.

When they'd stabled and tended their horses, Dodge and Miller built a fire inside the shack and sat hunkered down in the broken chairs around the small table, eating jerky and sipping coffee, waiting for the fire to beat the chill from the small, dirt-floored hovel that was rife with the sour, gamey stench of wild animals and mouse droppings.

Holcomb had built a line shack farther up the side of Baldy Butte, abandoning this one to all but those few saddle tramps and prospectors who happened upon it by accident. Dodge had stumbled over the place while elk hunting. As was the custom of the country, someone had left some split wood and kindling beside the sheet-iron stove, and a lone can of beans coated with a quarter inch of grime stood on one of the shack's three food shelves.

Apparently, it had been a year or two since anyone had overnighted here.

When he'd padded and warmed his belly with jerked beef

and coffee, Dodge grabbed his rifle and hat, and tramped outside for a look around. He returned satisfied that he and Miller were alone here in the box canyon. Snakehead and Lavoto must be tracking the buckboard wagon of the dead dove's father.

"Why don't you get some sleep?" he told Miller, tossing his high-crowned Stetson onto the table and dropping an armload of wood beside the ticking stove. "I'll keep the first watch. Wake you in a couple hours."

When Dodge had deemed the canyon clear, Miller had felt the tendrils of apprehension retreat along his spine. He could probably sleep now if he took a few deep breaths and kept his mind off that bean-eater, Lavoto's, flat black eyes and long pale fingers.

He leaned his rifle against a wall and sagged onto the room's single cot. There were no blankets, so Miller hunkered deep inside his coat, rested his head on his saddle, and rolled onto his side, drawing his knees up and facing the log wall through which he could feel the chill of the winter night.

He couldn't sleep. Behind his closed lids he kept seeing Boyd Shanley's slack-jawed face, saw the man's death-glazed eyes staring down at him from under heavy brows, the man's thick, chapped lips stretched back from his lips in a silent scream of agony.

Miller had thought, as his father had, that he'd make a fine deputy. He and his old man had run occasional bronco Utes and rustlers off their leased range south of Juniper Bend. But the down-at-heel reservation jumpers and Mexican long-loopers hadn't wanted a fight—just meat for their stewpots. These men out here in the Sawatch Range were wild as wolves, and, judging from how they'd treated Shanley, just as deadly.

A few times, Miller managed to partly clear his mind and start drifting into dozes only to be jerked out of his slumber by the creak of Dodge's chair or a log dropping in the sheet-iron stove. Dodge went out a few times, and came back, letting in waves of frigid air and smelling like pine smoke and tobacco.

He came in again now, and closed the door with a thud and a rasp of the flimsy latch doctored from leather, wire, and a pin from a water winch.

Miller pretended to be asleep. He didn't want the sheriff to know how afraid he was, how worthless he'd likely be if Snakehead, Little, and Lavoto came calling. Instead of triggering lead at the desperadoes, he'd likely piss himself before they blew both his eyes out the back of his head.

Oh, God. Oh, God . . .

He couldn't help giving a startled grunt when a hand closed over his shoulder. Dodge's deep voice said behind him, "Time to spell me, boy. All quiet so far."

Miller rolled over, dropped his feet to the floor.

"Absolutely. You got it, Sheriff."

He grabbed his rifle and sat in the chair while Dodge eased his heavy frame onto the cot, removing his spectacles, sighing and groaning wearily. "Don't fall asleep, Calvin. Don't wanna get caught flat-footed out here. Not with Snakehead and that pepperbelly out and about. They're likely miles down the trail, but no point in grabbin' the cat by the tail."

"I'm awake, Sheriff."

"Coffeepot's on the stove."

"All right."

In less than a minute, Dodge, lying on his back, fur boots crossed at the ankles and overhanging the end of the cot, was snoring. He had his rifle beside him, his high-crowned hat tipped over his ruddy, gray-mustached face. His glasses were on his chest.

He was sound asleep.

Miller was amazed. His pulse quickened. With Dodge asleep, Miller was on his own. Of course, Dodge would likely awaken at the first sound of trouble, but Miller was now his own and Dodge's first line of defense. He felt as brittle and insubstantial as a single stem of rye grass.

He leaned his rifle against the table then poured himself a cup of scorched java, and eased down in the chair beside the fire, the table angled on his right. Fatigue clawed at him, but the coffee and his jangled nerves kept him awake. So did Dodge's snores. They were spaced about five seconds apart though at times they died for nearly a minute at a time, until Miller was afraid the old lawman had kicked off and left him out here alone.

Likely Snakehead was a far piece from here. Maybe even running down that whore's father at this very moment. But Dodge had every intention of catching up with the man now that he'd murdered Boyd Shanley . . .

An hour passed. Miller got up and stretched a few times, peeked out the two frosty windows, went and stood outside for a few minutes, looking around and listening. He'd just gotten seated before the fire again when one of the horses in the stable whinnied.

Cold blood jetted through young Miller's temples. His chair creaked as his body tensed and he swung around and grabbed his Spencer. Dodge jerked his arms tight against his sides and his snoring faltered. Miller hoped the sheriff would wake up, but he only snorted, muttered, "A little lower there, Doreen. There . . . that's it . . ."

The sheriff let a sly grin slide beneath his trimmed gray mustache then settled back into his raucous slumber.

Miller stood and looked down at Dodge. He opened his mouth to speak to the man, but closed it.

No. He'd look the fool if he woke Dodge and it turned out the horse had only whinnied at a mouse or a bat. Miller was on watch. It was his job to check it out. In the unlikely event the horse had been frightened by Snakehead's men stalking the cabin, Miller would give a yell or fire a shot.

That was his job. He was a deputy, not some wet-behind-the-ears kid tagging along with the sheriff just for kicks and giggles.

Quietly, keeping his ears pricked, he donned his funnel-brimmed Stetson with the snakeskin band he'd tanned himself, and tied it to his head with his scarf. He picked up his rifle, glanced at the deeply snoring Dodge once more, watching the man's lips flutter, then quietly opened the door, peeked out, and then stepped on out into the frosty night.

So quiet he imagined he could hear the stars crackling high over the rocky, pine-studded ridges silhouetted against the sky. Patches of snow glowed in the darkness. One of the horses blew in the stable, and after a moment of looking around and listening for sounds of men walking toward him, he moved over to the stable doors. He shoved an ear against the weather-silvered wood.

Silence.

One of the horses huffed and shifted a hoof. From far away came the lonely hoot of an owl.

Slowly, Miller lifted the wooden bar from its iron brackets, and went inside the stable. He looked around carefully, finding nothing out of the ordinary. Both horses stood eyeing him obliquely. He wished they could tell him what one had started at.

Probably a rat. Maybe the owl had been winging around

the stable hunting mice. Horses were afraid of owls for some reason.

Miller went back outside. He was feeling better, lighter, more confident, but only because it looked as though the only two men in this canyon and probably within five square miles of it were himself and Dodge, whose snores he could hear even out here.

To prove to himself that he wasn't a complete coward, he walked a ways toward the mouth of the canyon. The rocky ridges around him were quiet. Occasionally snow sifted from an overburdened branch, twinkling in the starlight, and there was the faint cry of a night bird in the far escarpments. The air was stitched intermittently with the smell of pine smoke from the cabin.

Miller stopped.

Nothing untoward out here. He heaved a relieved sigh and headed back to the shack, his job done, his duty fulfilled. Fear no longer weighed like a yoke on his shoulders and water in his knees. He was proud of himself. He hadn't whimpered like a lost child and awakened the sheriff when the horse had whinnied.

He felt a grin lift his mouth corners. He kicked a rock across a hard, flat drift and lifted his boots high, setting his rifle barrel on his right shoulder as he headed toward the shack and stable hunched low against the back wall of the canyon, gray smoke skeining from the chimney pipe.

He lowered the rifle when he gained the cabin, and flipped the latch. He pushed the door open and stepped inside.

The candle burned low on the table, and firelight shone through the cracks around the stove door. Warm air pushed against him like the body of a sumptuous whore.

Whores.

Damn, it was going to feel good to get back to Juniper Bend and visit the Atlas for a night of sporting with Miss Carlotta's girls.

He leaned his rifle against the table and, untying the scarf knotted under his chin, looked at Dodge. The sheriff lay on the cot as before, chin dipped to his chest, fur hat over his eyes. Only he wasn't snoring. The glow from the stove's door cracks spread umber light across his right shoulder and the side of his hat.

Miller kept his gaze on Dodge as he dropped his scarf on the table and unbuttoned his coat collar. The apprehension he'd thought he'd exterminated was back, prodding his shoulder blades and nipping at his belly.

Dodge's chest wasn't moving.

Shit, the old boy hadn't kicked off, had he? Had a blowout in his brain or a heart stroke?

Miller stared down at the sheriff. He couldn't hear the man breathing. He looked like a statue lying there against Miller's saddle.

The young deputy whispered, "Dodge?"

Silence. The stove ticked.

"Dodge? You all right, Sheriff?"

Miller's heart swelled.

He leaned down, placed his right hand on Dodge's chest, and was about to call the man's name again, but stopped when he detected a warm slickness on his fingers. Looking close, he saw a large, dark stain on Dodge's quilted leather coat.

Miller lifted his fingers, rubbed them together. Heart thudding like a locomotive piston, he grabbed the candle off the table, and lowered it to about eight inches above the sheriff's chest.

The flickering yellow light shone on the rich red of fresh

blood. Miller's lower jaw dropped as he lifted his eyes toward Dodge's face and discovered the long, dark slash across the sheriff's neck.

"*Dodge!*" he heard himself scream as he stumbled back into the table.

Behind him, someone laughed. He turned to see the tall, black-hatted Mexican gunman, Luis Lavoto, standing on the other side of the door, leaning one shoulder against the wall behind it.

The killer held a bloody knife down by his thigh. He had the thumb of his other hand hooked behind his cartridge belt, near his deerskin, sheepskin-lined mittens wedged behind the belt. He laughed again, showing fanglike eyeteeth as he rocked his head back on his shoulders.

"Fool didn't even open his eyes," he said, chuckling through his teeth, "until I cut his throat."

Miller stared, lower jaw hanging to his chest.

Fury and terror hammered through him. He didn't know how he managed it—maybe it was seeing that the Mexican held only the knife, and that his six-shooters were still holstered, or maybe it was an unknown bravery rearing its beautiful head—but he found himself jerking his own walnut-gripped Remington from the soft leather holster on his left hip.

He was raising the gun, thumbing back the hammer, and screaming above the horrific tolling in his ears, when suddenly Lavoto had his own long-barreled revolver in his fine, pale hand thinly carpeted with sleek, black hairs.

Miller grunted, shocked to witness a move like that—so fast it couldn't be seen. But he had only a quarter-second to dread the end before Lavoto's gun roared, sprouting smoke and flames.

At nearly the same time, the door to Lavoto's right opened,

and Snakehead Dawson appeared, looking grim inside the blanket framing his face and letting a curl of hair drip down over his forehead. Miller was stumbling back into Dodge so he only glimpsed the Peacemaker in Snakehead's right hand before it, too, drove a .45-caliber chunk of hot lead through his heart.

Miller hit Dodge and the cot, rolled, and crumpled up on the floor, his young, loose limbs jerking with death spasms.

In the cabin around him, silence. The stove crackled and chuffed.

A floorboard creaked as Lavoto moved up to stand beside Snakehead Dawson, both men looking without expression at the two dead lawmen.

Snakehead sighed and slipped his smoke Colt into its holster. "Cold one tonight."

Lavoto nodded and holstered his pearl-gripped Colt. "Si."

Chapter 12

"Hold on, damnit." Yakima rose from his chair and clamped his big paw on the old-model Colt in Veronica Berryman's small, fine-boned hand.

She gave an indignant cry as, closing his hand tightly over the uncocked hammer, he jerked the gun from her grip. He stood, straddling his chair, and flicked the revolver's loading gate open.

"I've had enough of this hogleg." He raised the gun and spun the cylinder, and the cartridges tumbled onto the table, clinking and rolling. "You're liable to kill somebody."

"That's mine!"

"Where'd you get this thing?" He held up the old Colt conversion that was tarnished and rusty, its hammer loose and its action fouled with grit.

"None of your business. It's mine, damn you!" She said "damn" like she'd said it maybe twice before.

Yakima pocketed the cartridges, stuffed them into his pants pocket, and slammed the gun on the table before Veronica Berryman. "Take it. But quit trying to use it until you've learned how and you have something that needs shootin' at."

She opened her mouth for a saucy retort but closed it when another shrill whinny rose from the stable. She turned her head toward the window behind Yakima, raising her hand to her chest.

"There's someone out there, you idiot. And now you've gone and rendered me defenseless!"

Barstow had moved in his quiet, skulking way to the window, looking out. Now Yakima did as well. Barstow looked at him, apprehension in the honyonker's eyes.

"I'll check it out. Stay with the woman."

Yakima buttoned his coat, grabbed the Yellowboy, racked a cartridge into the chamber, and went out, quickly closing the door behind him to keep the heat in and to prevent himself from being outlined against it. He stepped to the left, putting the dark cabin behind him, and looked around.

He felt the gentle pelts of a slow, steady snowfall. The sky was murky. A few patches of near snowdrifts glowed in the wash of light from the window. He could smell the pine smoke. The only sounds were the gentle rustle of a slight breeze and the ticks of the snow against his hat.

Holding the rifle in one hand, he moved past the window, dropped off the porch, and, looking around and listening, tramped over to the corral. Except for his and Barstow's, he saw no human foot or horse tracks. He lifted the looped baling wire holding the rickety gate snug against a corral post, drew the gate open, and went into the stable.

He found Wolf and the mule as he'd left them. They seemed jittery, tense, and Wolf rippled his withers anxiously as Yakima ran his hand down the stallion's fine neck. The half-breed frowned, puzzled. He lit a lamp and investigated every corner of the stable. There was no one here, no sign that anyone had been here.

Yakima blew out the lamp and went back outside, closed the gate, and latched it with the baling wire. He took a deep, heady drag of the chill air then tramped lightly around behind the stable. He'd just turned the rear corner when a snarl sounded. The half-breed ducked as a gray blur of movement appeared ahead and above him, careening toward him from the low, gnarled fir growing up from a jumble of cracked boulders near a snow-dusted trash pile.

Yakima detected the sweet, wild fetor and then, dropping to his knees and twisting around, raised the Yellowboy to his shoulder. He saw the bobcat land just behind him with another, louder snarl and lunge away in its long, gliding stride through the rocks and boulders—a gray streak quickly diminishing in the darkness.

Yakima could have shot the beast, but stayed his finger on the Winchester's trigger. If the cat had been hunting him, he'd be on his back with the painter's fangs tearing his throat out. Likely the fir was its customary perch as it hunted rabbits and coyotes, and Yakima was the intruder here. The horses were safe in the stable.

Likely the cat wouldn't be back until the human guests of the shack were gone.

Yakima walked around the back of the shack and paused outside the front door, taking another look around. He turned and pushed the cabin door open. Barstow and Veronica Berryman were standing slightly crouched at the window. They turned toward Yakima as he closed the door and leaned his rifle against the table.

"Did you see anything out there?" the woman asked. Her face was pale and she clenched her empty hands in front of her belly. Her pistol was on the table.

"Just a cat."

"Painter?" Barstow grunted. "After our animals?"

"Maybe, but he's gone now." Yakima glanced at the woman who continued to regard him worriedly. "All quiet."

"Are you sure?"

It was warm in the cabin, and still humid. Yakima shucked out of his coat and draped it across the back of the chair by the window. As he moved around the table to the boiling stewpot, he kept his frowning eyes on the woman.

"What's got your neck hair up, Mrs. Berryman? Who you expecting?"

"No one," she said too quickly. Lowering her voice and sweeping a glance across the window once more, she strolled over to her chair by the fire. "I'm a woman alone in the wilderness. Isn't it understandable that I'd be cautious?"

Yakima kept his eyes on her as he sipped the stew broth. Her cheeks were mottled red. Cautious, sure. Bald-assed scared, no.

"Grub's done."

Yakima grabbed a leather swatch from the hearth and used it to pluck the pot from the fire and set it on the table. He dug some tin plates out of his saddlebags, and quickly slopped a portion of the smoking stew onto each.

The three sat at the table and ate in silence. Yakima was so famished that he rarely lifted his gaze from his plate. A couple of times when he did he glimpsed the woman's frightened eyes on him. She didn't eat as fast as Yakima and Barstow, who shoveled it in as fast as he could chew, grunting and groaning like a half-starved cur, his rickety chair creaking beneath him, but she was obviously hungry.

She flushed slightly as though embarrassed by it.

Yakima wondered how long it had been since her last meal. Puzzling, to find such a lady out here. And a frightened one at that. If she wasn't a society child from back

East somewhere—not that he'd known that many—he'd be a foal's mare.

Miss Berryman didn't finish eating until Yakima had gone out for more firewood and Barstow had wordlessly taken his and Yakima's plate outside to scrub them with snow. As he arranged the wood in front of the hearth, she rose from her chair in her stiff, uncomfortable way, and carried her plate with her cup and fork on it toward the door.

Barstow walked in just then, brushed her with his cow eyes that rarely told what the man was thinking, if anything, and stomped past her toward the table.

"Barstow," Yakima said.

The honyonker set the clean tins on the table, and returned the half-breed's look.

"Why don't you clean the lady's plate for her?"

Barstow's eyes acquired an annoyed cast.

Before he could say anything, Yakima said, "You gonna send her outside?"

Barstow chuffed, swung around, grabbed the woman's plate, and stomped outside.

"Thank you," she said when Barstow had closed the door.

Yakima shrugged, his back to her, as he banked the fire.

"You're a good cook, Mr. Henry."

Yakima kept his back to her. She was a damn good-looking woman but not one he was going to cozy up to tonight or any other night. Not that he wouldn't approve, especially on such a cold night. But there was no point in getting himself worked up.

He could tell she was waiting for a response, and when she didn't get one, she walked over to the room's single cot. "I'd like to turn in. May I take the bed?"

"First come, first served."

Yakima used a stick to poke the logs around then sat at

the table, plucked a quirley he'd already rolled from his shirt pocket, and lit it with the stick's glowing end. He drew deep and blew smoke at the fire. In the periphery of his vision, he saw the woman sit on the bed's edge, her eyes on him.

"You're half-Indian, aren't you?"

Yakima gave a wry chuff.

"That's all right," she said quickly, uncertainly. "I . . . I mean . . . I don't mind. Maybe a year ago I'd take umbrage, but I've been out here nine months now, and I've seen. . . ."

She let her voice trail off.

"You've seen your share of savages?"

"I didn't say that."

"I saved you the trouble, but I take no offense, Miss Berryman." His elbows on the table, he held the quirley in front of him, and swung his head toward her. "Or is it Mrs. Berryman?"

She looked down at her hands, frowning, flushing again. She parted her rich, full lips, and it seemed for a time she was going to say something but then closed her mouth and lifted her eyes to his, switching her thoughts.

"May I ride with you tomorrow?"

She paused. Faint beseeching sparked in her wide, hazel, firelit eyes. "My horse died out from under me about two miles away. I had to walk here and, as you can see, I have few provisions. You can drop me at the first village," she added quickly. "I'll buy a horse there and continue on my own."

"Continue where?"

Lines of incredulity stretched across her otherwise smooth forehead. "Are you in the habit of grilling people about their personal affairs, Mr. Henry?"

"Nope." Yakima shook his head. "But I am in the habit of

bein' curious, Miss Berryman. Especially about good-looking women in fancy fur coats stranded alone in the Rockies."

The door barked open behind Yakima. He reached for his Colt but stayed the movement when Barstow walked in with the plate. He'd likely been taking his ablutions, or checking on his mule and wagon.

Now he tossed the woman's plate on the table and doffed his hat. His thick shock of dark-red hair was matted down close to his skull. A sun line stretched across the top of his forehead above his broad, pitted nose. He brushed the ice from his soup-strainer mustache as he glanced over at the woman sitting at the edge of the bed. With an oblique grunt, he knelt to spread his blanket roll on the floor in front of the fire.

Yakima looked at Veronica Berryman. She met his gaze once more then slowly lay back on the bed, lifting her feet clad in fancy fur boots with high heels from the floor. She crossed her wrists on her stomach, and gave a ragged sigh.

Barstow worked himself down to the floor with much grunting and wheezing, and hauled out one of his bottles. He took a long pull then, offering Yakima none, set the bottle beside the food pouch he used for a pillow, yawned big, and closed his eyes.

"Cold one tonight," he said, smacking his lips.

Yakima took the last drag from his quirley and flicked it across the table into the fire. "Yep."

Chapter 13

Yakima slept with his back to the wall beside the door. Better to hear what was going on outside, and the cabin was plenty warm after his expert banking.

Twice he got up and walked around the cabin and stable. The woman was obviously expecting someone, but he would have gone out on the scout even if his and her paths hadn't crossed. It was in his nature, fortified by experience, to always expect trouble.

None showed itself, and when he woke at dawn, he flung his wool blanket aside, got up, stretched, and looked around the shadowy cabin lit by a milky window wash and the fire's dull umber glow. Barstow wasn't snoring but only breathing loudly with his mouth open. The woman lay curled on the bed, facing the room in a tight ball, her rich chestnut hair sprayed across her shoulders and screening her face. He could see her pink lips through it, swollen with slumber.

Loneliness like the sharp point of a bayonet blade poked at Yakima's knees. He remembered waking mornings in his Arizona mountain cabin, and rolling over and spooning his body against Faith's. Remembered her warmth and her suppleness on those cool mountain dawns, the caress of her legs against his thighs, how full and ripe her breasts felt in his hands as he gently ran his thumbs across her nipples.

Miss Berryman must have sensed his gaze. She stirred, opened her eyes. As she looked across the room toward Yakima, blinking and shoving her hair from her face and back over her head, he went over and stoked the fire. When he had it going good, he lightly kicked the still-sleeping Barstow awake, and got a pot of coffee chugging and sighing.

The three had a quick breakfast of corn cakes and leftover side pork, and then Barstow went out and hitched the mule to the wagon while Yakima fed and watered Wolf and saddled him. Ten minutes later, Barstow pulled the wagon out of the corral and stopped. Yakima had told him they had a passenger, and the two men waited there, Yakima on his black stallion, Barstow in the wagon, waiting and watching the cabin for the woman. Smoke continued to trickle from the broad stone hearth, feathering against the clear, soft-green morning sky.

Wolf gave a bugling whinny.

Yakima looked across the clearing toward the gap in the pine forest through which the trail curled. Four men rode through the gap, heading toward the cabin—bulky figures in heavy coats on horseback.

Steam jetted around theirs and their horses' heads. One man rode slightly ahead of the other three—a big bear of a man with a thick beard showing between the loose earflaps of his heavy wool cap. His stout legs, thick as grain sacks, were clad in heavy, patched dungarees, the cuffs of which were stuffed inside coyote-fur boots with drooping mule ears. From one of the boots the handle of a big knife jutted.

The cabin door rasped open. Yakima turned toward it.

Miss Berryman poked her head out, saw the four approaching riders, gasped, pulled her head back into the cabin, and quickly but gently closed the door.

As the four men came closer—none holding weapons though rifles jutted from saddle scabbards—Yakima held Wolf steady and said to Barstow out the side of his mouth, "I'll do the talking."

Barstow said nothing, only watched the newcomers with his dull, eternally perplexed expression.

As the four riders clomped toward the wagon, Yakima kept his right hand free and splayed across his thigh, within six inches of the horn-gripped .44 jutting above his tucked-back mackinaw flap. He said nothing as the four men, spreading out in a line before him, drew back on their mounts' reins. The big man was the oldest, and though it was hard to see much of their features concealed by their bulky cold-weather gear, he thought a couple of the younger riders owned a familial resemblance to the older one.

The older man regarded Cuno skeptically for a moment, taking in the gun jutting on the half-breed's hip. He raked his gaze across the casket in the wagon box and then across Barstow sitting the driver's seat, reins in his hands, elbows on his hips.

The old man returned his gaze to Yakima. He spoke in a deep but also faintly nasal baritone. "Mornin'."

Yakima nodded.

"Who's in the casket?" The older man, broad-faced under his shaggy beard, with deep-set eyes, spoke with authority in his deep, nasal baritone. He was a man used to giving orders and having them obeyed, and getting answers to impertinent questions.

Yakima curled a corner of his mouth as he said, "Don't see as how that's any of your business."

The man gave Yakima a hard look, as did the younger

men to either side of him. He seemed then to realize his usual hardnosed methods wouldn't work here, and he slackened his jaws. His mouth stretched a wry, faintly sheepish grin.

"Name's Fallon. Wilbur Fallon. These are my sons." Tossing his head toward the single rider on his right—a lean man, slightly older than Fallon's sons and with a brushy mustache and steel blue eyes under a snuff-brown Stetson—Fallon added: "This is Glen Plaza, my segundo. I own the T-Bar Cross down by Sapinero."

He pressed his lips together, impressed with himself in spite of his horse suddenly lifting its tail to plop apples onto the hard ground behind him.

Yakima told the man his name. "This is Barstow."

"You overnighted here, did you?" Fallon glanced at the cabin suspiciously.

"Why?"

Fallon's eyes flared again, and his chest rose. He took a moment to get his temper on a leash. "I'm wondering if you might have seen a woman out here. Alone. Pretty gal. Dark hair. Name's *Missus* Fallon, Mrs. Veronica Fallon. Was married to my oldest son"—his nostrils flared, and his ruddy cheeks flushed crimson—"until she murdered him."

Yakima thought he heard the muffled clomp of a heel in the cabin behind him. He kept his eyes on Fallon. "No one out here but Barstow and me. If we see the gal, though, we'll be sure to tell her you're lookin' for her."

Fallon looked around the canyon, as though he might see his quarry on one of the ridges. "We found her horse a couple miles up Sandy Wash. Blown out. Run to death. She probably froze to death soon after. A fragile thing from back East, never did take to this country. Or my son . . ."

"Reckon we oughta backtrack, Pa?" the younker sitting

a piebald to Fallon's far left inquired. He had a dumb, mean look sharpened by one wandering eye. "She's probably froze up in a drift somewhere in the woods."

"I hope she ain't," said the other Fallon offspring, a sharp-eyed younker with a scar on his chin. He ran a patched buckskin mitten across his snotty nose. "I wanna haul that bitch home and give her a proper hangin' in front o' Ma."

"It doesn't look good, boys. Not good at all, cold as it is." Fallon looked at Yakima, and gave an evil grin. "You see, Frank's mother simply will not rest until she's seen that uppity bitch hanging from one of our cottonwoods back to the home place. She never did take to the girl, just like the girl never took to Frank. Thought she was too good for him."

With that, Fallon spat and neck-reined his horse around. "Come on, boys."

The segundo, Plaza, stared hard at Yakima. "Maybe we oughta check the cabin, Mr. Fallon."

Fallon looked over his shoulder. "Why—you think he's lying?"

"Frank's wife's mighty pretty, Mr. Fallon."

Yakima hardened his jaws. "You don't know me well enough to call me a liar, Plaza. Maybe you better back water."

Both Plaza and Fallon looked at Yakima's gloved right hand resting palm down across his thigh, then at the horn-handled Colt jutting from his holster.

"Hold up, Glen," Fallon said. "We're here to find my son's killer, not start swapping lead with Indians dressed up as white men." The rancher glanced at Barstow. "You have an honest face, mister. Is the girl in the cabin?"

Barstow's shoulders tensed slightly. He glanced at Yakima. Yakima held the look, hard-jawed, his eyes flat.

Finally, Barstow turned back to Fallon, gave an unctuous shrug. "I seen no one else in there."

"Good enough." Fallon glanced at Plaza. "Come on, Glen."

He booted his horse into a trot back the way he'd come, and the others followed him. The segundo, Plaza, held his steely, suspicious gaze on Yakima until he and the others disappeared into the dark evergreens.

"Ay, yi, yi," Barstow clucked, staring after the riders.

Yakima swung his gaze toward the silent cabin. He sighed, stepped down from Wolf's back, and threw open the cabin's front door. The woman stood just inside, holding a chunk of stove wood in both hands in front of her, letting the club slag slowly toward the floor.

"Well, well, if it ain't Mrs. Fallon."

"It's Berryman," she said, cold fear trickling out of her eyes. "I'll never use the Fallon name again as long as I live!"

"That'd prob'ly be wise."

"You didn't tell him I was here."

"Maybe you're too pretty to hang," Yakima said, setting a hand on the door frame and leaning into it. "Or maybe I wanted to hear your side of it."

"I had no choice," Veronica Berryman Fallon said. "Frank Fallon was a brute! He came back to the ranch drunk after a three-day bender, and as belligerent as any teased bull. He had lip paint on his face and whiskey on his breath. I was tired of being pushed around, hit . . . forced to succumb to his goatish need."

Tears glazed her eyes, her upper lip quivered, and her voice shook. "When he chased me upstairs, I pulled an old gun out of the dresser. I warned him not to come near me. He laughed and lunged for me, and I shot him."

"You tell the old man that?"

"Does he look like the kind of man you can tell anything?" She leaned forward, digging her fingers into her thick mink hat on the table. Her hand shook. "I dressed as quickly as I could, gathering only a few things from the pantry. Then I ran out and saddled a horse. I was afraid someone had heard the shot—our cabin was just back of Mr. and Mrs. Fallon's house.

"No one must have heard, however, because I never did see anyone on my trail. I knew he'd come, though. Mr. Fallon. And I knew what he'd do once he found me . . . to placate Frank's hateful, tobacco-chewing old mother if for no other reason. She and Frank were cut from the same evil cloth."

Her knees buckled and she slumped forward against the table, her face crumpling. "Oh, I never should have come out here! Please, help me, Mr. Henry! Please help me get home!"

She dropped farther, barely holding herself up by the edge of the table. Yakima cursed and strode over to her, wrapped an arm around her waist, and pulled her up gently despite his impatience. At this rate, and with this many obstacles in his trail, he wouldn't make it to Crow Feather until spring.

"Can you stand?"

She sobbed uncontrollably, tears streaming down her face, a dam of pent-up terror and anxiety finally breaking.

Yakima cursed again and, bending, swept her up in his arms. "Grab your hat." He had to tell her twice before she threw her hand out to snatch her hat off the table. When she had it, and held it to her bosom, sobbing, he carried her out through the cabin's open door and set her up in the wagon beside Barstow.

The honyonker regarded her apprehensively, like she was some creature that had dropped down from the moon.

She continued to sob, bowing her head, her hands clutching the hat in her lap. The morning breeze jostled her long hair.

"Put your hat on," Yakima ordered.

"Why?" she cried. "Why did I come *out here*?"

"Put your hat on."

Crying, she pulled the fur hat down over her head, snugging it over her ears.

Yakima looked at Barstow. "Let's get outta here."

"What about that Fallon fella?"

Yakima stepped into his saddle and took up his reins. "What about him?"

"He ain't gonna like this."

"Can't say as I like it."

Yakima booted Wolf across the canyon, toward the pine forest dappled lemon with morning sunshine.

Chapter 14

Yakima kept an eye out for trailing riders hunting either Barstow or Veronica Berryman throughout the sunny mountain morning. They were up high, but the trail was relatively level, meandering through snowy beaver meadows and generally following the narrow valley of the West Fork of the Ute River.

The sky was broad and blue, the sun brassy and warm, painting the pine forest a deep, hazy green.

They passed a few prospector shacks and a small, remote ranch headquarters lamenting a single cabin, barn, and a horse corral of unskinned pine poles. Otherwise, it was a quiet ride, the only sounds the clomping of Wolf's hooves on the graded trail and the thudding, squawking of the wagon, with an occasional slam when Barstow hit a chuckhole and his daughter's coffin jounced and bucked on the wagon bed.

The sun was nearly straight-up when Barstow stopped the wagon suddenly. Yakima, riding ahead after scouting behind, halted Wolf and glanced along their backtrail.

"Break," was all the honyonker said, rummaging around in one of his tow sacks under the wagon seat.

A few seconds later he leaped off the wagon and, holding a handful of pages torn from a Sears & Roebuck catalog, shuffled off into a copse of pines and leafless aspens along the frozen river.

Yakima circled the wagon, inspecting the wheels for loose rims or cracked felloes. He rode up the side Miss Berryman was on, leaning out to inspect the undercarriage. The woman had removed her hat to soak up the sunshine. She leaned forward, running her hands through her long hair glistening in the golden light, then tossed her head back, letting the cinnamon tresses tumble across her shoulders.

Smoothing it down with her unmittened hands, she glanced at Yakima. "How did the girl die?"

Yakima looked at the coffin. The snow that had dusted it the night before had melted in the sunshine, leaving it moisture-stained. It sat at a slant amidst the sundry freight in the wagon bed, a shovel leaning against one side.

"She was shot."

Miss Berryman had hipped around in her seat to stare at the crude pine box. She frowned and switched her gaze to Yakima. "An unsatisfied customer?"

"A member of her beau's outlaw gang. Thought she knew the whereabouts of a secret stash of stolen loot."

Miss Berryman arched a brow. "Did she?"

"Couldn't tell you."

Her eyes acquired a pensive cast as she studied the coffin. "What a savage place this is."

Yakima put Wolf up beside the wagon, glanced at the copse in which Barstow had disappeared. No sign of the man, likely hunkered down to serious business.

"Where you from . . . if it isn't too personal?"

She swung her gaze from the coffin to Yakima. "New Jersey."

"How'd you end up marryin' into the family of Wilbur Fallon?"

She swung her head forward, rested her hands on the fur hat in her lap. "I . . . answered a newspaper ad. A man wanted a wife. I needed a husband. My father lost his business and his fortune due to the troubled times nettling nearly everyone back East, and hanged himself."

A tear trickled out from her right eye. She brushed it away and offered a brave smile. "We were destitute. I'd been going to school to become a teacher, but there was suddenly no more money. No money at all. Only paralyzing debt. You wouldn't think a family could be kicked out of their house, the only house most of them had ever known, only a day after they'd laid their poor, beloved father to rest. But they could."

"Seems to me you might have been better off with a man from your own neck of the woods."

"Oh, no." She shook her head, frowning. "Such misfortune, Mr. Henry, might seem to warrant sympathy. And it does warrant some sympathy, or pity, but mostly it's met with disapproval. Revulsion might be a more accurate term. Suddenly, everyone my family knew—had known for years—treated us as though we'd all contracted some horrible, contagious disease.

"No man within a hundred square miles would have anything to do with me or my sisters. Any man aside from dockhands or hod carriers, I mean. That's when I, perusing the *New York Times* and stumbled upon the ad placed there by Mr. Fallon for his son, wasted no time in answering. What a wonderful place to start fresh with a rugged, earthy man of the West! A western rancher, no less! 'A strapping, well-brought-up young man with a strong work ethic and iron-clad morals.' I'm quoting. Mr. Fallon's attorney must have written the ad—a man who missed his calling as a fiction writer."

"A little too rugged and earthy, was he?"

"Ha!" Miss Berryman clutched her arms as though suddenly chilled. "A drunken scoundrel. Spent most of his time drinking and gambling in the bunkhouse with his men. Threatened to chain me—yes, *chain* me—to the kitchen range while he traipsed off with his men to town every Friday night to fight and frolic with painted women, not to return until Monday morning! Not that I minded his absence, after we'd become acquainted . . ."

Yakima looked around. "Yeah, well, you've grabbed the puma by the tail, Miss Berryman. If Fallon doesn't run you down, he'll likely send bounty hunters. I can kinda tell when a man's serious, and Fallon looks serious." With an angry burn, Yakima remembered Bill Thornton, the pimp and roadhouse manager who'd sent bounty hunters after Faith. Eventually, they'd caught up to her, nabbed her from Yakima, and, while he'd tracked them, he'd been too damn late to save her . . .

"You won't let them take me, will you, Mr. Henry?"

He was staring off at a distant ridge. Her voice broke the reverie, and he turned to see her regarding him with pleading in her wide, hazel eyes.

"Let's just get you to the next town and get you on your way back East or wherever the hell you intend to go."

"I don't care where I go, as long as it's far away from Fallon. I'll go to Denver and get a job waiting tables in a restaurant, if it comes to that." Her voice dropped an octave, and her cinnamon brows furled. "And it very likely will."

Yakima jerked an annoyed look toward the river, and was glad to see Barstow tramping toward the wagon minus his handful of paper.

"Let's go!" Yakima called, beckoning. "I'd like to make Louisville before Christmas!"

Barstow threw up an arm but did not hurry his gait.

Louisville was the next village along the trail.

Yakima turned to Miss Berryman. She stared at him sympathetically. He'd been about to speak, but he closed his mouth.

"We're a burden to you, aren't we, Mr. Henry? I and Mr. Barstow."

He wasn't sure why, but her understanding gave him a guilt pang. He stared at her, saw the pain and fear in her eyes. What was one lost gold-guarding job compared with what she'd been through, and to what she probably had ahead of her?

"Ah, hell," he grumbled. "Tell Barstow to get moving. I'm gonna ride back and see if we got any shadowers."

He booted Wolf up the trail and into a lope. He glanced over his shoulder. She was watching him.

Glen Plaza said, "I told you we oughta checked the shack, Mr. Fallon."

"What is it?"

"It's her."

"Let me see."

Plaza handed the field glasses to Wilbur Fallon as they and Fallon's sons, James and Erroll, sat their horses just inside the pine forest at the base of a steep, shaded ridge. Fallon raised the glasses to his eyes and adjusted the focus.

The wagon heading up the trail nearly a mile ahead and on the other side of the Ute River fork swam into focus—

little larger than Fallon's thumb from this distance. There were two people in the box, their backs to Fallon. One was long-haired, and she wore a fur coat like the one he'd seen Frank's wife wearing around the ranch.

He couldn't see her face, but who else could it be? She'd found herself a couple of guard dogs—servants like the ones she'd obviously been accustomed to back where she'd come from. Big mistake, looking East for a woman for Frank. But no girl around here would marry him, and Fallon had thought that a woman with a little learning and big-city culture might soften the firebrand's thunder.

Instead, she couldn't cook and was afraid of dust and Mrs. Fallon, and abhorred Frank from the moment she'd laid eyes on him. Of course, it hadn't helped that Frank had been drunk when they'd met. But if she'd given the boy a chance, they might have ridden the river, and Fallon would have gotten some right sturdy grandchildren out of the deal. The girl might not have known her way around a ranch kitchen, but she came from good stock, Fallon could tell. She and Frank would have turned out a passel of whelps to put color in a grandfather's cheeks.

Instead, she'd shot him. Fallon's oldest. His toughest. The one most likely to keep the ranch going after Fallon was gone. The other two, James and Erroll, were too much like Fallon's brothers who'd amounted to nothing more than drunkards, sharpies, and hustlers, both turned toe-down by hot lead before they were thirty, one in bed with the wife of a Mexican horse-breeder in Santa Fe.

"Is it her?" James asked. The nineteen-year-old Fallon boy sat to Fallon's left. Erroll, twenty-one and born with a soft brain and one wandering eye, sat just beyond James, squinting stupidly after the wagon.

Fallon slid the glasses back away from the wagon to

scrutinize the big half-breed following about twenty yards behind on the black stallion. Fallon could see only the back of the breed's buckskin mackinaw from this angle, but he'd seen the horn-handled .44 the man had been wearing thronged low on his right thigh, in an oiled and trimmed holster. The holster of a man accustomed to pulling his weapon fast.

The green eyes Fallon had watched were the hawkish eyes of a man not to be trifled with. They spoke of long miles and high mountains, all of which the breed had crossed himself, alone, using his wits, his fists, and his guns. He was a survivor, and he'd survived at considerable expense. He wouldn't be taken down easily.

As the breed followed the wagon up a low hill, trotting the stallion, he glanced back over his shoulder, wary as a wolf. Fallon lowered the glasses.

He sucked a deep breath. "It's her." He gave the glasses back to Plaza. "It's her, all right."

Plaza, who knew his way around a shooting iron himself, smiled grimly. "How you want to do it, Mr. Fallon?"

"First thing we're gonna have to do, Glen, is kill that breed."

"Mr. Fallon," Plaza said, the pointed ends of his gray-flecked mustache rising higher on his saddle-leather cheeks, "I got a feelin' that breed's been needin' a big stone on his chest for a long goddamn time."

He started his horse forward.

"Hold on," Fallon said.

Plaza frowned.

"Don't be overconfident, Glen. That's not some blanket Indian."

"Ah, come on, Pa," James urged, running his gloved right hand along the big Remington jutting up from under his blue wool coat. "Us four can take that breed and the dumb bastard in the wagon box before they know what hit 'em. Then we can drag that murderin' bitch back to Ma, and . . ."

Fallon was scowling at the boy, deepening the lines on either side of his broad nose as though regarding fresh dog plop on the parlor floor. James hated that look. It always withered him, made him feel small, turned his guts to mush. At the same time, anger burned deep inside the boy, as though flaming kerosene were sloshing around in the hollows of his bones.

His father had never talked to Frank like that. He'd taken the whip to Frank plenty of times, but it was plain the old man had respected Frank's sand. But Fallon didn't think James or his older brother, Erroll, for that matter, were anything but hind-tit calves. Useless, cork-headed weaklings good for little more than stretching fence fire and mucking out the barns and stables.

They weren't even worth a little time in the woodshed.

"Did I speak to you?" Fallon snarled.

James lifted his hand from his gun, looked down at his saddle horn.

"Did I speak to you, boy?" Fallon repeated, louder.

James squirmed under the old man's bayonet glare. "No, Pa."

"Then you don't speak to me—understand?"

James licked his lip atop which he was trying to grow a mustache, and nodded. "Sorry, Pa."

Fallon looked past James to Erroll, who'd been looking at his hard-nosed father apprehensively. The look was all it took to turn the older Fallon son's gaze, and drop his shoulders a good six inches.

"Now, then," Fallon said with a sigh, turning to his segundo. "We'll follow that wagon for a few miles then work around them, get ahead of 'em, and take them at Slaughterhouse Pass, between here and Louisville. They'll be movin' good and slow and more worried about the wagon slippin' and slidin' on the trail than about an ambush."

Plaza nodded. "It's your call, Mr. Fallon."

"Yes it is." Fallon glanced at his two sullen boys. "Come on, girls."

Chuckling darkly, he booted his dun slowly forward.

Chapter 15

"Girls, huh?" James Fallon snarled. "We'll see about that, you old hog-wallopin' bastard."

He lay on his side, staring across the fire at his father and Glen Plaza. The two men were talking amongst themselves in hushed tones, thumbs hooked behind their cartridge belts, the picketed horses standing like dark statues behind them.

The Fallon party had set up camp when they'd watched the wagon leave the trail to hole up for the night against a high escarpment a mile east of Slaughterhouse Pass. James and his brother had then followed his father and Plaza into a wooded horseshoe bend of the swollen Ute River, where the river rose sharply toward the rocky pass. The boys had tended the horses then fetched firewood and started the fire over which they set coffee to boiling.

In other words, James and Erroll had done the slave work, while Fallon and Plaza conferred in private, expressions serious, voices hushed and exclusive. Neither made the Fallon boys privy to their plans.

James loins burned. It was just after he'd set the coffee to boiling that his idea had first presented itself as though sent down by God from heaven on invisible hawk talons. It was a brilliant idea and one which, after James had pulled it off, would likely make his bullish old father finally stand up and take notice of him, prove to the old mossyhorn that James was every bit as much of a man as Frank had been.

Maybe, just maybe, even more of a man than Frank.

He leaned his head back against his cold saddle and drew his blankets up to his chin. He closed his eyes, let himself drift into a doze.

After a time, he opened them. The fire had gone down. He lifted his head and looked around.

Erroll was snoring softly about ten feet away. His and James's father and Plaza were bundled figures on the other side of the banked, glowing coals, heads resting against their saddles. Plaza lay on his back with his legs straight out in front of him, so accustomed to the mountain cold that he'd covered himself with only two thin wool blankets from the bottom of which his patched socks protruded. James's father lay curled in a big, tight ball, puffing his bearded lips out as he snored.

James rose slowly, letting his blankets fall away from his shoulders. He kept his breath shallow to make as little noise as possible. He'd kept his winter boots on, so when he gained his feet he had only to reach down for his rifle. Keeping his eyes on Plaza, whom James knew to be a light, cautious sleeper—the man had once hunted buffalo in Comanche country—James backed slowly away from the fire. He'd planned his route before he'd gone to sleep, and had removed all obstacles.

Staring at Plaza, willing the man to remain sleeping, James backed into the woods until the fire was a pale glow before him. Suddenly, Plaza's head jerked.

James froze.

Plaza coughed. The segundo smacked his lips, snorted, then settled back into stillness against his saddle. James looked at his father. Fallon hadn't stirred. Erroll, too, remained a still, humped shape in the darkness at the edge of the wan firelight.

James felt the tension in his shoulders ease. He continued taking one backward step at a time, until he was a good twenty yards from the fire. Then, holding his rifle in both hands across his chest, he swung wide of the picketed horses and, moving quickly but quietly and avoiding down branches and snow patches, headed out of the sparse aspens toward the stage trail.

James knew this stretch of the Sawatch. He and his father and brothers had run cattle through here to the mining camps on the northern slopes. He knew exactly where the breed and the silent fellow driving the wagon had pulled off the trail. While he hadn't seen where they'd camped, he knew the best place to camp up there, at the rocky base of the pass.

He didn't follow the trail. He only crossed it and tramped up the broad slope through the forest, staying close to a stream that ran along that side of the canyon. It was a fast-moving stream through a steep bed, frozen in places, and the ice sounded like breaking glass tumbling over rocks.

It was a long, uphill tramp, and the forest was sparse in places, giving way to mountain sage and thin tufts of needle grass. The stars were bright, but there was no moon yet.

The closer he got to the place he figured the breed's camp would be, the faster, more persistently James's heart beat. His hands sweated inside his deerskin gloves. He could see the look on his father's face when he walked back into the camp, dragging Frank's kill-crazy bitch wife by her hair and told his father it wasn't all that hard. If you're quiet enough—quiet as a damn Injun—and can shoot a rifle, hell, all you need to do is sneak in close as you can, and squeeze the trigger a couple times. Two men, two shots, right?

Then he'd throw Frank's wife down in the dirt and pine needles by his father and, keeping a straight face—it was very important for James to look casual, like the whole affair had been no harder than riding down a calf and blazing a brand on its ass—he'd drop down into his blankets and tip his hat over his head, and start snoring.

That's sort of how Frank would have done it, anyway. And the old man would sort of look at him like he'd look at a dangerous bobcat—half-fearful, half-admiring. Not sure whether to shoot the son of a bitch or guffaw at his pluck.

Proud.

Of course, Fallon wouldn't say he was proud. He wouldn't say much of anything, but only snort and grumble and kick a rock, maybe. But he'd give that look, and that was all James really needed. To see that look directed his way just once.

Sure enough, the breed and the silent fellow had camped where James had figured—in a hollow spot in the rocks at the base of the pass. Hunkered on a spinelike ridge, he stared down at the fire's glow that silhouetted rocks and pines around it. The glow sort of pulsated, the fire banked well with wood chips, dirt, and needles. It was hard to see because of the trees and rocks between him and the fire, but James thought he could see figures stretched out around it. A ways off to his left he heard the dull crunch of grazing beasts.

The breed's horse and the mule were both a ways off from the camp. Good. Likely, if he stayed down breeze, they wouldn't scent him and give him away.

Squeezing his rifle in his sweaty, gloved hands, James stole quietly down the ridge, following a deer trail. A few minutes later, he hunkered down about thirty yards from the camp, staring through the dark trees at the fire. In front of the fire a dark figure lay sprawled under blankets and a dun fur coat. James thought he could see a swatch of light-brown hair peeking out.

Frank's wife.

James's heart hammered. His mouth was dry, and he tasted copper.

To the fire's right, the silent fellow lay against his saddle. Directly across the fire, the half-breed sat back against a tree, his blanket pulled up to his chin, a brown scarf wrapped around his hat and jaws. His coal black hair hung down from his hat, framing his broad, rugged face. A Winchester with a brass receiver leaned against the tree.

James was about to move, but he held his place when the silent fellow made a sound, then, rising to a sitting position, reached out from under his blankets to grab a bottle standing beside him. He uncorked the bottle and took a deep drink, his Adam's apple bobbing in his throat.

With a sigh, he shoved the cork back into the bottle and, as the half-breed lifted his head and poked his hat back off his forehead to watch the silent fellow dully, the silent fellow set the bottle down and snugged lower against his saddle, rolling onto his side facing James, and squeezed his eyes closed.

The half-breed studied the silent fellow for a time, green eyes blazing in the campfire's glow, then lowered his head and pulled his hat brim back down over his nose.

James waited until he was sure both men were asleep; then he stole around the fire, staying about thirty yards away from it. He came to the wagon sitting with its tongue drooping, and glanced inside.

The coffin sat wedged against tack, burlap bags, and odds and ends of tools and scrap lumber likely used for shimmying the wheels on uneven roads. He stared at the coffin. It looked pale in the darkness. He imagined the girl's body inside—probably frozen solid, her skin white as fresh snow. A cold hand touched James's back, and he shivered as he backed away from the wagon, then turned to approach the fire from behind the tree that the half-breed lay against.

Only, when he drew within six feet of the tree, moving toward it at an angle so he could see in front of it as he raised his rifle, the half-breed wasn't there!

James's heart stopped. His ears rang.

His wide eyes darted around in their sockets as he raked his gaze around the camp, seeing only the sleeping silent fellow and Frank's wife humped and curled beneath her blankets and fur coat on the far side of the fire.

James sensed something behind him. He wheeled.

A brick red fist flashed toward him out of the darkness, and everything went black.

As the kid stumbled straight back away from Yakima, the half-breed grabbed the kid's coat collar, drew his slackening body toward him, then stooped to pull the long-limbed, loose-jawed toe-head over his shoulder. The solid smack of Yakima's fist against the kid's face had rousted Barstow with a grunt, and as the kid's rifle hit the ground with a rattling thump, Miss Berryman lifted her head from her coat and blankets with a startled gasp.

"All's well," Yakima said, hauling the boy toward the fire. *"Just didn't realize we were gonna be entertainin' this evening."*

"Mr. Fallon."

Plaza's voice woke the rancher out of a dead sleep. He opened his eyes to pale dawn light washing through the trees. Plaza squatted beside Fallon's blanket roll.

The segundo hooked his gloved thumb over his shoulder and said grimly, "Boy's gone."

Fallon looked over to where James's blanket roll lay mussed and empty in front of the boy's saddle. Erroll stood looking dumbly down at the blankets then lifted his head toward his father, his wandering right brown eye rolling toward the right side of its socket, spikes of his yellow hair poking down from his soiled wool cap.

Fallon cleared his throat as he sat up, glowering toward James's blankets. "How do you know he ain't just off takin' a piss or a shit or something?"

"Been gone since I got up, pret' near twenty minutes ago?"

Fallon looked at Erroll. "Where's your brother?"

Fallon's oldest son, a corkhead, dropped his hand against his thighs and lowered his gaze again to the blankets, as though he thought his younger brother would somehow materialize from the wool army blankets.

Fallon heaved himself to his feet with a grunt and began buttoning his buffalo coat. "You yell out for him?"

"Didn't wanna alert the breed. I looked around, though. The boy's gone. He don't sleepwalk, does he? Maybe he wandered off and got himself lost."

Fallon looked at Erroll. "Does your brother sleepwalk, Erroll?"

"Don't think so."

Fallon scowled as he wandered out from the fire that Plaza had built up with feathersticks of dry pine, and stared out through the trees that were dark gray now at mid-dawn. Finally, he turned and came back to the fire, putting his big rump to it, warming himself against the brittle morning chill. "If he's not here by the time we finish breakfast, we leave him."

When they'd finished their bacon biscuits and coffee,

and James hadn't returned, they saddled up and rode out, with Erroll leading James's leathered mount by its bridle reins. They rode for a mile up Slaughterhouse Pass, noting the fresh wagon tracks in the trail. Neck-reining his big sorrel off the left side of the switch-backing trail and onto a game path that snaked off through the firs and aspens, Plaza glanced at Fallon.

"We'd best swing off the trail until we're around the wagon. I'd say it passed through here less than an hour ago. We'll beat 'em to the summit easy, then hole up and wait for him."

Fallon nodded and turned his horse after Plaza's, glancing back at Erroll urging James's mount along with sharp jerks on the reins. "Come on, Erroll, quit foolin' with yourself back there, boy!"

The sun shone for a time, angling golden light through the dense pine forest through which the Fallon trio rode nearly straight up toward the high saddleback ridge. An hour after they'd started out, leaden clouds moved in, and the temperature dropped.

Chickadees peeped and hawks cawed, their cries clear in the cloudy stillness. The horses clomped and tack squawked, bridle chains jangling faintly.

They were nearly out of the trees, near the summit of the pass, when both Fallon and Plaza stopped their blowing horses suddenly.

"What . . . ?"

Fallon glanced at Plaza, and the two men galloped their horses up a low rise, checking their mounts down in front of a lightning-topped cedar at the edge of the forest, the high, bald, rocky summit rising beyond. James stood tied to the tree, shivering inside his coat, cheeks red, teeth clattering under the brim of his hat. His nose was swollen to twice its normal size; it and his eyes were the color of ripe plums. Blood had dried on his thick, blue lips.

A rope was wound a half dozen times around the tree and the boy, so he couldn't move except to shiver. His expression was so obscured by the swelling from his broken nose that it was impossible to tell if he was terrified or angry, or both.

His rifle leaned against the tree to his right. Brass cartridges were spilled out on the ground around the butt and the boy's boots.

Fallon scowled down at the kid. "Christ!" He looked back at Erroll staring down at his brother, hang-jawed. "Cut him loose and throw him on his—"

There was a loud, rattling whistle. The bullet slammed into the tree the boy was tied to, spraying bark in all directions. The whip-crack of the rifle followed a half-second later, echoing around the ridges.

"*Jay-zuzz!*" Plaza hardened his jaws and looked around, holding his horse's reins taut.

Fallon hunkered low in the saddle, keeping his own fiddle-footed mount on a tight rein, and jerked a look toward the summit of the saddle a hundred yards beyond.

A rider sat a black horse at the top of the bald ridge, amongst a few spindly juniper shrubs and dirty snowdrifts. The half-breed was clearly outlined against the dirty gray sky. He held his rifle butt down against his thigh, the barrel in the air near his flat hat brim, and he was staring down toward Fallon.

His long, black hair blew out behind his shoulders in the chill breeze.

"That son of a bitch!" Fallon growled, slowly straightening his back as he glared toward the summit.

The half-breed stared toward the Fallon party for a few

more stretched seconds. Then he turned his head away and heeled his horse down the saddle's other side. The horse threw its tail out on the breeze, and then it and its rider slipped away as though through an unseen door in the clouds.

"*You half-breed son of a bitch!*" Fallon wailed.

He spurred his gelding cruelly. Before he'd lunged five yards, Plaza grabbed the bridle and dragged the horse to a skidding halt. "Hold on, Mr. Fallon!"

Fallon saw something in the segundo's eyes he'd never seen before.

Apprehension.

Plaza looked toward the vacant ridge then back at Fallon, his eyes sharp and narrow. "You were right about that puma. I do believe we got his tail, and we'd best let the fight die out of him a mite before we try him again."

Chapter 16

Veronica Berryman looked back across her shoulder as she sat in the jostling, hammering wagon beside Barstow. "Do you think Fallon found the boy?"

Yakima rode about twenty yards behind, keeping an eye on their backtrail and on the undulating hills and sparsely forested knolls on either side of the trail that dropped steadily toward the village of Louisville at the bottom of Slaughterhouse Pass.

"Yep."

She raked strands of hair from her face. "You saw?"

"Yep."

"So they *were* trying to get around us like you thought."

"Yep."

"To shrub-whack us."

Yakima snorted. "That's close enough."

Barstow looked back at Yakima, his gaze dark, vaguely worried.

Yakima said, "I sent a little message, a note about how maybe they oughta think about going home."

Miss Berryman turned forward for a time. She glanced

over her shoulder again. "What do you do for a living, Mr. Henry?"

Yakima hiked a shoulder and looked off into the firs along the trail. "This and that."

Barstow broke his customary silence. "This and that with his guns!"

The woman narrowed a skeptical eye at Yakima, as though wondering how many rungs up the half-breed was from the men pursuing her, then turned forward again and remained that way as the wagon continued down the last stretch of trail tumbling down from the pass above and behind them.

Below, Louisville sprawled in a broad basin almost entirely surrounded by stony, snow-mantled ridges. There were only a handful of log or whipsawed, unpainted frame buildings, some stock pens, and corrals—all together not much more than a brown blotch in the sage and short, wiry grass carpeting the valley. Beyond the small but sprawling village, the Taylor River ran along the base of the forested slopes rising gradually, and getting gradually steeper as they climbed, toward vaulting pinnacles obscured by dirty, billowy clouds.

Smoke gushed from stone chimneys and tin chimney pipes, fluttering windily over the town like a dozen ragged kites. As Yakima and the wagon approached, leveling out on the basin floor, a dog's barks grew louder. Above the whistling wind there rose the faint tinkle of a piano.

The trail cleaved the town in two neat halves, false-fronted business buildings and low, log cabins falling back away from the trace as though making way for cattle drives. The rickety structures creaked and sighed against the wind's battering. There was enough room between each one for two more.

No one appeared out and about this windy day, except

for the dog barking unseen, and a half-dozen saddle horses and one spring wagon standing at hitchracks. The pattering of the piano continued, originating from up the street somewhere.

The only movement was tumbleweeds shepherded this way and that by the brittle wind. The drug store on the street's left side, about halfway through town, was basted with the prickly balls of Russian thistle.

"There's the stage office," Miss Berryman said, pointing to a low, log structure on the street's right side. A shingle jutting over the boardwalk announced FRANKLIN EXPRESS COMPANY.

Barstow pulled in, and the woman climbed down the right front wheel.

Barstow looked at Yakima. "I'll head over to the saloon, get a drink under my belt."

The wind whipping his mustache, he sniffed, whistled to the mule, and jerked away at an angle toward the saloon, a long, low, sod and board structure that the green lettering over the front identified as THE SAWATCH—BEER AND WHISKEY. Smoke from two gushing chimneys obscured the place. In the back of the wagon, the coffin slid and slammed as the wheels hammered over the many deep, iron-hard ruts, drowning out the poorly played piano.

Yakima put Wolf up to the hitchrack fronting the express office.

He stayed in the saddle as the woman, her ankle-length mink coat fluttering about her legs, stepped onto the boardwalk and knocked on the door under a little overhang on the building's right side. She waited then knocked again. After another wait the door opened and Yakima saw a sleepy, unshaven male face peek out.

The woman said something that Yakima couldn't hear beneath the moaning wind and the creaking of the posts suspending the express office's shingle above the street, but he heard the man say gruffly, "Everyone knows the stage don't run up here but every other week in the winter, and it just ran last Saturday. Now, if you wanna come in and keep me warm in the old mattress sack, I'll be glad to oblige you. Otherwise, run along, little honey, and let me sleep!"

The door slammed in Miss Berryman's face. She stepped back as though slapped and turned a worried look to Yakima.

He raked a hand across his jaw. "Had a feelin'."

Dismounting, he beckoned to the woman. "Come on."

She remained in front of the closed express office door. "What am I going to do?"

"I don't reckon you have much choice than to keep on with me and old Barstow. Unless you wanna hole up here and wait for the next stage."

She turned her head slowly back toward the pass, the summit of which was hidden in the sooty clouds. "He'll catch up to us. Eventually, he'll catch up to us, and he'll take me."

Frustration and impatience nibbled at Yakima. If she was going to start sobbing like a schoolgirl who'd had her braids dipped in ink, he'd leave her here to try her luck with the express agent. She wouldn't likely find a ride until they hit Rolette, where there was a spur railroad line, and at the time they were currently making, they wouldn't hit Rolette until late next week.

"Come on," Yakima growled. "Let's get Barstow and pull foot. I don't have time to stand here while you wail like a goddamn coyote."

"You don't understand," she said, turning to Yakima, tears

streaming down her pale, tapered cheeks. "I'm not from here, and I don't want to die here! Fallon's going to haul me back to his ranch and . . . God knows *what* he'll do!"

"That's what he'll do, all right. God knows. Now, you comin', or you wanna stay here and salt the boardwalk until he gets here?"

Yakima turned and started to lead Wolf at an angle across the street, toward the saloon. Behind him, the girl cried, "Wait!" and he heard her running footsteps. She gave a cry, and he turned to see her twist her ankle in an iron wheel rut, and fall in a fur-clad heap on the frozen, dung-littered street.

"Ah, Jesus." Yakima grabbed her arm, and pulled.

"My ankle!" She was sobbing hysterically now. "I twisted it and . . . and . . . it *hurts!*"

"Ah, Jesus," Yakima repeated. He released her arm and knelt in the street beside her, holding his reins in one hand. Wolf lowered his long, blazed snoot curiously toward the woman who'd closed her mouth and her eyes to cry in shaking, quivering, tear-streaming silence.

All Yakima needed was to have to carry her around like a damn lap dog.

"You didn't break it, did you? In them damn high heels, I wouldn't doubt it. Can't imagine how you walked two miles on them crazy stilts."

"It hurts!"

"Let me see."

He wrapped his hand around her right ankle, and squeezed.

"Ouch!" the woman cried.

"Ah, hell," he said, manipulating the woman's foot. "If it was broken and I moved it like that, you'd say more than 'ouch.' It's just twisted. Come on."

"What . . . ?"

Yakima gained his feet and, stooping low, pulled the woman unceremoniously over his right shoulder.

"Oh!" she cried, as he straightened. "What are you doing?"

"I'm skinnin' the damn cat!"

"Put me down!" As Yakima hauled her across the street on his shoulder, Wolf clomping dutifully along behind him, the woman punched his lower back halfheartedly with her mittened fists. "Oh, you savage! You don't carry a woman this way! Put me down, Mr. Henry . . . *this instant!*"

"All right—there you go," he said as he plopped her down on the wagon seat.

She lifted her injured foot and, clutching the edge of the wooden seat with her mittened hands, glared at him through her tears. "I'm not a sack of wheat, you brigand!"

"Wait here."

Yakima walked around the front of the mule and, leaving the woman sobbing in the wagon, mounted the saloon's low, ice- and manure-rimed porch. The piano had fallen silent, so there was only the woman's sobbing, the creaking of the building, and the howling wind.

He opened the heavy plank door and, as he stepped inside, quickly raked his eyes across the room whose murk was only enhanced by several gas lanterns swaying from softly singing ceiling chains. A big iron stove whooshed and rumbled about ten feet in front of the door, but Yakima's eyes were drawn to four men sitting around a table another ten feet right of the stove.

Three, wearing open coats, scarves hanging loose from their necks, were gathered around one man, Barstow. The honyonker sat with his back to the stove, his shoulders slumped. His billed watch cap was on the floor, near the boot of the long-haired man squatting down beside him, with his back to Yakima and shoving his face up close to Barstow's as though to share a secret.

Another man stood on Barstow's other side, resting one hand on the table. As Yakima had entered, this man's other hand was just dropping from the side of Barstow's head, and Barstow's thick, matted hair was stiffly falling back into place after the man's slap.

Directly across the table from Barstow, a rangy, black-bearded, hollow-cheeked Mexican in a wolf coat and black hat sat up high on a chair back, boots on the seat of the chair, elbows on his knees. In both hands, he held a silver-plated Colt Peacemaker, and as he stared across the table at Barstow, his black eyes bright with reflected light from the smoky lamp hanging above the table, he absently turned the .45's cylinder with slow, menacing clicking sounds.

He glanced toward Yakima then, dismissing the half-breed out of hand, returned his gaze to the honyonker whom the squatting man was addressing in hard, threatening tones.

". . . so don't try to tell us you don't. *Comprende, amigo?* That's only gonna make us mad. Now, one more time . . ." The man's voice dropped lower as he shoved his head up closer to Barstow's. Long, thin, sandy hair fell from his rabbit hat, and he wore a green-striped blanket coat.

Yakima brushed his hand across the handle of his .44 jutting above his coat flap, and sauntered casually toward the bar. There were three other men in the place, on the room's left side, and they cast occasional, cautious glances from their game of stud to the lobos and Barstow, and spoke amongst themselves in hushed tones.

The barman—a big man with long, uncombed hair and a face as pitted and dented as a coffee tin that had been used for target practice—stood idly drying a glass as he watched the festivities that were now behind Yakima.

"What's yours?" he asked the newcomer dully, keeping his gray, skeptical eyes on the tense foursome near the stove.

"Ale." Yakima flipped a nickel onto the counter then leaned a forearm on it as he turned sideways to look behind.

Again, the man who now stood with his back to Yakima, smashed the heel of his right hand against the back of Barstow's head. The honyonker winced as his head shot forward, his dark-red hair forming a ragged rooster tail where the standing man had cuffed him.

Barstow shook his head, keeping his stubborn cow eyes on the table before him, and spoke slowly. "Nope, I tell ya. She didn't tell me a thing, friend. You're barkin' up the wrong tree here."

The Mexican gunslinger jerked his gun straight out in front of him, loudly thumbing the hammer back and pressing the barrel against Barstow's forehead. "*Mierda santa— ¡Voy a soplar su de mierda me distraigo!*"

Yakima brought his .44/40 up in a blur of fluid, expert motion. The gun roared like a cannon in the cavernous room, the bullet punching through the Mexican's wrist, just back from the pearl grip.

The Mexican screamed, and as the cocked Peacemaker fell to the table, it discharged, sending a slug careening into the saloon's front wall but not before carving a notch from the right ear of the long-haired, ferret-faced man who'd been hunkered down next to Barstow, whispering threats.

Long Hair leaped to his feet, touching his ear and then looking at his hand while the Mexican dropped off his chair to shuffle around, crouched forward and squeezing his bloody wrist and casting an exasperated, black gaze at Yakima.

"What the hell you think you're doing, sonofabitch!" screamed the long-haired gent with the bloody ear.

The man who'd been slapping Barstow wheeled. He was the only one not wearing a hat but only a blanket over his head, as though in some grisly imitation of the Virgin Mary. Brown curls licked over his forehead, and a patchy beard darkened his heavy jaws. He looked more shocked than afraid as he glanced down at Yakima's smoking pistol, eyes bright with a growing delight.

"The man wants to die," the Mexican grunted, now clutching his wrist to his belly, the blood staining the front of his wolf coat. "Any man does this to me wants to die in a very bad way, amigo. Maybe you'd best oblige him, Snakehead," he added to the man closest Yakima, the man without the hat.

His shiny, obsidian gaze slid back to Yakima, and he gave an icy smile through large, gritted teeth.

"Man's a friend of mine." Yakima glanced at Barstow who sat up straight now, looking at Yakima wide-eyed, relieved but also cautious, waiting to see how things played out. "And you were about to put a bullet in his head." He waved his gun at the Mexican's freely bleeding wrist. "You made out better, if you ask me."

"We didn't ask you," said the man called Snakehead, chuckling with incredulity, facing Yakima full and holding his hands out away from his exposed walnut gun handle jutting from a tied-down holster on his right thigh. "Our little conversation ain't none of your business, see? And I don't think you know who you're dealin' with here, but I'm Snakehead Dawson and that there chili-chomper is Luis Lavoto. My friend whose ear you just pierced is Phil Little."

Glaring, the veins in his forehead bulging and throbbing, Snakehead moved slowly toward Yakima, clenching his fist above his gun. "We're bad fellas. Really bad hombres, if you get my drift, and what you just did here got you killed." He took another step and jutted his chin at Yakima like a wedge. "You understand me, you two-bit, dog-fuckin', half-breed son-ofabitch!"

Yakima lowered his Colt and blew a ragged hole through the pointed toe of Snakehead Dawson's right boot. The hardcase stopped and, tightening his jaws so that Yakima could hear his teeth cracking, lifted his face to the ceiling and bellowed like a pole-axed bull.

When the bellow died down, Yakima's voice rose in a low growl: "I never fucked a dog in my life, and I'd resent it powerful bad if you spread it around that I did."

Snakehead dropped his head to look down at his boot. The ragged hole had turned red. The blood bubbled up out of it and was dribbling over the soft, worn sole and onto the floor. Snakehead, continuing to stare down at it, made a short, high-pitched gasping sound—an expression of boundless grief and frustration.

He looked over at the Mexican still glaring and gritting his teeth at Yakima, then at Phil Little who stood a ways back of Snakehead, in belligerent, brooding silence. Snakehead gave another gasp as he whipped his scarf-covered head back toward Yakima, eyes red with hammering fury. Sweat dribbled down his pale, unshaven cheeks. His lips parted as though he were about to say something, but he said nothing, just glared.

His exasperation was palpable.

Yakima glimpsed movement behind Dawson, and turned his cocked .44 on Phil Little, who'd begun sliding a hand inside his coat. Yakima clucked.

Little stopped his hand, and his face crumpled as he stumbled backward, crouching forward and dropping his hands over his crotch—"Don't shoot nothin' off'n me, you crazy Injun bastard! I was just goin' fer my cigarette makin's!"

Yakima waved his gun at the door. "You three hook-worms best clear on out of here before I start blowing ears and peckers off."

The Mexican grunted and looked down at his wrist that was dribbling blood onto the floor between his high-heeled black boots. Little had backed against the front wall, lifting a thigh to cover his crotch. He looked ready to leave.

Snakehead didn't want to leave. He wanted to draw his gun. But it was obvious even to his dull, killer's brain who was calling this dance.

He narrowed an eye, his cheeks ashen behind his patchy beard. "This is far over, breed. Far, far from over."

With that he turned and, dragging his injured foot side-ways and smearing a trail of blood, headed for the front door. The Mexican stared at Yakima for a few stretched seconds, following Snakehead's promise with a few silent threats of his own, then, squeezing his injured wrist in front of his bloody wolf coat, tramped to the front of the room and followed his two compatriots outside.

Barstow was staring at Yakima. He grabbed a bottle off his table and, with shaking hands, splashed whiskey into a glass and threw it back.

Behind Yakima, a deep voice said, "Those are tough ene-mies to have, mister."

Yakima turned to the bartender who regarded him darkly. "I've had worse."

He picked up his ale schooner and drained it in a single, long pull. He ran the back of his hand across his mouth, nodded at the stud players regarding him stonily. They'd stopped playing when Yakima had drilled a hole through the Mexican's wrist, and now they resembled statues sitting with their cards fanned in their hands. Cigar smoke spooled lazily upward.

Setting the empty schooner on the bar, Yakima started toward the door.

"Come on," he told Barstow. "Didn't know you were gonna take all day."

Chapter 17

Snakehead Dawson cursed and snarled as he dragged his injured foot eastward along St. Louis's main street, heading for a large, frame building announcing MERCANTILE across its front and with a small shingle off to the side reading: LIONEL M. PURDY, M.D. A smaller shingle below that one advertised: GENERAL MEDICINE AND TOOTH EXTRACTIONS.

Phil Little followed Snakehead about ten feet back, with the Mexican, Luis Lavoto, walking stiffly while holding his bloody wrist to his belly, his face bleached with the misery he weathered in silent agony and barely contained exasperation.

The sky was even grayer than before, and small, dandruff-like snowflakes stitched the air. The three outlaws, walking single file along the street, angling toward the doctor's office, were the only people out and about, the locals all huddled by their fires and cooking ranges. Snakehead left blood in the scuffed snow and in the bare patches of frozen ground behind him.

Lavoto followed up the smudges with large, dark-red droplets oozing out from the fingers of his left hand wrapped taut around his bullet-torn right wrist.

Phil Little held his right hand to his notched ear, but the small groove had all but stopped bleeding though the long-haired outlaw with a domelike forehead gritted his sharp teeth against the burning pain that clawed up into his temples and which was aggravated by his rage at the half-breed's remembered disrespect and insolence.

Imagine a down-at-heel half-breed Indian cutting into him and Snakehead and the notorious Luis Lavoto, who owned the respect of nearly every pistolero in northern Mexico and Arizona. Snakehead's reputation was known all across the frontier, while Little himself was building a name for himself beyond his native Texas. A few more killings, and he'd likely start reading—if he learned to read, that was—his own name in dime novels and illustrated newspapers!

Snakehead dragged his bloody boot onto the boardwalk fronting the doctor's office, and knocked on the door, making the sashed windows in the door's upper panel ring.

"Come on, Doc. Open up, goddamnit. You got business!"

Snakehead rammed his fist twice more against the door, and then a shadow passed behind the glass, and the lock clicked. The door opened six inches, and two yellow-brown eyes set above a thin, pale nose, gray mustache, and goatee looked out. The eyes darted around Snakehead and his compatriots standing behind him.

Snakehead rammed his shoulder against the door, throwing it wide while the mustached gent stumbled straight back with a yelp, regarding Snakehead and the other two men moving in behind him with fear and incredulity.

"Oh, for mercy sakes!" he exclaimed, noting Snakehead's bloody boot and the wrist Lavoto was holding against his bloody, snow-dusted wolf coat.

"No mercy in it, Doc," Snakehead said, plopping down in a chair against the far, papered wall, and lifting his bloody boot above the floor, puffing his cheeks out as he breathed. "Bastard showed no mercy. Not a bit. And me an' the boys ain't gonna show him none, neither, once we've run his savage ass to ground.

"But first I'm gonna need some stitches where one or two of my toes used to be. The bean-eater there's gonna need some attention to his wing though Lucky Phil made out with only an ear crease, the cowardly sonofabitch!"

Snakehead looked at Phil Little holding his ear as he stood with his back to the closed door, and the sawbones stood regarding all three with a sour, disapproving expression. "You piss yourself, Phil? While you was beggin' for your life instead of doin' something conclusive!" Snakehead laughed raucously as blood dripped from his boot suspended a foot above the floor. "Bravest gunnie west of the Brazos, your big sis told me. My ass!"

"Shut up, Snakehead!" Little shouted, bunching his lips and jutting his chin toward the trio's unofficial leader. "The breed was obviously crazy, and I was tryin' to buy some time, distract the bastard, so I could get one of my own pistols out and blow his green-eyed head off!"

"One of your pistols out, uh?" The Mexican moved toward Little, releasing his bloody wrist to reach for his big Peacemaker. "You're a coward, amigo."

Little jerked backward, reaching for one of his own guns. The doctor stepped between the two, throwing his arms out to separate them. "Did you men come here to get your wounds looked after, or to kill each other? Either leave your guns in their holsters and sit down, or get out of here!"

When neither the Mexican nor Phil Little made any further offensive moves but just stood scowling at each other, the doctor looked at the blood dripping onto his floor from Lavoto's ruined wrist. He grabbed the Mexican's left arm and pulled and pushed the bigger man over to a wood-framed, leather-upholstered examination table beside a spindly potted palm tree near Snakehead.

"Get over there and sit down before you bleed all over my floor." The sawbones tossed Lavoto a towel. "Wrap that around it, and let me get my stove stoked." He turned, stopped to stare down at Snakehead's boot and the blood pool growing on the worn puncheons beneath it. "Men shooting each other on Christmas Eve! What's the world coming to?"

The doctor limped to a doorway, drew the blanket curtain back, "Jessie! Get in here! We got customers!" He started to turn away then poked his head through the curtain again. "Fetch a bucket of water!"

He went over, cuffed Phil Little's hand away from his ear for a quick inspection, then, sighing and shaking his head, went to a stove in a corner near a cluttered rolltop desk, and began stuffing split pine logs into it from the peach crate beside it.

"It's Christmas, huh?" Little said, smiling with the realization. "You don't say."

The doctor gave a dry snort and stood over Snakehead Dawson, planting his fists on his hips. "Can you get that boot off?"

"I can if you'll pour some whiskey down me."

"You don't think you've had enough already?"

"No, I don't, Doc," Snakehead said with a wild, pain-racked laugh. "No, I truly don—!"

Dawson cut himself off when a young woman walked into the room, bent forward over the bucket of water in her hands. She was about five-two or -three, with thick, curly hair tumbling onto her shoulders and framing a waifish, blue-eyed face with bee-stung ruby lips.

Full breasts pushed at her man's blue-plaid shirt, the tails of which hung down over the thighs of her baggy, faded blue denims. Her bare feet below the rolled cuffs of the denims were small, stubby-toed, and pink.

"Holy shit!" Snakehead said after he'd loosed a raspy whistle. "Where in the hell did you find your little helper there, Doc?"

The girl glanced at Snakehead, as did the doctor, rolling his eyes. "Put the water on the stove, Jessie."

The girl held her gaze on Dawson for a stretched, co-quettish second then hefted the tin bucket onto the humming stove by the desk.

"While I tend the wrist over here, why don't you help Casanova over there with his boot? If you can't pull it off, cut it off. You'll find scissors in the cabinet."

While the doctor tended Lavoto at the examination table, the girl grabbed a scissors from a cabinet, and a handful of towels, then came over and spread the towels under Daw-son's bloody boot. She gave the outlaw another coquettish glance through those sky blue eyes, then knelt on the floor in front of him.

"Who shot ya?" She looked up at him again, sweeping her thick, blond curls away from her eyes. The front of her shirt billowed out, giving Snakehead a good enough look inside to see that she wasn't wearing a camisole or anything else under the shirt. Her breasts sloped out— pale, firm, and pink-tipped—from her chest.

She followed the desperado's gaze into her shirt then jerked a coy, faintly reproving look at him. She left the shirt hanging open, however.

"Injun," Snakehead said, laughing. "Big one. Big, mean Injun, girl."

"He wasn't all that big, amigo," Lavoto said, taking a long pull from a bottle the doctor had apparently given him while Dawson was staring at Jessie's chest.

"He was damn big," Dawson said. "Biggest damn Injun I ever saw, and, Miss Jessie my sweet, he was better with a forty-four than any man I ever seen. Hey, Luis, toss that bottle over here before you drain the damn thing!"

"He wasn't better," Lavoto said, his Spanish-accented voice thick from the several pulls he'd taken from the bottle while the doctor cut his sleeve away from his wrist. "He just had it aimed at me before I could aim mine at him. Before I realized he was crazy enough to do such a thing. He ambushed me, the loco Indio bastard! A coward like *mi amigo* Phil over there!"

"Goddamnit, Lavoto," Phil objected, sitting in a chair at the doctor's desk and holding a towel to his ear. "One more time, and . . . !"

"Shut up, both of ya!" the doctor shouted in exasperation. "I done told you where you could take your disagreement, and see if I care if you bleed to death out there in the cold street." He glanced through a gray window by the door. "Looks like we got another damn storm rollin' in, too."

"As fer me," Dawson said, studying Jessie's thick curls as she dropped her head to inspect his boot, tugging lightly on the heel, "I'm gonna cozy up with Miss Jessie tonight. I got me a feelin' she's the place to be on a frigid Christmas eve."

The girl scowled up at him. "I ain't no *place!* I'm a girl!"

"Yes, you are, Miss Jessie. Ouch! Easy, there, girl—can't you see that little hole there in the toe? That's a real hole, not a damn tobacco stain!"

The doctor scowled over his shoulder as Lavoto tossed

the bottle across the room to Dawson, who snagged it out of the air with one hand, and plucked out the cork with his teeth. "How's it coming, Jessie?"

"It ain't, Doc," the girl said, giving the heel another tug and causing Dawson to jerk his head back and suck a sharp curse through his teeth.

"Cut it off with the scissors, if you can. If not, use a knife."

"Never did like to see knives in the hands of . . ." Snakehead let his voice trail off. He studied the girl's face down beneath her shifting curls. "Hey, don't I know you from somewhere, Miss Jessie?"

"No, you don't know me from nowhere," the girl growled as she started trying to cut down through the top of Snakehead's boot with the large shears.

"Why, sure I do," Snakehead said. "Weren't you working for Miss Alma down in . . ."

The girl jerked her hard-jawed face up toward him while poking the point of the scissors into his shin.

"Ow!" Snakehead howled. "Oh, now . . . no I reckon you just *look* like a girl I knew that worked down in Taos for a spell . . ."

"That must be it," Jessie said, giving up on the shears and moving over to the cabinet near the doctor's rolltop desk.

The doctor himself was inspecting the bullet-torn wrist of Luis Lavoto, who lay back on the examination table, his head resting on the sack of parched corn that the doctor provided as a pillow. The sawbones had lit a lamp hanging above the table, and he held the Mexican's wrist up to the flickering light, shaking his head as he studied the bloody wound.

The woodstove chugged. Outside, larger flakes of snow

were ticking against the gray, frosted glass. By the door, Phil Little sat forward in his chair, elbows on his knees, his right hand covering his ear. He stared at the floor, his eyes bright with fury and shame at the fool he'd made of himself back in the Sawatch Saloon.

As the girl came back with a bone-handled knife in her small, pale hand and a disapproving expression on her waifish face, Snakehead regarded Little, the Texas pistoleer, with a sneer, and chuckled at the man's lack of pluck when the chips were down, as they'd been a few minutes ago at the saloon. You learn a lot about man in a situation like that.

He looked down as he felt the girl begin to hack away at his boot. "Easy, girl, easy. Go slow. Looks to me like your blade there's pretty damn sharp."

"Oh, it is," Jessie said, continuing to work, her thick curls sliding around her cheeks and forehead. "It's very sharp. I just sharpened it this morning, matter of fact. I could gut a chicken before it even knew it was dead."

She sucked her rich upper lip, smiling.

Snakehead chuckled with only a little mirth at the girl's thinly veiled threat. He spied movement in the upper periphery of his vision, and lifted his head, frowning, to face the window behind Phil Little. He saw an arm clad in heavy blue wool and part of a glove, and then the glove was raised, and a soft knock sounded on the doctor's door.

"Oh, for heaven's sake," the doctor said, glancing at the door.

Two men stood on the other side of the door's sashed pains, one behind the other, the nearest one crouching to look inside.

"What is it?" the doctor yelled.

The door opened. Jessie paused in her work to watch, as

did Snakehead, the two men in bulky, wool, snow-dusted coats—one blue, one black—stumble in out of the cold and close the door behind them. The one in the blue coat was shorter than the one in the black coat, and he had a full beard, while the taller gent sported only trimmed sideburns and a long fringe of brown whisker hanging down from beneath his lower lip. A long scar ran from his hairline to down across his long, red nose. He also wore a red wool cap, while the shorter gent wore a battered plainsman hat tied down with a shabby gray scarf.

The shorter gent said in a halting, clipped-voweled Midwestern lilt, "We're here to see Mr. Snakehead Dawson and his partners."

The doctor only chuffed his exasperation as he returned his attention to Lavoto's wrist while Jessie continued hacking at Snakehead's boot. Dawson regarded both newcomers, who stood dully, shyly looking around the room in their ragged clothes and cracked leather boots, the ends of soft leather holsters showing beneath their coats.

"If you're bounty hunters," Snakehead said through pain-gritted teeth, wincing as the girl hacked down along the sole of his blood-soaked boot, "you're dead men. You know that, don't you?"

He glanced at Phil Little sitting behind and right of the two shy strangers. Little had quietly drawn his Remington revolver and rested the butt on his knee, thumb on the hammer, ready.

The two shy strangers followed Dawson's gaze, and, as one, they lifted their mittened hands not quite chest-high, their dark eyes showing alarm. "Oh, no," the shorter man said from inside his thick, black beard. "We're not bounty hunters. No, sir. We're not here looking for any trouble."

"Quite the opposite, in fact," said the taller man with the

scar. Unexpectedly, he spoke in an accent that Snakehead Dawson knew to be British, having run into a limey here and there about the Western frontier. "We're here to . . . to . . . well, to help you in exchange for you helping us."

Dawson looked at Little then over at Lavoto who was staring past the sighing, groaning doctor at the two shy strangers, his mud black eyes incredulous, faintly annoyed. He'd slipped his left-side gun from its holster, and Dawson could see the tip of the barrel sticking up above the Mexican's flat belly.

"Well, as you can see," Dawson said, "we ain't in any kinda position at the moment to help ourselves much, much less help you boys."

His cold gaze strayed to Little. "Except Phil over there. He's just fine. Made out like a bandit though he done pissed in his boot. He'll be able to help you two boys get your cat down outta the tree, though what you're gonna do for us, I'd like to know. You ain't carryin' any whiskey as I can see, nor totin' any whores."

He looked down at Jessie. She met his glance with a cool one of her own. She'd cut his boot loose and, while Snakehead grunted and jerked around in his chair from the pain shooting up and down his leg from the raw, burning ache in his foot, had started pulling it off his heel.

"Oh, Lord o' mercy there, Miss Jessie—go slow there, girl!" Dawson urged, gripping the edges of his chair in both hands and arching his back, stretching his lips far back from his tobacco-crusted teeth.

As the girl continued to slowly ease the boot from his foot, he sucked air through his teeth, and the two newcomers, the tallest one removing his wool cap respectfully, inched forward to look over her shoulder. Their eyes were wide, and their faces were pale. Phil Little rose from his chair to stand over the girl as the boot slipped down and away from Dawson's foot, clad in a wrinkled, blood-soaked sock.

"Jeepers, Doc," Jessie said.

"How bad, Jessie?"

The girl dipped her head low to look at the top of Dawson's quaking foot. Above Snakehead's own grunts and sighs, she said, "Looks like he lost about one and a half little piggies—the top of the one next to his big toe and there ain't nothin' but bits and bloody little pieces of the one beside it."

"*Isn't anything*, Jessie," the doctor corrected the girl's English. "Please—your grammar."

The girl glanced over her shoulder and rolled her eyes at the sawbones, who was finishing up with the Mexican, having wrapped a large bandage around the man's cleaned, cauterized wrist. The smell of scorched blood and skin permeated the air, and Lavoto lay back against the sack of parched corn, glaring straight up at the ceiling.

"Ah, gawd—I'm gonna kill that half-breed sonofabitch!" Snakehead bellowed, jutting his chin toward the door. "I'm gonna blow all his toes off, and then I'm gonna shoot his fingers off, and that's just to get me started!"

"Clean the blood off that foot as best you can, Jessie." The doctor was crouched before the stove door, holding a long-handled iron object inside. Over his shoulder, he said, "I'll have the wounds cauterized in just a minute."

As the girl gently cut the sock away from the cursing, grunting Snakehead's foot, the shorter of the shy newcomers stepped close to Snakehead, and said, "That's what we come here to talk to you about, Mr. Dawson."

When Snakehead just looked at him through fever-bright eyes, the shorter, bearded man said, "We come to throw in with you in the matter of that half-breed, Yakima Henry. And the money that Pedro Camargo done told the whereabouts of to the whore, Rosie Dawn."

Snakehead was in too much agony to ask the question himself, so Lavoto asked from the examination table, in a pain-pinched but steady voice, "Who the hell are you, amigo?"

The shorter man looked at the Mexican, and flushed.

The taller man said with reproof, "This is Lars Larson. The drunken fool who shot Rosie Dawn."

Chapter 18

As storms will in the mountains, this one moved in quickly on Yakima, Barstow, and Veronica Berryman. The sky kept dropping, and the snow kept coming down harder, until Yakima, riding ahead and looking for a place to hole up, could see no more than twenty yards in front of him.

The wind howled eerily, thrashing the pine tops along both sides of the trail in the narrow canyon they were traversing. Branches fell, crashing to the forest floor. The slender pine trunks creaked and groaned. The wind pelted Yakima's face with the cold waves of snow, until he felt as though he were being shot with steel pellets from a shotgun at mid-range.

Behind him, Miss Berryman hunkered low in the seat beside Barstow, holding a scarf to her face. The honyonker hunkered even lower, bellowing at the mule that couldn't make up its mind if it wanted to simply stop or turn and run back the way it'd come. Both Veronica and Barstow were so plastered with the heavy snow that they looked like statues carved from white marble.

Yakima rode a quarter mile ahead, desperately looking for cover—a notch cave, a heavy stand of trees. At this point even a hollow at the bottom of a stone scarp would do.

As he rode over a low hill, the forest on the trail's right side showed a gray, open patch in the blowing snow. He rode into the gap, Wolf shaking his head and snow-crusted mane, and reined the horse to a halt. Ahead, something brown shone amidst the gray-white, and the half-breed's heart quickened.

He toed the horse ahead and discovered a large, burned-out cabin standing on stone pilings. Behind the cabin and between waves of blowing snow, he thought he could make out the ruins of an old stamping mill. Just left of the mill was the brown patch he'd spied earlier.

A barn.

Yakima rode up for a closer look. The barn was intact—a large, frame structure with two side-sheds, corrals extending out from the sheds. Apparently, the fire that had consumed the mine office and stamping mill hadn't spread to the barn, which looked solid and tight, its big double doors closed.

Yakima didn't bother to find a way in. First, he'd fetch Barstow and the woman, and then he'd find a way into the barn for him and his fellow travelers as well as for Wolf and Barstow's mule.

He booted Wolf back through the driving snow. The horse lunged through deepening drifts, and as Yakima gained the main trail he saw that his own tracks were nearly filled in. Wolf drove hard, snow flying up around the stirrups. Yakima kept his head down, his hat brim over his eyes. He turned a long bend in the winding canyon trail and spied the brown blur of the mule and the wagon thirty yards ahead, behind an ever-thickening veil of snow.

Barstow was a dark stick figure standing beside the mule, bent slightly backward. The mule's muffled brays penetrated the wind's howling. As Yakima approached, he saw that the wagon was hung up in a drift and that the mule wasn't budging but only shaking its head, thrashing its tail, and loosing its shrill, indignant cries.

Veronica Berryman sat the driver's seat looking frozen under all that mink fur and the scarf covering all but her eyes that regarded him pleadingly.

Yakima jumped down from Wolf's back, and ran around beside the wagon. Barstow's shouts were incoherent beneath the wind's howling, the mule's braying, and the thrashing and cracking of the trees all around. Yakima inspected the left side wheels. They were half-buried, and the rear axle was hung up so that the left rear wheel wasn't getting any traction.

Yakima ran around Barstow and the mule. "I found a barn! Unhitch the mule!"

"I'm not leaving the wagon!"

"Leave it!"

Jerking his skitter-stepping stallion along behind him, Yakima ran up to the driver's seat where the woman sat, stiffly crouched forward. Without ceremony, Yakima reached up, grabbed her under the legs and behind her back, pulled her off the wagon, and half-tossed, half-set her onto his saddle, the horse lunging sideways at the unexpected rider.

She cried and lunged forward to grab the horn.

Yakima grabbed a couple possible bags from beneath the wagon seat, and tossed them up to her. She grabbed them clumsily, and held them across the saddlebows as Yakima turned again to Barstow who was continuing to try to pull the mule and the wagon out of the drift.

"Unharness the beast!" Yakima shouted at the tops of his lungs.

Barstow ignored him, shouting curses at the braying mule.

"You're on your own, stupid bastard!" Yakima leaped up behind Veronica Berryman and, holding his arms around her, booted Wolf down the trail, following his own rapidly disappearing tracks in the growing drifts. He looked back toward Barstow. The man was behind the mule, and it looked like he was unhitching the beast from the doubletree.

Yakima waited.

When he saw Barstow moving toward him, pulling on the braying mule's reins, snow splashing up around the hon-yonker's thighs, he continued down the trail, bent forward and wincing at the icy flakes pelting his face like wind-driven sand. Wolf whinnied and pulled at the reins, lurching back and sideways at the intermittent wind blasts. Yakima held the reins fast and continued trudging forward, glancing back to see Barstow and the mule following about thirty yards behind.

Several times the wind blasted so hard, hammering Yakima and Wolf with so much snow, that the half-breed's progress stalled until he could catch his breath and coax the stallion into continuing. He had several anxious minutes of looking for the trail back into the clearing where he'd spied the barn, before he glimpsed part of a single hoofprint branching off the main trail and through the firs and aspens hugging the narrow, gray gap of a frozen snow-covered stream.

He'd crossed the frozen stream and made his way through the trees on the far side, when Barstow shouted something behind him. The sound was ripped away on the wind, so that it sounded little louder than a murmur. A half-second later, Veronica gave a cry.

Yakima looked around, bewildered. He glanced over his left shoulder, and his gut tightened. Long, gray, lunging figures slanted toward him from the dark line of the trees behind. Yakima heard the mule's wild brays as he wheeled and, holding Wolf's reins in his left hand, fumbled under his coat for his .44.

The first wolf was within ten yards before Yakima got his Colt out, and his cold, gloved hand worked awkwardly as he cocked the hammer. Swinging the gun up and out, he dropped to a knee and, as the wolf lunged toward him—so close that Yakima could hear the ragged snarls and see the bared teeth and gleaming yellow eyes—squeezed the trigger.

The wolf yelped as it slammed into Yakima's right shoulder, throwing Yakima backwards. The wolf hit the ground nearby, snarling and rolling, scissoring its legs as it died from the heart shot.

Another was right behind it. Yakima fired from his back as the animal started its lunge. He saw fur at its belly part as the bullet punched through the large, rangy beast's lower middle. The wolf yowled loudly as it landed atop Yakima, snarling and gnashing its teeth before the half-breed slammed his left elbow into the wolf's right shoulder, casting the wolf into the snow beside him.

He shot the wounded beast again and bolted to a knee as three more wolves ran more slowly, suddenly cautious, toward him and the horses. They were flanked by several others still running out of the trees.

Wolf was pitching and trying to pull his reins from Yakima's still-taut grip. Barstow was running toward Yakima with his mule in tow, holding a double-barreled shotgun in one hand. As two wolves closed on him and the mule, Barstow stopped suddenly, took the mule's reins in his teeth, and dropped to a knee.

He raised the shotgun. The report was barely louder than a pistol crack amongst the wind's howling, the mule's braying, and Wolf's neighing. One of the wolves was thrown straight up in the air then back and sideways, piling up in a red-speckled, charcoal-colored heap. The other stopped as though tugged from behind by an invisible leash, and stood snarling at Barstow with its hackles raised.

Yakima glanced up at Veronica. She'd dropped both the possible bags that he'd given her, and she lay slumped against Wolf's neck, barely clinging to the horn of the leaping, sunfishing stallion whose reins Yakima had somehow managed to hold through two wolf attacks.

Barstow triggered his shotgun's second barrel, and the wolf that had been glaring at him wheeled and ran. Somehow, Barstow had missed with his twelve-gauge barn blaster, but the wolf was running off with its tail between its legs, past several others still holding their ground with malicious humps in their backs, sort of sidestepping, holding their heads down, their growls ripped and torn by the wind.

Yakima reached over Wolf's neck for his Winchester. Cocking the rifle one-handed, he turned to Barstow, who was pulling the mule up toward him while warily regarding the stalking wolves.

Yakima shouted, "Take my horse! Head for the barn!"

Barstow grabbed Wolf's reins, and suddenly both the horse and the mule were running ahead of him, so that they nearly pulled him off his feet in their haste to head for the safety of the brown blur of the barn ahead. Barstow dropped his shotgun but managed to hold the animals' reins as he was half-dragged through the snow.

Several wolves raced forward. Yakima shot one, wounded another, then turned and ran after the horses himself, jacking out the second empty shell casing and racking fresh. Three more wolves, emboldened by their fleeing prey, lurched forward in long, ground-eating strides, two heading toward Yakima from his left flank while a third angled ahead of him toward Barstow and the horses.

Yakima wheeled and fired a shot at the wolf running toward the barn. His bullet blew up snow beyond the lunging, gray beast. Racking a fresh shell, he tracked the animal with his Winchester but held fire, as the wolf was now between Yakima and Barstow and Veronica, both of whom were now in front of the barn, the honyonker holding fast to the reins in his fists and the woman tumbling down from Wolf's back with a scream.

"Get inside!" Yakima shouted and began to run forward.

Snarls and crunching snow sounded behind him. He wheeled, leveling the Winchester at one of the two wolves who'd bounded within ten yards and was closing fast. His rifle roared. The wolf on the left swerved away with a yip, but the other thrust off its hind legs and, stretching out, snarling fiercely, slammed is head into Yakima's chest.

As the half-breed hit the ground on his back, he managed to raise his rifle between him and the wolf's chest. The snarling, convulsing beast sunk its teeth into Yakima's left shoulder. Yakima ground his teeth together as the Wolf bit him under his arm, then thrust up and out with the rifle. The wolf gave a louder, enraged growl as it righted itself.

Before it could lunge atop Yakima once more, the half-breed snaked his Winchester out across his chest and fired.

The bullet caught the beast through its right eye, snapping its head back and twisting its body up and around and backward, where it piled up in a bloody heap on a bare patch of frozen, sage-tufted ground.

As Yakima leaped from his knees to his feet and lunged toward the barn, Wolf loosed a shrill whinny as the third wolf jumped at the horse's left hip. Barstow had let go the mule's reins, and the mule was bounding off around the side of the barn, three more wolves that had materialized out of the flapping white snow curtains yipping and yowling in savage pursuit. Wolf's reins dangled loose as Barstow, with the woman tight beside him regarding the wolf with terror-bright eyes, tried to slide the big left door open.

The stallion leaped up against the door, narrowly missing the woman with its slashing front paws, and then the horse fishtailed around to face the wolf slashing at the horse's hooves and legs with its long snout and flashing white, razor-edged teeth.

Yakima ran up to within ten feet of the wolf, shot it, then leaped to grab Wolf's reins before the horse could run off to be the pack's second helping after the mule. He'd just grabbed the reins when he heard a thunderlike rumble, and saw the left door slide left, opening a dark gap between it and the other one. Barstow fell to his knees—the door had unexpectedly given way while he'd been pushing and shoving—and Yakima wasted no time in leading the nickering, blowing horse into the barn behind the girl.

He wheeled, yanked Barstow into the dark shadows by the man's arm, then stepped out and slid the door closed behind him, swinging his rifle around, looking for more wolves. Several milled amongst their dead between the barn and the trees.

Yakima lunged around the barn's north front corner—he didn't know what they'd do if they lost the mule—but the animal's shrill scream sounded before he'd run ten yards, and he could hear the wolves snarling and mewling savagely a ways off in the blowing, swirling snow that caused a near total whiteout.

The mule was finished.

Lowering his head against the wind, Yakima tramped back around to the front of the barn. He shoved the left door open, slipped sideways through the narrow gap, snow blowing in around him, and jerked the door closed. He sensed trouble before he heard the scuffing and stumbling around in the dusky shadows before him, and Wolf's anxious nickers—before he smelled whiskey and the sour smell of bodies, and he tripped over a yielding object on the floor in front of him.

Barstow was out cold, slumped on his side, blood showing above his left ear. His cap lay a couple feet away, smashed flat against the hay- and straw-covered floor, the shape of a heel showing in the crown.

"*Yakima!*" the woman screamed.

He jerked a look straight ahead, saw several bulky masculine figures shuffling around the woman they seemed to have down on the floor, tearing at her clothes. Yakima's heart thudded and he lurched over Barstow's still frame, bringing his rifle up in both hands.

He hadn't quite gotten the Winchester raised before something hard smashed against the back of his head. His arms and the rifle dropped. He fell to his knees, fought to keep his head up.

The barn swirled around him. Somewhere in the dark, swirling figures he saw a woman's pale, naked ass, then the woman's long, chestnut hair, and he heard men laughing and grunting and whooping while Veronica Berryman screamed, "*Nooooo!*"

Yakima collapsed.

The scream died.

Chapter 19

The girl's screams and the men's laughter helped Yakima win the war against unconsciousness. Less than a minute after he'd passed out, he climbed up out of the black soup trying desperately to pull him down, and, wincing against the bells tolling in his ears and the hammering pain in the back of his head, lifted his chin from the barn's cold, earthen floor.

"Oh, for cryin' out loud, Angus!" someone said beside him.

A figure moved past him, holding the axe handle the man had apparently used to trim Yakima's wick, as well as Yakima's own Winchester. The figure, clad in a long bear coat and fur hat from which yellow-blond hair hung down to the middle of the man's broad back, headed toward where three others were circling Veronica.

Somehow, she'd gotten away from them.

Her coat and hat had been torn from her body; she wore only a ripped camisole, pantaloons, and fur boots. Her entire right breast and all but the nipple of her left were exposed by the torn undershirt. Her hair hung in a loose mess about her face and shoulders, framing her terrified eyes. She'd gotten ahold of a pitchfork, and, sobbing, she was trying to fend off her attackers with the fork's three, rusty tines, holding the fork's business end out in front of her as she sobbed and begged to be left alone.

She and the four men were silhouetted against a corrugated tin washtub behind them from which flames leaped and wavered, sending smoke and sparks wafting toward the rafters. Yakima pushed a foot up beneath him. He must have made a noise; the men near Veronica glanced back at him, and widened their eyes.

"The breed's gettin' up, Fletcher."

The long-haired man wheeled toward Yakima, stretched his lips back in a beaver-toothed grin. He swung his right foot back then hammered it forward toward Yakima's chin. Suppressing the pain in his head, Yakima thrust his hands forward, caught Fletcher's fur boot in his arms. Lunging from his knees to his feet, he pitched Fletcher violently backwards, off both feet, and Fletcher's head smashed against a wooden stall partition with a bang.

Fletcher groaned and lay back against the base of the partition, slowly shaking his marbles back in place as the other four men turned from Veronica to Yakima, their eyes bright with challenge. They were big, bearded men in blanket or fur coats, and pistol grips and the handles of hunting knives jutted above their coat hems.

The man farthest right grinned largely, showing two gold front teeth, and slipped a big bowie knife from the sheath belted outside his three-point capote.

"Hey, maybe the breed needs a haircut!" he bellowed, little gray eyes sparking challenge. He saw Fletcher reach for Yakima's own Colt .44, which Fletcher had wedged behind his wide, brown leather belt. The man with the knife threw a hand out at Fletcher. "No! I'm gonna give him a haircut—me an' my cousins. Right, boys?"

"Let's do it, Sal," said the largest of the five, a huge bear of a lantern-jawed gent with a patch over his left eye. "I'll hold him while you give him a trim. Turn him into a white man right here an' now, then throw him out to them wolves he made so mad."

As the man with the knife and the other two cousins moved slowly toward Yakima, fanning out around him, the big man moved in quickly, working his way around Yakima to get at the half-breed's back.

Veronica stood behind the men now, regarding Yakima anxiously, the pitchfork hanging slack in her hands.

When the big man was directly left of Yakima, moving toward Yakima's flank with a grin on his broad, square face, Yakima bolted toward him. The man wasn't ready for the sudden onslaught, and Yakima had punched him twice with both fists before the man gave a raging bellow and staggered straight backward, just now starting to raise his fists defensively.

Knowing how to use a man's size against him, Yakima was not afraid of men bigger than he.

He punched him twice in the belly, quick but savage blows delivered from Yakima's own center of gravity. As the big man's knees buckled, he lurched forward to bull Yakima over. Yakima sidestepped him, twisted around, grabbed the man's head in both arms, and snapped his neck.

The man groaned and dropped like two hundred pounds of dry freight.

Yakima whipped around to see the other three bolting toward him, reaching for their own knives. Their eyes were shocked, vaguely wary. Using his Eastern fighting skills, Yakima kicked up and through the wrist of the man in the middle. The man cursed shrilly and looked up to see his knife careening end over end in the barn's high, dusky shadows.

"Son of a bitch!" The man on the right lunged with his knife toward Yakima's belly. The wickedly up-curved tip of his skinning knife flashed in the gray light pressing through the cracks between the barn's whipsawed boards.

Yakima lunged backward while making a chopping motion with his right hand against the attacker's wrist. The man's knife hand jerked down. At the same time, Yakima leaped off his left foot and buried his right boot in the man's crotch.

The man grunted as he dropped his head, and Yakima, still moving fluidly but quickly and savagely, smashed his left knee up into the man's face, feeling the man's nose break, saw blood painting the floor.

The man to his left lunged toward Yakima with his own knife extended. Yakima whipped the back of his right elbow against the back of his attacker's knife hand, and the blade plunged hilt-deep into the ear of the man with the broken nose.

Broken Nose screamed, "WHACHHHH!" and dropped to the floor and rolled around wildly, clawing at the handle of the knife protruding from his ear and around which blood welled thickly. The man, whose knife had been used to kill his cousin, grabbed for the Remington holstered outside his hooded fox coat, whipping the hood back from his bald head, revealing a silver ring dangling from his right earlobe.

Yakima was on him in a half a wink, smashing the man's face twice with his fists and sending him bellowing and sprawling. Sensing another attacker moving toward him from behind, Yakima wheeled.

The man had replaced the knife Yakima had kicked out of his hand with a horn-gripped, .45-caliber Colt. The gun belched smoke and flames but not before Yakima had thrown himself to the floor between him and the shooter.

As the bullet screeched over his head and the bald gent gave an agonized yowl, Yakima turned a complete somersault, bringing his legs up and forward as he heard the man cursing and ratcheting his Colt's hammer back. Yakima's heels slammed into the man's chest and shoulders, throwing him straight back toward the barn doors as the man's Colt flashed and belched once more, the bullet hammering the high ceiling between the two balconied haylofts.

Yakima sprang off his heels.

The shooter, thrusting himself back away from the doors and toward Yakima, leveled the pistol once more. Yakima kicked the Colt out of the man's hand, whipped around in a complete circle, and smashed the back of his left fist against the man's face, driving his nose into his skull with a sickening crunch. He slumped back against the door, dead before he hit his knees.

A gun barked behind Yakima. The bullet tore a gobbet of wood from the door.

The half-breed wheeled. Fletcher stood facing him from ten feet away, a smoking Remington in his right hand. He scowled out through the long, mussed blond hair hanging in his face, chin down, lips pooched with barely contained fury.

"Them's my boys, you rancid savage!"

Fletcher cocked the Remy but before he could pull the trigger, he jerked as though with a start. His eyes widened. He lowered the Remy and took two steps forward and sideways, swinging around to reveal the ash handle of the pitchfork jutting from his back.

Veronica Berryman stepped back away from him, raising her hands to her mouth, her eyes wide with revulsion. Fletcher triggered the Remington into the earthen floor, blowing up dirt chunks and straw.

He chuckled with amazement and incredulity. "B-bitch . . ." He dropped to his knees, rolled onto his side, farted, and shook as he died.

Veronica Berryman sobbed behind her hands.

Yakima looked at the bald man who lay prostrate on the floor with his head against a stanchion door. He clamped a hand over the bloody hole in his chest. "Hep me, breed." His voice was thin and ragged. "Hep me . . . we was just . . . funnin' with the girl. . . ."

Yakima raked his gaze from the dying man to Barstow, who'd gained his hands and knees and held his head down, shaking it. The attackers' five horses—the men were likely market hunters laying up out of the weather—stood stalled in the barn's far left shadows. Wolf stood against the far right wall, between two small windows, nickering, blowing, and tossing his head, the stallion's eyes ringed with fear.

"Thanks for the help," Yakima grunted at the mount.

Wolf shook his head.

Yakima slid the right door open about three feet and looked outside. The snow was coming down hard, causing a near whiteout, but several furred, canine faces regarded him from the swirling whiteness that grew grayer as the day waned.

Yakima reached down and dragged the broken-nosed man outside into the storm. He left him about twenty yards from the barn, then went back inside, and soon he'd dragged the other dead men out. When he stood over the bald, chest-shot gent, the man stared up at him in horror.

"You ain't . . . you ain't gonna . . . ?"

He gave a defiant shriek as Yakima reached down and grabbed the hood of his coat and began to pull him toward the open door. "You're wolf supper, pard."

Yakima pulled him outside and left him with the others. Hearing the man screaming and yowling, Yakima went back inside the barn and closed the door. Barstow stood holding his hand over his ear and regarding Yakima and the door behind him dully.

Behind Barstow, Veronica Berryman had pulled her coat on and regarded Yakima skeptically. "You're going to leave him out there?"

"What do you think they were going to do with you—after they'd finished?" Yakima walked past her to add more wood to the fire in the tin washtub. "Besides, them wolves are hungry, and I got a feelin' they're already done with the mule."

Outside, a wolf howled. Another one barked madly. More beasts snarled, and there were panting and growling sounds, the quick thuds of many padded feet.

The bald man's shriek was ripped and torn by the wind.

Veronica gasped and turned away from the front doors.

Yakima tossed chunks of pine logs into the tub. "They're still hungry, all right."

With the mind control his Shaolin friend George had taught him while they'd laid track together, Yakima had been able to suppress the pain in his head to do battle with the goatish market hunters. But now that the fight was over, the throbbing pain resumed, and he could feel now, too, the burning wounds where the wolf had bitten him about the chest and shoulders.

When he'd unsaddled Wolf and stalled the mount a ways off from the hunters' horses, he moved heavy-footed over to where Veronica Berryman and Barstow sat by the fire, near the barn's rear wall.

Barstow leaned back against some feed sacks, dabbing at his cut ear with a cloth and taking deep pulls from a bottle. The woman knelt in front of the washtub, staring at the leaping flames as though she might find sanctuary there from all her travails, not the least of which was nearly being raped by five men in a cold barn, snowbound deep in the Rocky Mountains.

Yakima had no more time for either of them. He was aching and exhausted, and he wanted some time to tend his wounds and gather his thoughts. But a question had been chewing on him.

He adjusted the saddlebags and canteen strap on his shoulder, grabbed Barstow's whiskey bottle out of the man's hand, and threw back a drink. He lowered the bottle, swallowing, and stared down at the honyonker looking up at him skeptically.

"Since we're ridin' together," he said, "I figure it's my business whether you know where that money's hid."

Barstow stared up at him, wincing as he dabbed at his ear. "I done told you . . . I don't know nothin' about no money. Even if I did, it'd be the devil's loot . . . now, wouldn't it?"

Yakima looked at him. Outside, the wolves could be heard snarling and mewling between wind blasts. The barn's walls quaked and shuddered.

Yakima took another deep drink from Barstow's bottle, returned the bottle to the man, who frowned with concern as he said, "My girl . . . she's out there in that wagon. Wouldn't want the wolves gettin' her."

Barstow's relationship with his daughter was none of Yakima's business. But he was aching and foul and he only wanted to be alone and to rest, so he said, "Seems to me you threw her to the wolves a long time ago, mister."

He swung around, and he did not meet Veronica Berryman's gaze as he climbed a rickety wooden ladder into the loft.

Chapter 20

Yakima heaved a deep sigh as he dropped down into the hay near a small window in the loft wall. He shoved his saddlebags and canteen aside and leaned back into the hay.

He could feel the heat from below; since heat rises, it was probably almost as warm up here as down by the tub. A few sparks rose on the heat waves and smoke. The way his luck was going, the fire would probably set the barn ablaze, and he couldn't have cared less.

He closed his eyes against the throbbing in his head and the burning wolf bites. He didn't think the bites were deep, but he could feel the cold blood running under his coat and shirt. In a minute, after a doze, he'd shuck out of his duds and clean himself, then nibble some jerky. Only fools smoked in barns, but he craved a quirley and a cigarette was no more of a hazard than the burning washtub.

Listening to the snapping flames and Barstow's grunts beneath the howling wind and creaking barn timbers, he closed his eyes. He'd just drifted off when he heard the ladder creak and complain. Opening his eyes, he saw Veronica step into the loft.

She held her coat closed as she moved toward him, sort of crouching, setting her high-heeled boots down softly. She was favoring the left one a little. She wasn't wearing her hat, and her thick hair hung down as before.

Her trepidation and arrogance had leached from her features, and now her face owned a haunted look. Unadulterated fear and befuddlement.

She knelt down beside him, frowning at him but saying nothing.

He sat up slightly. "How's the ankle?"

She shook her head as if to dismiss the question. "I'm sorry I acted so childish." She lowered her head and chuckled without mirth. "It's just that I thought, when I discovered I couldn't take the stage, that it couldn't get any worse than that. But now I watched you kill four men, and I rammed a pitchfork into the back of another . . ."

She lifted her gaze to his, shaking her head and licking her lips.

"Yeah, it can always get worse."

"I've lived a pampered life."

"Yep . . ."

She nodded at his coat, torn and bloody where the wolves had bit him. "You're bleeding."

"It's not bad. I'll tend it in a minute."

"Take your coat off."

Annoyance lanced into his fatigue. "I said I'll tend it in a minute."

She reached for his canteen, and shook it.

"Frozen," he said.

"I'll fetch some snow."

"Can't you hear those wolves devouring your friends?"

She shivered and looked at him distastefully. "I'll crack the door." She rose and started toward the ladder, but she stopped to toss him a sharp look. "I don't blame you for being tired of me. Us. But I'm tending that wound whether you like it or not, Mr. Henry."

She disappeared over the side of the loft, and Yakima heard the ladder creaking beneath her weight. "Contrary bitch."

He chuckled, though in his fatigue and pain he wasn't sure what was funny. Maybe it was his current predicament or his life's experience with women which, aside from a few whores including the beautiful Faith whom he'd love until they turned him under, had never gone well. Now, here he was leading a dead whore in a wooden overcoat, the whore's half-mute father, and an Eastern Jane across the snow-choked Rockies on Christmas Eve.

He'd given up on the gold-guarding job. Now he just wanted to get out of the mountains alive. He didn't care so much about Barstow—the man was a copper-riveted fool—but he wanted to see the honyonker's daughter, Rosie Dawn, safely planted. He felt obliged to see Veronica Berryman out of her travails as well, since she was nearly as helpless and de-fenseless as the dead whore.

"What are you chuckling about?" the woman asked when she returned with a cup of snow water she'd apparently heated over the fire below. Barstow was grunting and sighing down there by the tub, and between wind blasts Yakima could hear the honyonker's bottle slosh as he pulled from it.

"Just addled, I reckon."

She knelt and started unbuttoning Yakima's coat, her face only seven or eight inches from his, so that he could see every faint skin blemish and rare freckle and the fine veins just beneath the smooth, flour-white skin at her neck. "I saw him hit you with that axe handle. I thought he'd killed you."

"I reckon he thought so, too." Yakima reached for his

saddlebags but stopped the move when she opened his coat. He sat up, and she helped him shrug out of the garment before he dug around in his saddlebags for a bottle.

He popped the cork with his teeth, spit it out, and extended the bottle to her.

"No, thanks. I'm trying to get your shirt off, Mr. Henry."

"We've only known each other a couple of days, Miss Berryman. Are you sure the folks back home would approve?" Yakima threw back a long drink and winced as the liquor that he rarely indulged in hit his throat and belly with a searing but soothing burn.

"Very funny." She took the bottle from him, set it down, and then began to dutifully untie the neck of his buckskin tunic.

He stared up at her, soothed by the liquor and a little heated up by the beautiful woman's closeness—by the smell of her, and the faint caress of her hair ends dancing across his chest—as he raised his arms so she could pull the tunic over his head, and drop it atop his coat and saddlebags. She looked down, vaguely troubled, at his threadbare balbriggan top that, shrunk from washings in half the rivers and streams on the Western frontier, clung like a second skin to his broad, slab-muscled chest.

She swallowed, colored a little, as her eyes played across his shoulders. Yakima reached up and touched a faint mole just off the right corner of her long, perfectly shaped mouth.

She frowned, raising her eyes to his. "Please, stop. Can't you see I'm trying to help you?"

"You're a good-looking woman."

Ignoring him, she canted her head low to inspect the bloody holes in his shoulder and the others just beneath his left armpit. "Take your top off so I can get at those wounds."

Yakima gave a grunt as he sat up again and peeled the

undershirt down his shoulders and arms, until it was curled over his cartridge belt, and his torso was bare.

"Good lord," she softly intoned, raking her eyes across his rugged frame. She touched a knotted white scar on his right pectoral. "How did you get this?" She shuttled her shocked gaze around his chest and belly starred with scars of many shapes and sizes. "All of . . . these . . . ?"

"Knives. A few bullets. Broken whiskey bottles. Even a wagon spoke, if you can believe it."

Veronica looked at him as though he'd suddenly become a jaguar before her eyes. Then her expression grew pensive, empathetic. "You've lived a hard life."

"You throw a boot across a saloon out here, you'll hit a hard-luck sonofabitch. I'll have the whiskey bottle."

"Hold on." She splashed some whiskey into the cup of snowmelt then handed the bottle to Yakima, drawing her mouth corners in with disapproval. "Don't you go getting amorous on me, Mr. Henry. I've had enough of lusty men. You've taken me under your wing now, and I trust you."

Yakima tipped the bottle back, brought it down with a loud slosh, and smacked his lips. "Injuns and drink don't mix, so here, you best take my pistol." He shucked his Colt from its holster and set it down near her right knee. "Go ahead and use it if you have to. Throw me out with the wolves."

She looked down at the gun as she opened her coat and tore off one of her pantaloon cuffs. "You know I will, too. You've seen me use one of those."

"Scared pure hell out of me."

"Hush, now." Biting back a grin, she dipped the wadded cloth in the snowmelt whiskey, and dabbed at the tooth marks on his shoulder. Yakima jerked as the whiskey bit into the gouges like acid. "Easy."

"You've been shot, stabbed with any number of sharp objects, and this hurts?"

"You gonna work or yak?" He threw back another shot.

Sitting back in the hay, he set the bottle beside him and watched her work. Several times she glanced at him, incredulous, then turned back to her work.

The wind continued to hammer the barn with violent, shuddering blasts. Drafts fluttered her hair about her finely tapered cheeks. Between blasts, Yakima heard the wolves snarling as they ripped and tore, devouring his enemies. The girl glanced toward the front of the barn a couple of times, swallowing with revulsion, before continuing to dab the blood from Yakima's wounds.

"A couple are deep," she said, wringing the cloth out in the cup for the last time, glancing at his scarred chest once more. "But I gather you're good at healing."

"They'll be gone in no time."

She set the cup and the cloth down, but did not move away from him. She sat beside him, her legs curled under a hip, a hand on the floor, the other in her lap. Her coat had opened, and he could see a good bit of the deep, creamy valley between her breasts.

She looked around, listening to the wind and the wolves with a troubled expression. The only light was the umber of the fire below the loft, and it shaded her face attractively.

Yakima set his hand on hers. She looked down at it then furled her brows at him.

"Come here," Yakima said, giving her hand a gentle tug.

Her frown deepened. "No."

"It's Christmas, and wolves are on the prowl, Miss Berryman."

"You're not going to frighten me into . . . laying with you, Mr. Henry."

"Might freeze to death. It's cold."

"You'll keep the fire stoked, I'm sure."

"It's stoked." He reached up and caressed her neck.

Even in the shadows he could see her cheeks mottle red. She swallowed, parted her lips. Her breasts rose and fell heavily behind her torn camisole.

She shook her hair from her eyes. "Are you drunk, Mr. Henry?"

He splayed his fingers across the back of her neck, and pulled her head toward his. "What difference does it make?" He closed his lips over her mouth. She did not pull back, but her body remained rigid in his arms. She placed both her hands on his chest and pushed away from him— but not far away.

She stared at his mouth, and her breasts rose and fell more heavily. A sort of snarl played across her upper lip, and then she threw her arms around his neck, pressed her warm, moist mouth to his, and kissed him with savage passion. She mashed her breasts against his chest and dug her fingers into the ridged muscles defining his shoulder blades.

Yakima reached into her camisole, cupping a breast, rolling his thumb and index finger over a nipple at the end of the full, firm orb, feeling it harden and pebble, hearing her groan hungrily as she sent her tongue into the far reaches of his mouth.

The wind gusted, quieted. A wolf howled while another yipped and another snarled furiously.

Veronica jerked with a frightened start. Groaning, she pressed her body even harder against Yakima's.

After a time, he pushed her down to the floor and removed the remaining strap of her camisole from her shoulder, running his hands down her slender arms and staring down at her heaving, swollen breasts.

"Please don't take advantage of me," she whispered. Her hair was sprayed out across the hay beneath her head, and her open mouth made a perfect, dark circle.

"All right."

Staring down at her, his own breath coming short, desire making his loins ache, he shucked out of his jeans and balbriggan bottoms. He snaked his arms under her knees and hoisted her legs over his shoulders, positioning her hips with his hands, mounting her.

The wind blew and the wolves snarled and the loft creaked with each thrust of Yakima's hips.

"Oh, you bastard!" she howled, digging her fingers into his bucking hips and closing her mouth over the bite marks in his shoulder.

When Yakima had brought himself and Veronica to grunting, moaning climax, he pulled on his balbriggans and stoked the fire in the tin washtub near which Barstow lay under several blankets, mouth wide, a bottle resting on his chest. The fire blazing, Yakima stole back up the ladder. He lay down beside the girl and pulled her heavy coat over them both.

Veronica spooned her body against his, snaking her arms around him and pressing her hands to his chest. She kissed the back of his neck, sighed, and slept.

Chapter 21

Snakehead Dawson dreamt that his feet were on fire.

It was a long, agonizing dream. No matter what he did he could not put out the fire, or, just when he'd gotten it out, it would return and he'd try in vain to run from the flames or to stomp them out while yearning to dip his toes in a snow-drift or a frigid snowmelt river.

He was mercifully called up out of the dream by carnal growls, a girl's hushed voice, and the sighs of straining bed-springs.

Snakehead opened his eyes and looked around, slow to get his bearings but finally recognizing the few sticks of roughhewn furniture of the musty hotel room that he, Luis Lavoto, and Phil Little had rented over a saloon near the doctor's office in Louisville, Colorado Territory.

As the sounds of lusty frolic continued, Snakehead looked to his right, where he'd last seen the doctor's helper, Jessie Fine, after she'd managed to take his mind off the misery of having one and a half toes blown to pulp inside his right boot. Only rumpled blankets over there, and the indentation of the blond girl's head in the far end of Snakehead's striped moisture-stained pillow that smelled as though a rodent had crawled inside and died.

Gritting his teeth against the raw, gnawing pain in his right foot jutting above the blankets toward the cool, soothing air, he lifted his head and looked across at the bed beyond his, abutting the far wall. Dirty dawn light was just beginning to push through the room's burlap curtains, so all Snakehead could see was a large, dark shape atop the bed that Lavoto had rolled into last night, cursing his bullet-torn right wrist.

The murky figure on Lavoto's bed rose and fell quickly, making the bed springs squawk like a long-dying chicken.

A girl's pinched voice said, "Oh . . . oh . . . *oh* . . . *!*"

Snakehead clamped his jaws together hard. That was Jessie's voice. On the other side of the room, near the sheet-iron stove, Phil Little was snoring.

But Snakehead stared hard at the figure before him and which he now recognized as Lavoto's long frame humping up beneath sheets and quilts. He could see the back of Lavoto's black head at the bed's far end, glimpse Jessie's blond curls spread across the pillow beneath the Mexican gunslinger.

"Hey," Snakehead grumbled, rising up on his elbows. "What the hell you two think you're doin' over there?"

While the girl continued sighing and groaning and Lavoto continued making the bed squawk, the Mexican pistoleer chuckled. "I'm screwing your girl. What does it look like, amigo?"

Snakehead wasn't sure what disgusted him about that. He, Lavoto, and Little had shared women before. Somehow, Snakehead had figured Jessie had been more than a mere whore for him last night, since she hadn't taken much coaxing to get her away from the sawbones' dive, and she hadn't asked for money despite Snakehead knowing she'd been a whore in Taos at one time.

Also, she hadn't looked like a whore—not in those tomboy clothes and with all those blond curls and eyes blue as cornflowers.

She'd reminded him a little of a girl Snakehead had known long before he'd become "Snakehead" but was still only Milton Earl Dawson from Tunnel Hill, Georgia—back before the carpetbaggers had moved in from the north, bought up all the farms for back taxes, and Milton Earl, his three brothers, six cousins, and his father had gone to a town meeting one night and shot six of the shit-lizards, as his father had called them, with bird guns.

Yessir, Jessie sort of looked like Noreen Brindle, the little girl from the farm near his family's cabin and whom he'd planned to marry someday before fleeing west and continuing to kill people for money because it's what he'd fallen into and what he'd discovered with a vague, long-faded horror that he was good at.

"Goddamn you, Lavoto, you cooch-stealin' sonofabitch!"

Phil Little stopped snoring, and Lavoto suddenly stopped hammering away between Jessie's legs to grab the pistol hanging from the holster on his left front bedpost—the man was as fast as Snakehead had ever seen even with his left hand—and aimed the Colt back across his bed at Snakehead.

Snakehead froze, stared at the quarter-sized black maw yawning at him, and knew a rare moment of terror. Lavoto was faster than Snakehead, and Snakehead was fast, but he'd been in so much pain last night he hadn't even hanged his pistol on his bedpost. Too late to reach for the gun now. Lavoto had him.

Snakehead said nothing. On the other side of the room,

Little lifted his head to look around in sleepy confusion between strands of his long, sandy hair. "What . . . what's goin' . . . ?" He saw the gun and let his voice trail off.

Beneath Lavoto, the girl groaned and wrapped her arms around his neck, tugging at him. "Come on, honey," Jessie said in a whiney little girl's voice—the same one she'd used with Snakehead a few hours ago. "Forget it, now, huh? Play with Jessie."

Lavoto continued to stare down his gun barrel at Snakehead, and Snakehead continued to stare back, knowing he was on the razor edge but also knowing if he showed fear, he'd get a bullet through an eye. Fear was a tonic to Luis Lavoto, and a call to bloody murder.

"Come on, honey," Jessie said.

Finally, Snakehead saw a flash of white between the Mexican's mustache-mantled mouth, and he heard the Colt's hammer click as Lavoto depressed it. "You can have her back when I'm finished." He winked, dropped his Colt back into its holster, then lowered himself over the girl and continued to make her groan and the mattress sing.

"Forget it," Snakehead snarled. "Got more important things on the docket today."

He felt foolish for having thought she was anything but a whore in the first place—and not even one that charged but only wanted a man, or men, between her legs. That humiliation somehow kicked up the burn in Snakehead's foot, and, ignoring the girl and Lavoto, he swung his legs over the side of the bed and gingerly set his right foot on the floor.

He looked down at it, made a sour expression. The second toe was capped, the third one gone entirely, leaving a half-inch gap. In the lousy light, the dried blood looked black, and the bruising and swelling reached up across his foot to nearly his ankle.

He cursed loudly and bounded up from the bed to grab a bottle from the cracked washstand, and threw back a long, soothing shot of busthead.

"How's your foot?"

"Shut up, Phil."

He dressed quickly, trying to blot out the sound of the mattress dance that was getting louder and louder, but did not put on his right sock and boot. Instead, he carried the boot and the whiskey bottle into the hall, closing the door on the sounds behind him, and limped to an outside door.

He had to shove the door open with his shoulder, as ten inches of fresh powder mantled the top of the outside stairs. He shoved his right leg through the opening and buried his foot in the snow.

He winced, and his heart fluttered at the nearly unendurable chill. At the same time the frigid cold relieved some of the searing burn. Holding his foot there in the snow, he groaned and sighed, and then he pulled the raw, aching appendage back into the hotel and drew the door closed with a wooden grate and a thud, plowing a small mound of powder inside the uncarpeted hall.

Snakehead held the tender, swollen foot about six inches above the floor. It was now mottled white, and it quivered there at the end of his ankle. The outlaw gave a single sob of misery spiked with fury, and grunted, "You will be avenged."

He grunted and groaned some more as he pulled his sock on and, with painstaking gentleness, pulled his boot on, setting the heel on the floor to carefully work it snug. Dragging the foot down the hall to the narrow stairs, he clomped down the scarred wooden steps, using both railings to keep as much weight as he could from the mangled limb, which he could feel throbbing fiercely inside his suddenly too tight boot.

He glanced over the left rail. The saloon was dusky and nearly empty, most of the chairs still tipped over tables for sweeping. A table near the bottom of the stairs was the only one occupied, by the two strangers who'd visited the doctor's office yesterday—the short bearded man, Lars Larsen, who'd shot Rosie Dawn, and his partner, the tall, scar-faced Englishman who'd introduced himself as Logan Blyster.

Half-empty beer schooners stood on the table before the two men, near two empty shot glasses. Broken eggshells filled Larsen's shot glass, and as Snakehead dragged his foot over to the men's table, he saw an egg yolk bobbing around at the bottom of Larsen's beer schooner. A brown-paper quirley smoldered between the man's fingers wrapped around the schooner, while Blyster sat back, packing a silver-tipped briar pipe.

Both men studied Snakehead with dull expectation as well as a distinct wariness.

"Hollis," Snakehead said, glancing at the bartender who was sweeping at the far end of the room, near the two closed doors with their winter-frosty panes, "I'll have what Whore-Killer's havin'."

Hollis—a chunky man with a mustache and a few sparse hairs greased back on his nearly bald pate—stopped sweeping. "Which one's Whore-Killer?"

"This man right here," Snakehead said, curling his upper lip distastefully at Larsen. "The Swede."

"All right." The barman ambled toward the counter running along the room's right wall, under an enormous elk head whose antlers sported several bullet holes as well as a pair of frilly black panties.

Larsen dropped his eyes to the table, then lifted his quirley to his lips, inhaling deeply. As he exhaled and as the barman filled a beer schooner, he lifted his gaze again to the outlaw. "How's your foot?"

"I don't wanna talk about it."

Larsen slid his eyes nervously toward the Englishman, who was puffing his pipe to life and causing his burning match to flame intermittently. Smoke wafted around his long, savagely scarred beak. Around the pipe stem, Blythe said in his English accent, "Did you have a chance to think about our proposition, Mr. Dawson?"

Snakehead propped his right boot on a chair beside him and said with dull skepticism, "You wanna throw in with me and my boys as we go after the loot."

The two men said nothing. The Englishman merely lifted his mouth corners slightly, removed the pipe from his mouth, and blew smoke at the low rafters.

The barman set a beer schooner on the table. Beside it he set a shot glass with an egg suspended over the glass. "And why the hell would we want the company of a couple of cork-headed, grubline-ridin' saddletramps like you? Especially you, there, Swede, ya miserable whore-killer. Don't you know only pussies shoot whores? And don't you know that ain't the best way to get any information out of the girl? Shit, you just made the job tougher for all of us."

Snakehead was getting heated up due in no small part to the returning fire in his boot. "You know, there, Swede, it ain't too damn far off target to say you're responsible for me getting a toe blowed off."

"How in the hell is that?" the Swede said, incredulous.

"I wouldn't be out here in the first place, chasin' Rosie Dawn's pa around the Sawatch in the middle of a cold goddamn winter, if you hadn't shot the bitch."

The bearded Larsen narrowed a dull, brown, belligerent eye slightly, flushing, and took another drag from his cigarette. "She wasn't gonna tell nobody where that money was. But she knew where it was, all right. The girl couldn't lie for shit."

"I'd have gotten it out of her."

Larsen gave a dry chuckle and rolled his eyes.

"Gentlemen," Blyster said, "this is getting us nowhere. Lars knows he made a mistake. He was drunk and he gets crazy when he's drunk. Crazy-mad. It's not his fault. The girl should not have provided him with liquor."

"Helluva big mistake," Snakehead said. "Now we gotta hope she spilled the beans to her pa. If she didn't, we're all out here on a wild-goose chase, and I got a mighty big hole in my boot for my trouble."

"That's why we're here." Larsen looked at Snakehead's boot propped on the chair.

Snakehead's bloody sock showed through the ragged hole in the boot's pointed toe.

The Swede said, "To help you fellas track down that half-breed, and pistol-whip the whereabouts of the loot from the whore's old man." He hiked a shoulder and sat back in his chair, his stubborn eyes careful. "For a percentage, o' course."

Snakehead cracked his egg into his beer and threw back his entire shot. He slammed the glass down on the table and stared hard at the Swede. "What makes you think we need your help, Whore-Killer?"

"Because you have an injured foot," the Englishman said, holding his pipe in front of his chin. "And Senor Lavoto has an injured wrist. His shooting wrist."

"Shit, Lavoto's as good with his left wrist as he is with his right one. Hell, he can shoot them pistols with his feet."

"But tracking in this weather—him with an injured wrist and you with a hole in your foot—won't be an easy task. Of course, Little has only a scratch on his ear. But the man who shot you, Mr. Dawson, is no down-at-heel, grubline-riding half-breed. That was Yakima Henry."

Snakehead stared at the scar-faced Englishman through the wafting pipe and cigarette smoke. "Who?"

"We seen his work down in Mexico," Larsen said. "Mercenary work. Cold-steel work for a couple of rich brothers who had 'em a silver mine in northern Chihuahua. The breed went in to help 'em get their silver out when they got pinned down by banditos. He left enough dead Mexicans to fill three cemeteries."

Snakehead looked at his foot that was quivering slightly as it throbbed—he imagined a thumping red heart wedged in his boot—and threw his head back on his shoulders with a pained sigh. "Well, I saw fer my ownself that he knew his way around a six-shooter. Not to worry, though, boys. Me and Luis can handle six of them Henry fellas, and . . ."

He let his voice trail off when he heard footsteps on the stairs behind him, and turned to see Luis Lavoto descending the steps erratically. The tall Mexican wore his black, silver-banded hat and wolf coat, and he held a bottle by the neck in his left hand. His bandaged right wrist was suspended over his chest by a belt sling.

"She's all yours, Snakehead," the Mexican drawled thickly. "I took my pleasure, if you could call it pleasure. She's too skinny and makes too damn much noise. If a girl's gonna make that much noise, she better be a helluva lot better than *that!*"

Lavoto stumbled at the bottom of the stairs, as though he'd been expecting another step, then staggered over to the bar. He took the last swig of whiskey from the bottle then set it on the bar top, tipping it over then watching with drunken amusement as it rolled off the bar and shattered on the floor behind it.

"Hey, what the hell!" the barman yelled from where he was sweeping under a table near the player piano. He turned toward the bar, and his eyes widened. "Oh, it's you, Senor Lavoto."

"I'd like another bottle," the Mexican snarled.

"Right away, Senor!" The barman tripped over a table leg as he scurried across the room.

Snakehead watched Lavoto standing there, waiting for his bottle, swaying from side to side and staring down at the bar top as though reading a paper. Snakehead looked at the Mexican's blood-spotted bandage, saw the fever-sweat pasting his black hair to his forehead.

Lavoto's cheeks were bleached out and hollow under his thin black beard. Blood poisoning, maybe. He might be able to shoot with his left hand, but they had a long, cold ride ahead of them. If the Mex didn't make it, it would be just Snakehead and Little against the half-breed. That wouldn't be a problem if Snakehead himself wasn't feeling like a fall leaf in a howling gale, and if Little hadn't shown his true cowardly colors.

No way Snakehead would consider letting the money go now. Nor the half-breed . . .

Snakehead glanced at Blyster and Larsen. Larsen lifted his quirley to his lips, took a deep drag into his lungs.

"Can you boys shoot?" Snakehead glowered at Larsen. "I mean shoot somethin' besides whores?"

Larsen flushed again, and his nostrils expanded, chafed at the riding he was taking. "Banks're our specialty, but we lost most of our gang in a shootout in Kansas. Lost the booty, too. We might not be as fast as you fellas, but we can track and we can shoot. The five of us has a better chance of bringin' down that breed than you three alone, in your conditions. And better than just me and Blyster here, too."

"And we figure fifty-six thousand dollars is enough to spread amongst us," Blyster put in with a cautious edge to his inflected voice. "No need for anybody gettin' greedy . . . and trigger-happy."

"Ah, no of course not." Snakehead smiled.

He hooked a thumb toward Lavoto standing shamble-footed at the bar, carefully lifting a shot glass to his lips. "Best let me break the news of the five-way split to Lavoto over there." He kept his voice down and eased his bad foot to the floor. "Ole Luis is the most independent cuss you've ever heard of. If I don't ease him into the idea, he's liable to shoot you fellas outright."

As Snakehead wheezed and groaned to his feet, Larsen and Blyster shared a wary look.

Chapter 22

Yakima awakened in the cold barn and looked at the woman cuddled against him for warmth, her cheek pressed to his belly, her chestnut hair sprayed across his chest.

He gently slid a lock of hair from over her right eye, revealing the pale, brown-lashed lid. Remembering such mornings with Faith, in the cabin of their horse ranch at the base of Bailey Peak, a pang of loneliness swept through him—that futile yearning for the dead that sinks like molten steel from the throat to the toes, searing everything in its path.

Veronica made a sound.

Yakima let her hair fall back into place as she lifted her head, blinking groggily. She looked at his chest, frowning as though unsure of where she was, who this man might be. She slid her befuddled gaze up Yakima's chest to his face, and, blinking her heavy-lidded eyes, flushed and rose up on her arms. She looked down at her bare, swinging breasts, and closed her hands over them.

"Ohh," she said, looking around with chagrin, understanding washing over her. "You must think me quite depraved."

Yakima curled his upper lip as she pulled back away from

him, casting her gaze across her clothes. "There's worse things."

Sliding her hands from her breasts to her arms, covering her chest with her elbows, she regarded him with beseeching. "I'm not . . . like that. I . . . I was . . . I was *frightened!*"

"Don't worry about it. Our secret." He threw her coat off his naked body, and closed it over her shoulders as he started to rise. "I'll stoke the fire."

As she lay back down, drawing the heavy coat over her so that only her head was revealed, Yakima dressed quickly in the barn's frigid chill, his breath frosting before him in the barn's dusky shadows. Curled on her side, she watched him. He didn't look at her. He swept his long hair back with his hands, donned his hat, and grabbed his saddlebags, canteen, and rifle. He tramped across the loft to the ladder.

"Yakima?"

He glanced back at her. She rose onto an elbow, letting the coat slide off a shoulder. "I wasn't that frightened."

Yakima continued down the ladder and walked over to the tin washtub. A bed of coals glowed at the bottom. Barstow's blankets and possibles lay nearby, but Barstow himself wasn't here. The indentation of his body remained in the hay and straw near the tub.

Yakima looked around. "Barstow?"

Yakima tossed a couple of split pine logs into the tub then went to the front doors. If Barstow had gone outside to tend nature during the night, the wolves might have gotten him. Snow lay inside the closed doors. Yakima threw the right door open, and more fresh, downy snow tumbled across his boots.

He looked out into the gray shadows, saw the mussed snow and dark stains and bits of cloth where the bodies of

Veronica's attackers had been. Fresh boot tracks angled out away from the barn, skirting the remaining carnage.

Yakima stepped out and, hefting his rifle, called for the honyonker. Dense wintery silence was the only reply. To Yakima's left and right, dark, craggy ridges vaulted skyward, shedding the forest that thinned out high amongst the stony fissures and the steeples flecked with clinging snow. A hawk called in the far distance.

Yakima went out, pulled the door closed, and followed Barstow's tracks back toward the main trail, his fur boots crunching loudly. The clouds were low, but no snow currently fell. The pines lining the frozen stream and the trail hung heavy under the thick, white mantling.

A shout rose ahead of Yakima, beyond the stream. He stopped suddenly as the echoes rolled back from the canyon's sheer, rocky wall. He looked ahead through the pines toward the wagon, which he couldn't see for the trees.

"GODDAMNIT!" The shout echoed again, shrill with frustration and agony.

Yakima jogged ahead through the trees, snow rolling up around his knees. He crossed the stream and, as the pines and firs fell back beside him, he saw the brown shape of the wagon sitting where they'd left it, hung up on the snow-covered trail between the stream on the left and the canyon wall on the right.

"GODDAMNIT TO HELL!" Barstow's voice rose again, the epithet's clear echoes dwindling slowly, as though someone on the canyon rim were aping the honyonker's angst.

"Barstow?"

Yakima moved around the wagon as the honyonker rammed his mittened fist against the closed tailgate. His face was red, and his mustache was frosty. Tears made his usually dull brown eyes sharp as he turned toward Yakima.

"How am I supposed to get home without the mule?" Again, he rammed his fist against the tailgate. "Tell me that! How am I supposed to get my girl home without the mule?"

Yakima opened his mouth to speak but stopped when Barstow clamped his mittens against his face, sobbing. A bottle lay in the snow nearby. His voice was hoarse, thick with agony. "*Damnit!*" he cried. "I never did right by her. I never did a good thing for her while she lived, and now . . ."

Barstow wheeled angrily and stomped around the far side of the wagon. Yakima saw only the man's head with his billed watch cap and the craggy, red face and brushy red mustache all twisted in misery.

The man faced Yakima, enraged, and pounded the top of the wagon's side panel. "I expected her to work like the boys, but she wasn't made for it. Her ma told me. The boys told me. I wouldn't listen. And after the girl turned six years old, she never had another word for me! Not a word!"

He pounded the side panel again, tears now flowing freely down his cheeks, mucus bubbling out of his nose and onto his mustache. "I tried beating it out of her. A 'Good morning, Papa,' or a 'Good night, Papa' . . . *anything!* I whipped her, and I locked her in the woodshed, but she never had another word for me. Not one fuckin' word!"

He wheeled miserably, and his head dropped down behind the wagon, out of Yakima's sight. The half-breed walked around the back of the wagon and saw Barstow sitting in the snow, his back resting up against the wagon's half-buried rear wheel, head hanging.

Suddenly, hardening his jaws, he bellowed, "And now I can't even bring her home to her ma to bury her!"

He dropped his head again, punching his thighs and sobbing.

Yakima tramped over to the man, looked down at him,

frowning. The man's agony was so poignant that Yakima could feel it in his own chest. He squatted down beside the honyonker, placed a hand on the man's jerking shoulder.

"Barstow," he said softly. "We'll get her home. We got five extra horses in the barn."

"They ain't pullers!"

"They won't pull as well as the mule, but they'll pull." Yakima slipped behind Barstow, snaked his hands under the man's arms, and heaved him to his feet. "Come on."

The man's own sadness, coupled with the sadness Yakima had awakened with, remembering his own dead, was a heavy yoke on his shoulders. As much as to buoy his own spirits as Barstow's, he slapped the honyonker's back. "Let's go get them horses. We'll get one or two hitched up. There's plenty of tack in the barn."

The night before, in a ranch cabin east of Louisville, the birdlike old woman who owned and operated the Beartooth Ranch pulled a hot poker out of the large stone fireplace, and turned toward where Wilbur and Erroll Fallon and their segundo, Glen Plaza, held James Fallon down on the heavy pine-plank eating table under a sputtering oil lamp.

"Hold him down good and tight." Emma Karlsrudd crossed her eyes in their wizened sockets as she gazed at the glowing end of the poker. "This is gonna hurt like hell and then some."

James Fallon looked at the glowing poker and its reflection in the old woman's close-set eyes, and shot a horrified look at his father who leaned over, holding his head down with his heavy forearms and bunching his lips with the effort. "Don't let her do it, Pa!"

"I'm sorry, boy," the old woman said, moving toward the

table. "That beak of yourn is broke on the inside and the outside, and this here's the only way to set it and cauterize it."

"Ah, shit!"

"Don't you cuss in my house, youngun."

"Just get it over, will ya, Emma?" Wilbur Fallon urged. "I'll whip him later."

"Steady, now!"

Fallon gave a grunt as he pinned James's head to the table. Plaza and Erroll Fallon each did the same as they held his legs.

"Nooo!" James screamed, and then he felt the heat of the glowing poker and smelled the glowing iron, and then the old woman rammed it far up into his right nostril. James's mouth was wide open but for some reason no scream sounded anywhere but in his own head.

Screaming internally, he stared glassily at the low, soot-and grease-coated ceiling beyond the lamp, feeling his fingers twitch and his toe tingle.

The woman slid the poker out of the right nostril then, with a sadistic grit of her chipped yellow horse teeth, jammed it into the left nostril, where it sizzled and sputtered and filled James with a pain unlike any he'd ever felt before—a pain that couldn't really be described as pain but maybe the monolithic fury of a dark god delivered to him personally or, more specifically, to the soft tissues of his inner tender, aching, swollen nose.

Even before the old bird removed the poker from his left nostril, the pain died.

"He's out," Fallon said, releasing James's head.

"Most of 'em are out by now. Don't know how many noses I've doctored over the years—fifteen, twenty, I'd say—when I still had a bunkhouse full o' punchers."

"You all alone out here now, Emma?"

Plaza and Erroll released James's legs. Emma Karlsrudd set the poker back in its rack by the fireplace. "Hell, yes. I'm pret' near eighty. Outlived four husbands—buried 'em all out yonder. Ran off all my younguns. Hebert Nordstrom runs my herd now, in exchange for my water, and I just run a few chickens and goats of a summer."

She looked at Plaza and Erroll, and canted her head toward a half-open door on the other side of the kitchen. "You can dump the patient in yonder. He'll likely be out for a while. If he comes around, I have something that'll knock him out."

Fallon kicked a chair out from under the table and shrugged out of his heavy, quilted-leather coat. "If he comes around, it'll serve him right to suffer. The cork-headed moron made a damn fool o' himself tryin' to show off."

As Plaza and Erroll carried James toward the door that the woman had indicated, Fallon draped his coat over the chair back and looked at Mrs. Karlsrudd severely under the guttering gas lamp. "I don't know what to do with him, Emma. I might have to send him to college."

"When they're no use on the ranch, there ain't much else you can do, Wilbur. I didn't have the money to send mine to school, so when they all showed themselves to be nothing but cowardly dogs too weak to dig a post hole or muck horse dung, much less run rustlers off, I packed 'em a day's worth of grub, let 'em saddle a horse o' their choosin', and pointed 'em down the road."

Fallon sank back in his chair, wagging his head.

Plaza and Erroll came out of the room in which they'd deposited James. They hadn't removed their coats yet, as they'd all just arrived at the Karlsrudd Ranch less than a half hour ago, after the storm had nearly stranded them out on the trail, and they'd tended their horses before tending to James's broken nose.

"You boys look hungry," Mrs. Karlrudd said, rising creakily from her chair. A corncob pipe jutted from the pocket of her plaid wool shirt she wore with the shirttails drooping down over her shapeless, grease-stained skirt. "You throw your coats down by the fire and sit up to table. I'm gonna heat you some antelope stew, take the cold out of your bones."

"You don't go to no trouble on our account, Emma," Fallon said.

"No trouble a'tall. I ain't sat down with a tableful of men in a coon's age. I might even pack down some more vittles my ownself. This cold makes an old woman hungry." As she stoked the cast-iron range, she slid a sly glance at tall, rangy Glen Plaza who stood behind a spool-back chair, doffing his hat and digging his makings sack out of his shirt pocket. "Makes her right chilly, too. Makes her think all kinds o' nasty thoughts, like curlin' up to some long, tall drink of a cowboy for a little warm and randy frolic."

Plaza tossed his makings sack onto the table and shrugged out of his coat, wincing a little but otherwise not reacting to the old buzzard's flirtation.

As Erroll sat down in a chair beside his father, Fallon scowled at their hostess, and said, "You leave my segundo alone, damnit, Emma. You're like to plant him back with your other men, and I need him for the trail tomorrow." He looked at Plaza, a fire returning to his eyes as he tugged at his shaggy beard. "Need him for some gun work."

The old woman came out of a side room with a black pot, heading for the range. "Gun work? What kind of gun work you got, Wilbur? Strange time of year for rustlers to be workin' these parts."

"We ain't after rustlers." Fallon packed his pipe as Plaza

sat down across from him and started building a quirley. "This is damned embarrassing, Emma, but tragedy has befallen my range. Frank's dead. His wife killed him. It's her we're hunting."

Mrs. Karlrudd looked sharply over her shoulder as she stirred the stewpot with a long-handled wooden spoon. "What did you say, Wilbur? I must be goin' deaf as well as loco."

"Frank's dead. His wife, that girl from the East, shot him in their own damn bedroom."

"That's what I thought you said." Mrs. Karlrudd turned around. The coffeepot she'd filled earlier was chugging hard, coal black brew boiling up out of the spout. "Holy Jesus and Mary, your Frank's *gone*?"

"Two days ago. She shot him and ran, and we're gonna run her down and haul her back to the headquarters."

Mrs. Karlsrudd shook her head as she hardened her jaws and narrowed her eyes, pointing the wooden spoon at Fallon. "Turn her over to Ruthie. She'll know what to do with her. Only a mother knows what to do with the killer of one of her boys. Especially one like Frank—a good, strong child from the get-go."

"That's what we're gonna do," Fallon said.

Erroll said, "We're gonna hang her in front of Ma. Maybe even let Ma slap the horse out from under her."

Fallon glanced at his idiot son in disgust. "Shut up, Erroll. You stay out of this. Me and Mrs. Karlsrudd is talkin'."

"Wish I'd had one like Frank," the woman said, turning back to the stew. "Why'd she kill him?"

"Who knows? She was an uppity bitch from the start. I shoulda known better than to send back East for a gal to marry Frank. It's just that he scared off all the girls of marryin' age in the Sawatch."

Mrs. Karlsrudd chuckled as she slammed the lid down

on the pot and turned to grab some mugs from a shelf. "That he did, that he did. A hard young man, that Frank, but that's what it takes to run a ranch out here. Some women just don't understand that. You gotta give your man plenty of leash in these parts, and don't expect him to be a tea-drinker, if you get my drift. If he slaps you around a few times of a winter, well, that's just him keepin' in trim. You take the horns with the hide, is how I see it. My problem is I never could find a man stronger than me, and I ended up killin' 'em one way or another."

With a hearty chuckle, the old bird set filled coffee mugs in front of Fallon and Plaza then grabbed a bottle off a shelf. She splashed liquor into each man's mug then set the bottle on the table. "Yessir, that's a cryin' damn shame, you losin' Frank. What're you gonna do now, Wilbur? Can either of these other two wear his boots?"

Fallon looked at Erroll, who was picking at a callus on his right hand, brows bunched in concentration.

"Not by a long shot," Fallon grouched, cuffing the back of the boy's head.

Erroll did not react but only kept on picking at his open palm.

Mrs. Karlsrudd filled a coffee mug and sat down beside Plaza, reaching for the whiskey bottle. "Who busted the other one's nose for him?"

"The half-breed with Frank's wife."

Mrs. Karlsrudd lifted the bottle from her cup, frowning across the table at Fallon. "She ran off with a half-breed?"

"Don't know if they had it planned or if she just ran into him along the trail. But the sonofabitch lied about havin' her, and when James got cocky and tried to sneak into their camp, the breed busted his nose. Tied him to a tree where the worthless younker damn near froze to death so I'd be stuck with only one worthless son instead of two. Not sure how big a loss it would have been, but the whole affair told us we gotta treat the breed like a coiled diamondback. He's wily, that one. Must be half-Apache, maybe Comanche."

"Cheyenne."

Fallon and Plaza looked at the woman sipping her whiskey-laced java.

"He's half-Cheyenne," Mrs. Karlsrudd said, lowering her steaming mug and smacking her lips. "Name's Henry. Yakima Henry. And you're right, treat him like a panther, cause that's what he is mostly."

Plaza dribbled cigarette smoke from his broad nostrils as he said in his soft, deep voice, "Ma'am, you know this fella?"

"Not personal. But an old woman learns a lot from entertainin' travelers from along the road such as yourselves. I've heard of this Henry feller. A kill-crazy half-breed Cheyenne. Pistol for hire, some say. Some say he don't fight less'n he's provoked, but from what I've heard it don't take much to provoke him."

Mrs. Karlsrudd sipped her brew then got up to check the stew.

"A fella came through here last summer—he chopped firewood through July—and he told me about meetin' up with Yakima Henry in the Spanish Mountains last winter. Seems Mr. Henry didn't like it when a bartender told him he didn't serve half-breeds, and he kicked the holy livin' shit out of everyone in the whole damn saloon, includin' the fella I talked to. Poor fella's only been fit for cuttin' firewood ever since. Sent a couple flyin' outta that saloon and straight to their rewards."

The woman pulled four tin plates down from a shelf over the range. As she began ladling the smoking stew, she gave Fallon and Plaza a pointed look over her shoulder. "You fellas tread easy if this is the man you're following—if it's Yakima Henry you gotta pry that killin' devil-woman away from. You hear?"

Plaza looked at her over his chair back, smoking. Nodding, he turned to his boss. "Looks like you was right, Mr. Fallon. He ain't your average saddle tramp."

Fallon narrowed his eyes as Mrs. Karlsrudd set a steaming plate down in front of him. "Tread light, bullshit. Pardon my French, Emma." He looked at Plaza. "Well, now we know who we're dealing with."

"Yessir," Plaza said. "How you wanna proceed, Mr. Fallon?"

"With care, like Emma said." Fallon forked a chunk of charred antelope into his mouth. "And we do whatever it takes to get the woman."

Chapter 23

Yakima booted Wolf up a low hill. He skirted the knoll's shoulder, so he wouldn't skyline himself, and reined the stallion to a halt on the southeast slope.

From here, he could see a good stretch of his backtrail, the wagon and horse tracks spooling around bluffs, buttes, low mesas, and fir-clad mountain slopes, for nearly ten miles across a lower elevation. The clouds had parted, and the sun had come out here on the Sawatch's northwestern flank, and the sun reflecting off the snow felt like a million miniature javelins in the half-breed's eyes.

He squinted, bringing five riders into focus.

There were three men in the lead, with two more following, as the group traced a long bend in the trail. They were five ant-sized figures moving around a stony shelf and now beginning to disappear around a steep, rocky hillside. The front three disappeared, leaving only the two riding drag.

Movement behind the drag riders caught Yakima's attention, and he lifted his gaze to about another mile behind the first group. Another group was making its way along a small, flat stretch of snow along the stream that had cut this broken valley countless millennia ago. From this distance, the second group was half the size of the first group, so it was impossible to accurately count their number, but, squinting hard, Yakima thought he could see four.

That they were after him or Barstow or Veronica Berryman, there was little doubt.

He hipped around in his saddle to stare northwest, where the pleats and folds of the snowy Sawatch dropped and tapered out to a tawny, snow-dusted plain stretching between low hills.

He could just make out the village of Rolette nestled amongst that high prairie's sage-covered knolls and clay-colored shelves. The false-fronted buildings of the main street and the stock corrals poked above the sage, with the steel tracks of the rail spur showing like two thin, glistening silver threads at the far northern edge. The whole town including outlying shacks was little larger than Yakima's thumb from this distance.

Rolette was probably only ten miles away as the crow flies, but still half a day's pull for Barstow's wagon. Yakima's group would find little refuge there, no matter when they arrived, but he might at least be able to get Veronica on the train or the stage headed for Denver. Then he could deal with his shadowers unleashed by concerns for her safety.

Shit . . .

He looked southeast again, then northwest, and caressed the stock of the Winchester resting across his saddlebows.

As his horse clomped along the snowy trail, Snakehead looked down at his bloody boot hanging free of its stirrup, and wheezed a curse. He'd thought the cold would numb the pain, but it only increased it—a fist-sized heart pounding right behind where his toes had been before the half-breed had shot them off.

He cursed again as he reached back and pulled a bottle out of his saddlebags.

"Why are those three so damn far ahead?" Luis Lavoto growled. Riding beside Snakehead, the Mexican hunkered low in his saddle, holding his bullet-torn wrist taut against his belly. The bandage around his wrist was dark with frozen blood.

"Hadn't noticed."

"I don't see why we need them, anyway, amigo. I really don't see it, *usted entiende*?"

"I can appreciate and understand your reservations, Luis." Snakehead half-laughed and half-sobbed as he straightened in his saddle, raking his gaze from his torn, bloody boot. "But I look at things hard and clear. I'm practical that way, and whether you see it or not, you and me ain't in the best of conditions. Now, even you have to admit you've felt better. Come on—admit it, Luis."

Lavoto took a pull from the bottle in his hand, and grimaced but said nothing. He stared straight ahead at the backs of Phil Little, Lars Larsen, and the tall, scar-faced Englishman, Logan Blyster, who conversed in a desultory way as they followed the wagon tracks. They'd fallen into what appeared a friendly relationship if not a partnership—one that may or may not exclude the two slower, wounded riders.

Snakehead took a pull from his own bottle. "You see— them two and Little are gonna make up for what we ain't got. Namely, our health. They're gonna keep us going, keep us on the trail, and do the thinkin' for us. And when we catch up to the half-breed, they're gonna help us take him down if only to distract him while you and me exact vengeance on the loco sonofabitch. Blow his toes off and a couple other things before we kill him."

Snakehead wheezed a mirthless laugh then tossed a conspiratorial look at his Mexican partner. "Afterwards, when we don't need 'em no more, we'll shoot 'em—all three—and throw 'em down the nearest privy pit."

As their horses rode up and over a snow-covered rise, Lavoto looked at Snakehead. "You don't think they've thought of that?"

Snakehead stared at the three men in front of him, riding easily down the rise. "Sure, I do." Again, he pulled on the bottle, and smacked his lips. "And that just makes it all the more interesting."

Just then, Phil Little glanced over his shoulder at Snakehead and Lavoto. Turning forward, he muttered something to his two new compatriots, and booted his horse into a trot through the wind-drifted, sugary snow rumpled by the tracks of the wagon and its single outrider.

"See there?" Lavoto growled. "They're gonna try to lose us!"

He booted his own horse into a shambling gallop, and Snakehead, cursing when his grieved right foot inadvertently slapped his horse's ribs, sending a shudder of agony all through him, did likewise.

It was an agonized, loping ride over the parts of the trail the wind had cleared of snow, but he and Lavoto managed to stay within fifty yards of the three healthy riders. After nearly an hour of hard pulling through the glistening, new-fallen snow, Snakehead looked up to see the three growing large before him. His brain fuzzy from pain and drink, he was slow to realize that the three had stopped in the trail, the fiddle-footed horses blowing, their breath puffing visibly in the cold, crystalline air.

Lavoto drew his own horse to a halt beside Snakehead as Phil Little said, "What in the hell do you suppose he's doin', anyway?"

Snakehead followed the others' gazes ahead along the trail that rose and curved steeply before them, between two sheer walls of pitted and fissured sandstone. It was a long, narrow gorge.

On the top of the hill that rose up out of the gorge, three hundred yards away, a man sat a black horse sideways to the trail, holding a rifle straight up on his right thigh. He was a long ways away, but his silhouette told Snakehead that he wore a black, flat-brimmed hat, and black hair hung straight down to his shoulders.

Snakehead glowered. "He wants to finish it right here."

"He's too damn far away for accurate shooting," Little said.

Their horses stomped, blew, and nervously shook their heads, sensing the riders' tension.

"Even for rifles," Lars Larsen said.

Lavoto spat. "He wants us to come ahead."

"Sure, so he can tear us all to pieces in this narrow canyon." Blyster slid his rifle from its saddle sheath. "He has the high ground. Ups his odds right nicely."

"We'll wait him out," Snakehead said. "If he wants to fight, we'll fight him at a point of our own choos . . ."

He let his voice trail off as the half-breed suddenly raised his rifle to his shoulder. Snakehead and the others in his party all jerked with starts, holding their reins taut and jerking up their own rifles defensively. The half-breed aimed his rifle straight at them, angled down the hill, but then he swung it suddenly to his left, aiming almost parallel with his position at the top of the steep hill.

Snakehead saw smoke puff and flames stab from the barrel of the half-breed's repeater. A second later, the whipcrack of the rifle barreled through the canyon, echoing flatly.

One of the horses whinnied. Lavoto's steeldust reared slightly, and the Mexican whipped its ass with his rein-ends, cursing in Spanish.

"What the hell . . . ?" Phil Little said as the half-breed's rifle crashed twice more.

The third shot was still echoing when the breed lowered the rifle butt to his thigh and turned his head toward the canyon. As the rifle's echo dwindled, a rumbling like that of a distant, oncoming train rose to replace it.

Snakehead and the others glanced around at each other, incredulous. Snakehead felt fingers of apprehension pinching his back as he cast his gaze up canyon, where the wall fell back behind a jutting shoulder.

And that was when he saw the boulders tumbling down from the canyon's lip, on the other side of the knob—flashes of tawny rocks and white snow chunks.

"Ah, shit!" he bellowed, as the rumbling grew louder and the ground began to shake.

Little screamed, "*Rockslide!*"

As he and the others, including Lavoto, reined their horses around sharply and booted them back the way they'd come, Snakehead cast one more look up canyon. The half-breed had disappeared down the other side of the hill, and the snow and boulders were smashing into the canyon just below his previous position.

Smashing and rolling straight down toward Snakehead, because there was nowhere else for them to go, there were tons of rock and snow that would seal the canyon tight as cork in a whiskey jug.

Forgetting the pain in his right boot, Snakehead batted both heels madly against his horse's flanks. Horse and rider bolted down canyon behind the others. Dawson felt his horse's hooves slipping in the snow, and his heart hammered as he silently begged the mount to stay on its feet. As the dun stretched out over the ground, sending the fresh white down cascading up around its rider's stirrups, Dawson shot a glance behind.

The rocks and snow were bounding toward him in a jumbled mass pinched together by the canyon's sheer, steep walls. The slide roared and rumbled like a fire-breathing dragon or a runaway train, dust and snow blowing up around it like smoke.

Snakehead ground his spurs into the dun's flanks and hunkered low, screaming, "Come on, you miserable Cayuse. *Ruuunnnnn!*"

As he followed the others through the narrow canyon that began opening a hundred yards beyond, he had only to turn his head slightly to see the mountain of snow and bouncing boulders growing quickly behind him, causing the ground to leap and pitch beneath his horses' scissoring hooves. The others were bucking blurs just ahead, and they too were screaming and yelling and glancing wide-eyed behind as the rumbling grew to a ringing roar.

Snakehead felt the wind kicked up by the slide blowing its cold, sour breath at his back.

The canyon wall continued high on his right, but the left, fir-studded wall dropped gradually away to the stream angling white through barren aspens, with open ground beyond. The riders ahead turned toward the trees and the stream. Dawson followed suit, whipping his horse savagely with his reins and gouging it with his spurs.

As the trees grew before him, he cast another horrified glance behind.

The first of the boulders and snow chunks were within a few yards, smashing and crashing so loudly that he couldn't hear his own frightened breaths or the thudding of his own horse's hooves. Rocks and snowballs pelted his back and the back of his neck. The brittle wind chilled him right down to his bones and sinew.

Snakehead's horse lunged after the others, all racing to get behind the left ridge wall. The bare aspens loomed large before him, growing larger by leaps and bounds.

An enormous boulder cleaved in two as it hammered toward him as though thrown by an invisible, giant hand. Dawson ducked and automatically threw up an arm, sure the rocks would smash him somewhere around the horse's left hip.

Then he bounded behind the fir-carpeted ridge wall. The rocks that had been about to smash him disappeared but reappeared a half-second later, rolling on past him, straight down the canyon to be pulverized under the rest of the massive, hammering, raging slide.

He turned forward in his saddle. As several aspens swept past him on both sides, he hauled back hard on the dun's reins, throwing all his weight into both stirrups. The dun slid to a grinding halt, nickering wildly.

The other riders halted their own mounts—all except for Phil Little who was clubbed from his saddle by a low-hanging aspen limb to hit the ground behind his horse with an indignant grunt. It was a soft landing in the deep snow, and Little turned in a drift to peer back at the canyon, as did the others.

The rocks and snow chunks rolled and bounced on down the trail, a few slithering out toward the stream a safe distance from the riders, the ragged mass gradually slowing until it stopped with a few last belching grinds and clacks and a couple more final thundering booms echoing up the canyon.

Snow, dust, and cold air wafted. A few boulders shifted

positions. Rocks dribbled through cracks in the humped rubble that now rendered the trail impassable for anyone but bird or climbing beast.

Suddenly, silence.

A horse blew.

Another stomped.

Snakehead stared at the heaped rubble, and, feeling the ache in his boot kick up again, he spat sourly. "That sonofabitch!"

On a high, windy ridge a mile behind him, Wilbur Fallon, staring at the plugged canyon through his field glasses while Glen Plaza, James, and Erroll sat their horses to either side, echoed the outlaw's sentiment.

Chapter 24

Yakima drew up in front of the Rolette Federated Livery and Feed Barn and turned to look behind him.

The wagon was coming along the street that was all shadows now at dusk. The mud and rut puddles that had formed when the day's sunshine had melted the snow—only a couple of inches appeared to have fallen at this lower elevation—had frozen solid with the fast approach of night.

The two saddle horses that Yakima and Barstow had harnessed and hitched to the wagon came on hang-headed, hooves clomping loudly on the hard street, the cold dry wheel hubs squawking. The coffin slammed around in the box.

Veronica sat beside Barstow, a blanket across her lap, her breath steaming around her fur hat. It seemed even colder here on the high-prairie flats where there was little to impede the wind than it had even several thousand feet higher. As the wagon drew up to the barn, Veronica looked cautiously behind to see if they'd been followed out of the mountains.

To Barstow, Yakima said, "We'll hole up here for the night. Why don't you tend the wagon and the horses while me and Miss Berryman find out when the train's due?"

Barstow glanced over his right shoulder with much the same expression as Veronica's.

"Oh, I 'spect they'll be along when they find an alternate route out of the mountains," Yakima said. "I think I bought us some time, though."

The honyonker raked a mitten across his jaw. "I'm only eight miles from home . . ."

"It's gettin' dark," Yakima said. "But you might make it."

Barstow glanced behind again. "Wouldn't wanna get run down on the trail, though." He looked at Yakima, his eyes doleful. "Alone."

Veronica was looking across the broad street to a small log building silhouetted against the jade sky and whose jutting shingle identified as the sheriff's office. Smoke pushed from the cabin's single chimney pipe. A silhouette shone in the window right of the front door.

"Maybe we should go over and talk to the sheriff," she suggested.

"And tell him what? That the prominent rancher whose son you shot is hound-dogging your trail? Fallon probably plays cards with the that badge-toter over yonder when he comes to town to ship beef." Yakima glanced at the solemn honyonker. "You might be able to find help over there, Barstow. Tell the sheriff you got men on your trail who think you know where stolen money is . . ."

Barstow looked toward the office, and made a face. "I reckon Ray Noble wouldn't be much help to me. Like you say, he's friends with the bigger ranchers. Don't give half a hoot for us ten-cow operaters.

Veronica, too, stared toward the sheriff's office. Her bangs slid around on her forehead. "I hope there's a train through here soon."

Yakima dismounted and helped her out of the wagon. As Barstow headed up the livery barn's ramp and through the open front doors toward a guttering umber light, Yakima swung around and headed on up the street toward the depot.

The woman fell into step beside him, glancing past him. He followed her gaze to the sheriff's office. The silhouette had disappeared from the window, but another one—this one the shadow of a tall figure—stood out on the front stoop, leaning against an awning post. A cigarette glowed in the darkness.

Veronica looked at Yakima. "What if he—?"

"We're just passin' through."

The railroad tracks appeared, red as blood in the sun's last light. The depot was a long, low building at the far end of the main drag, with telegraph wires snaking off to the left and right, over the rails that ran east and west, as well.

A brick walk led to the door and the wooden platform around the depot, and there was a large overhang with several benches under it. No one sat on the outside benches. Although a light shone inside the building, and smoke gushed from a chimney, Yakima could see no passengers waiting in there, either. Not a good sign a passenger train was imminent.

He hoped a combination would pull in and leave before Fallon's group came down out of the mountains. He wanted Veronica out of here, heading east to wherever the hell she'd decided to try next. That would save Yakima the trouble of dealing with Fallon but only with the five shadowers he'd left in the canyon.

He'd hoped the landslide would convince the desperadoes there were easier ways to make a living, but it wasn't likely. Brigands like them didn't learn easy. Yakima probably should have waited to trigger the landslide when they were farther up the trail, and buried them under several hundred tons of rock.

He'd likely pay for giving them one more chance.

He tied Wolf to the hitch rack fronting the depot then led Veronica along the brick path to the front door. Warm air rife with the smell of human sweat, tobacco, and woodsmoke heaved against them as they pushed inside the little building then quickly closed the door on the chill breeze.

As Yakima had thought, the place was abandoned except for a man fumbling with a soup pot on the depot's boxy stove on the other side of the varnished wooden benches. A slate timetable flanked the man, and after Yakima deciphered the chalked dates and times, looked at the stoop-shouldered gent turning toward him and Veronica from his bubbling soup kettle.

"The next train's not due till tomorrow?"

The man sucked soup from his wooden spoon then ran the back of a grimy blue sleeve across his salt-and-pepper soup-strainer mustache, smacking his lips. "That's what it says."

"Will it go to Denver?" Veronica asked hopefully.

"By way of Laramie, yes ma'am." The station agent studied the unlikely pair curiously behind twinkling spectacles, and gave a little shake of his head as though to clear his befuddlement. "Take you three, four days to make Denver. On account of the slow mountain grades and a layover in Wyoming."

He bunched his shaggy brows once more, presumably trying to imagine what a big, long-haired half-breed with a pistol on his hip could be doing with such a polished length of mink-coated city woman. "You both goin'?"

"Just the woman. She'll take a ticket."

Yakima turned to look out the window at the street behind him, where a few oil lamps were being lit while the windows of most of the business establishments, excepting the saloons, were going dark.

"All right, then," the agent said, dropping his spoon into his soup pot, rubbing his hands on his blue wool trousers, and tramping toward the teller's cage, "that'll be three dollars and fifty cents, less'n you're wanting a sleeper."

"Coach will be fine," Veronica said, and Yakima could hear her voice quaking hopefully and desperately as she followed the man over to the cage.

Yakima kept an eye on the street while the agent wrote the woman a ticket, accepted her money, and warned her not to be late. "The engineer's a Luthern, don't ya know," the agent chuckled. "And keepin' a timetable to him is as important as following the Golden Rule. That spur combo'll be pullin' outta here at eight o'clock sharp!"

As Veronica shoved her small leather purse down into her coat pocket and turned toward the door, Yakima regarded the agent now returning to his soup kettle. "Can you recommend a hotel?"

"There's only one hotel in town, young man," the agent said, not looking at Yakima. He stirred his soup. "You passed it if you came in from the mountains. The Point Bluff Inn. Tall red building. I won't guarantee they'll rent a room to a mixed-blood, but you can try. Business has been off of late on account o' the cold weather."

"Obliged."

"Don't mention it."

As Yakima and Veronica headed back to the barn, she said, "Maybe we'd better see if we can stay in the livery stable. I have only a little change left in my purse. I could find only enough in the house for a few days' worth of food." Her voice dropped a notch. "Frank spent all his cash in the saloons."

"Don't worry about money. We'll be stayin' at the Point Bluff on Cisco Dervitch."

"Who?"

"Never mind."

They walked up the ramp and through the livery barn's open doors. Yakima paid a young man in a heavy scarf and torn gloves to grain and water Wolf, and to give him a good curry. The kid was already tending Barstow's horses while Barstow himself sat on the back of the wagon, his legs hanging down over the tailgate.

"Only hotel in town's the Point Bluff," Yakima told the honyonker. "Let's go live it up a little."

"I don't have money for no hotel stay."

"I do."

Barstow looked reluctant. He was sipping from another bottle. He jerked a thumb over his shoulder as he said, "I best stay with my girl. We're almost home. Wouldn't want anything to happen to her now."

"Nothing's gonna happen to her. The kid'll watch the wagon."

Yakima had grabbed his saddlebags and rifle, and he hefted them now as he and Veronica headed toward the barn's open doors. He glanced back. Barstow was staring at the pine coffin behind him. It was heartbreaking how the gent had suddenly found some feeling for the girl only after she was dead. Finally, he grabbed a toe sack and slid off the wagon, closed the tailgate, and turned to the boy removing Yakima's saddle.

"You keep a close eye on my rig, now, y'hear, boy?"

The boy nodded. Reluctantly, holding his bottle and toe

sack, Barstow followed Yakima and Veronica out the doors, down the wooden ramp, and into the street. The hotel was on the other side of the street and about a block back the way they'd come. As they headed that way, Yakima glanced across at the sheriff's office. A dull lamp glowed behind a curtained window. No sign of anyone watching the three mismatched strangers.

The Point Bluff Inn was a tall, narrow building with a crude gallery on its first floor and a rickety-looking balcony on its second. It was painted barn red, and there were a couple of horses tied to the hitch rack out front. Inside, six men—saddle tramps by the look of them, and a couple of traveling soldiers in cavalry blues beneath buffalo coats, and drummers in ragged suits and bowler hats—sat smoking and playing cards, three groups at separate tables. It was a dark place, and cold in spite of two grumbling woodstoves—one at the front, one at the back, near the short pine bar.

All faces turned toward the three strangers as Yakima led the way to the back, his fur moccasins scuffing along the puncheons flecked with sawdust and tobacco spit.

There was a silent piano against the wall to the left. A middle-aged dove with feathers in her hair sat on the bench before the piano, her legs crossed as she filed her nails with a restive air, bouncing her foot. She was chunky and red-haired, and she wasn't wearing much more than black stockings and a purple corset, which was likely why she sat close to the roaring stove.

A sloppy blond gent in a soiled apron stood behind the bar, leaning forward against the planks, his eyes so heavy-lidded he appeared about to fall asleep. Yakima asked for two room keys. The man looked the half-breed up and down, then raked his eyes slowly across the woman, and then across Barstow.

He nodded at Barstow, whom he obviously knew, and said, "You bring your girl home, Mr. Barstow?"

Barstow sighed and nodded. "I'll have a bottle of that special of yours, Ed."

Continuing to lean heavily forward, the blond bartender cast his glance at Yakima and Veronica once more. "Who're your friends?"

"We traveled together out of the mountains. She's pretty cold up there; my wagon—she gets stuck."

As though that answered the question, the blond gent gave Yakima a disapproving look then said with a tone of extreme tolerance, "Two dollars a head."

Yakima tossed a silver cartwheel onto the bar. "That's for the rooms and the bottle. You serve food?"

"Not in the winter." The barman reached under the bar for an unlabeled bottle, set in it on the counter in front of Barstow. "There's a cafe just north of here, back by the wash. Barstow knows it."

Yakima set his saddlebags on the bar. He grabbed Barstow's toe sack out of the honyonker's hand and set it on the bar beside his saddlebags. "We'd like our possibles hauled up to our rooms. The lady's with me. We'll pick up the keys when we return from supper."

The barman slid his gaze back and forth between Yakima and Veronica with mild amusement. Barstow glanced at Yakima, narrowing an eye and lifting his mouth corners. Veronica kept her own gaze on the bar, apparently understanding the half-breed wasn't being presumptuous but merely practical. It would be a hell of a lot easier to keep an eye on her if they were in the same room together.

Leaving the silver cartwheel on the bar, Yakima turned away and, taking Veronica by an arm, led her back toward the front of the room. He heard Barstow clomping along behind him, popping the cork from his bottle.

As Yakima passed the two soldiers playing cribbage, one leaned toward the other and said just loudly enough for Yakima to overhear, "Did the breed say the lady was with *him*?"

Yakima opened the door and let the woman and Barstow walk out ahead of him. He followed them out to the narrow gallery, and Barstow took the lead, angling eastward across the main street, casting another cautious glance toward the mountains that humped darkly against the purple eastern sky.

The cafe, simply called Food, huddled on a side street at the north edge of the town, between a haberdashery and a boarded-up saloon. The wind swept across the darkening plain from the northern mountains and blasted the place with blowing snow and dust.

Light shone in the windows. Three horses stood at the front hitch rack. As Yakima walked in, he hesitated slightly when the first man he saw was a tall gent perched on a stool at the lunch counter, twisting around toward the door so that his sheriff's star flashed in the wan light offered by several hanging oil lamps.

He was a rangy man, mid-thirties, with neatly cropped but stringy yellow hair falling down from his shabby brown bowler. A red mackinaw was draped over the stool beneath him, and he wore a checked wool shirt under a cowhide vest. A blond mustache curled down over his broad, bemused mouth.

Walking in behind Yakima, Veronica gave a start. Yakima grabbed her arm and pulled her over to a table, with Barstow following and nodding dully at the badge-toter, who swung his head around to follow the trio to their table half-way down the room's right wall.

When Yakima's party had taken their seats, Yakima meeting the badge-toter's amused, faintly curious gaze with a level one of his own, the sheriff turned toward the counter to resume eating. Veronica looked at Yakima worriedly. Yakima gave her a reassuring smile and, glancing at the menu card resting against the wall at the left edge of the table, leaned back in his chair, enjoying the warmth of the wood-stove hunched and wheezing nearby.

He was happy to see the half-breed waitress. Maybe that meant he wouldn't have any of his usual trouble trying to get a meal amongst white folks. He'd had all the trouble he needed for a while.

If all went well, and it turned out he'd lost their pursuers, tomorrow he'd see Barstow off in his wagon, put Veronica on the train, and head on up the trail for Crow Feather.

Neither he nor Barstow or Veronica said anything as they sat sipping their coffee. Yakima felt the eyes of the room on him, and he could sense the incredulity of the lawman who sat with his back toward him, just beyond a square-hewn ceiling joist, as the badge-toter ate and sipped coffee. Light from a nearby hanging lamp spread soft yellow light across the man's broad, hunched shoulders, glistened off his cracked leather vest. The lawman had a Schofield revolver with worn walnut grips thronged low on his right thigh.

The half-breed girl, who looked harried and was being yelled at by an unseen man in the kitchen, came and scribbled their orders on a notepad. She returned with their food a few minutes later, and Yakima and Barstow plowed into their food while Veronica Berryman ate a few hungry bites and then started to pick.

When the half-breed girl had refilled their coffee cups,

Barstow furtively lifted his fresh bottle above the table, and tipped a jigger of the liquor, likely brewed in the Point Bluff's backroom, into his coffee. Yakima noticed the man's hands were shaking. Veronica seemed to notice it, too. She slid her eyes from the man to Yakima, a faint question in her gaze.

Yakima was half through his pile of gravy-drenched pork roast and potatoes when the sheriff yelled his thanks to the man in the kitchen, and slid off his stool at the counter. Adjusting the angle of his bowler with both hands, he turned toward Yakima's table.

Veronica gave a soft gasp, and turned her head quickly forward, dropping her eyes. Barstow forked a chunk of his own roast into his mouth, chewing and rolling his eyes nervously around in their sockets as the lawman stared across the width of the room at him.

Slowly, kicking his boots with a self-important flourish as he shrugged into his mackinaw, the rangy lawman strolled toward the trio's table. He stopped near Veronica's right elbow.

"Mr. Barstow," he said in greeting.

"Sheriff Noble."

Noble pinched his hat brim at Veronica. "Ma'am."

He did not look at Yakima, who continued to eat in spite of the lawman's presence. He was hungry, and the lawman had no reason to cause trouble unless he had a natural aversion to mixed bloods. Anyway, Yakima had never known a lawman he couldn't take from a sitting position.

The sheriff gave Veronica a smoldering appraisal before sliding his gaze back to the honyonker, who in the lawman's presence looked as uncomfortable as a soiled dove at her first church wedding. "You bring your girl back home—did you, sir?"

"That's right," Barstow said, a forced smile making his gravy-stained mustache twitch as he smiled unctuously up at the lawman. "Brung her down out of the mountains. Gonna take her on back to the ranch first thing tomorrow, put her in the ground soon as the ground thaws."

The lawman stared at him for a few beats. "She belonged down here all along, didn't she?"

"That she did."

"I hope you had a good trip. Heard the mountains had some snow of late."

"It went all right," Barstow said, his eyes flickering toward Yakima.

The sheriff turned his head toward the half-breed, his eyes hooding with cold disdain. He sniffed, bit at his long mustache then turned back to the honyonker.

"Mr. Barstow, pardon me for askin' this at such a hard time, but that girl of yours, Rosie Dawn—"

"Her name was Rose Alice," Barstow corrected the man, suddenly putting some steel in his voice. "That was her name. I didn't know no Rosie Dawn."

"Okay," the sheriff allowed reasonably. "All right, then. Sorry, Barstow. Rose Alice it is." The sheriff squinted an eye and cocked his head to one side. "She never really did know where ole Pedro Camargo hid that stolen loot, now, did she?"

Barstow stared up at the local badge-toter, gravy on his lip. He shook his head. "If she did know, she took it with her, Sheriff."

The sheriff nodded slowly as he stared pensively down at Barstow. Suddenly he switched his gaze to Yakima and leaned over the table, extending his right hand and staring brashly into Yakima's eyes. "Sheriff Ray Noble."

"Yakima Henry," the half-breed said, shaking the lawman's hand over Veronica's plate.

"Please to make your acquaintance, Mr. Henry." Noble gave the half-breed's hand a resolute pump.

"Likewise, Sheriff. Nice town you got here."

"I try to keep the lid on. You gonna be visiting long?"

"Can't really say," Yakima said. "Would there be a problem if I was?"

"Oh," Noble said, smiling. "I reckon that'd be up to you."

Yakima returned the smile.

Noble adjusted his hat again and smiled once more at Veronica, who sat frozen, fork in hand, staring down at her plate. "Ma'am, I do hope your stay here in Rolette is a pleasant one. You let me know if there's anything I can do to make it so, now—hear?"

With that, Ray Noble raked his eyes coldly across Yakima as he turned and strode to the door and on outside into the cold, blowing night.

Chapter 25

When Yakima, Veronica, and Barstow had finished their supper, they headed on back to the Point Bluff Inn. Veronica and Barstow went up the stairs at the back of the main saloon hall, while Yakima stopped at the bar to order a bottle.

He was glad to see only the men who'd been here earlier—the two cavalry grunts, the drummers, and the saddle tramps. To a man, they were a little drunker, a little more involved in staying warm and playing cards and drinking whiskey. The whore was sitting on the lap of one of the saddle tramps who was laughing and jabbering as he stared dreamily down her cleavage.

The sleepy-eyed barman set a bottle on the bar and waited for his money.

"You got any coffee?"

"See that pot on the stove yonder? That's a coffeepot."

Yakima looked at the pot on the stove near the end of the bar. "Got a cup?"

The barman stared at him dully with the kind of mindless animosity that made Yakima's shoulder blades tighten and that forced him to resist the urge to do something that would likely get him thrown in jail and counting the bricks in a cell block wall for the next week and a half. Finally, the barman turned to a shelf behind him, grabbed a tin cup, and set it on the bar.

"You fixin' to stay up tonight?"

"I don't sleep well when I sense hostility."

"Coffee ain't gonna help that."

Yakima paid for the bottle, flipping three coins onto the bar top where they leaped and clattered. "You a doctor?"

He grabbed the bottle, filled the cup, and trudged up the steps, feeling the eyes of the men and the whore in the room behind him.

He found his room just beyond Barstow's, on the second floor. Two candles guttered in wall sconces, revealing the soiled floor runner, several cracks in the plastered walls, and moisture stains on the stamped tin ceiling. He rapped on the door, shoved his face close to the panel, and said wryly, "Don't shoot—it's me."

He heard the tap of bare feet. She opened the door and stood before him barefoot, the mink coat draped over her shoulders. She'd already gotten the room's squat stove going, and the fledgling flames leaped and cracked at the yellowed dime novel pages and kindling sticks.

Veronica arched a brow at him. "You took my bullets away—remember?"

"Better safe than sorry," he said as he moved into the room, kicking the door closed and looking at her feet.

She backed up to the single bed, which sloped sharply down in the middle, and sat on the edge of it. "My feet were sore from the boots. I'm going to warm then in front of the fire."

Yakima crossed the room and with his rifle barrel swept the curtains back from the window over the dresser. A few townsmen in suits and heavy coats moved along the street, smoking and talking, heading for a saloon most likely.

"What if they come?"

Yakima released the curtain and turned to Veronica, who now sat with one bare foot atop the other, hunched forward against the cold. He set his bottle and his coffee on the dresser, leaned his rifle against the wall, and shoved a hand into his coat pocket. He held out his hand to her and dumped six .44-caliber shells into her raised, pale palm.

"We kill 'em."

She bit her upper lip. "Do you think we can expect any help from the sheriff? I mean—you and Mr. Barstow?"

"No."

He shrugged out of his coat. Hanging his coat on a door hook, he went over to the stove and shoved several sticks inside. When he turned back to her, she was fumbling with the gun and the bullets, wincing as she tried to thumb the loading gate open.

Yakima sat down beside her, took the gun and the bullets, loaded the gun, spun the cylinder, and gave the gun back to her. "Be careful. Be certain who you're shooting at, aim for the heart, grit your teeth, and shoot the sonofabitch."

She looked down at the heavy piece in her hands and nodded. She glanced up at him again, brows furrowed. "Why are you helping us?"

Yakima doffed his hat, threw it onto a chair, and ran his hands through his hair. "I reckon I'm just a sucker for a pair of bleeding hearts."

"You could have ridden away from the danger. Now you've made enemies of not only the men after Mr. Barstow but those after me. And the man who rides with Mr. Fallon, Glen Plaza, is a cold, cruel man. One, I've heard, who's very good with his guns."

Yakima met her doleful gaze. "When you can help someone, you help 'em," he said.

"I bet you haven't been helped all that often—have you, Yakima? I can tell by the way men talk to you, treat you."

"I've been helped enough times by enough good people to know what's right and what ain't right, who's good, and who needs killin'. Those men after you are in that last category. Same with the ones after Barstow."

He patted her hands that held the heavy gun. "Now, go over and warm your feet by the fire before you catch the chilblains and limp around like a stove-up mountain man the rest of your life."

Her lips quirked a smile and she leaned toward him and planted a gentle kiss on his cheek. She set the gun down on the bed, walked over, grabbed the slat-back chair, and sat down in front of the crackling stove, holding her bare feet up near the door.

When Veronica had rolled into the bed and, judging by her long, regular breaths, had gone to sleep, Yakima sat in the chair by the door, facing the window above the dresser on the opposite side of the room. He'd just finished his coffee laced with whiskey when hooves clomped in the otherwise silent street outside the hotel.

He got up and, automatically laying a hand across the holstered revolver on his right thigh, moved quietly over to the window, and slid back the curtains. Beyond the frost-mottled glass, five riders rode into view from the east. The street was dark now after midnight, so all Yakima could see were five bulky silhouettes on horseback.

The horses' hooves thudded loudly on the frozen, wheel-rutted street.

Yakima watched as the group, all riding slouched in their saddles, angled off into the shadows on the street's far side, toward the same livery barn where Yakima had stabled his own mount and Barstow had stabled his wagon with his daughter's coffin. In a few minutes, the gang would have no doubt that they'd come to the right place.

Since the Point Bluff Inn was the only hotel in town, they'd head here after they'd seen to their horses.

Yakima looked at Veronica lying curled beneath the bed-covers, hair spilling across her pillow as she faced the wall. Her breaths were regular and deep, but occasionally she gave a troubled groan.

He considered waking her, to have her crawl to relative safety under the bed, but, judging by the heavy way their stalkers rode in on shamble-footed horses, there was a chance they'd wait to make their play until after they'd slept. Two of the group, after all, were sporting grievous wounds on which the cold had probably wreaked seven kinds of hell.

The cold and the rockslide.

Yakima couldn't help but twisting a devilish smile when he remembered how those boulders had fallen away from the cliff face and chased the gang down canyon. The grin faded, his features flattening out severely, as he stared through the window.

He should have waited another five minutes before loosing those boulders, and sealed those curly wolves up for-ever under a cairn. They'd be out of the way, and Yakima would have only Fallon to worry about.

Yakima turned his head to peer east, toward the inky line of the Sawatch Range shouldering against the shimmering stars. Unless the rancher had decided his dead son wasn't worth avenging after all, his group would be along soon as well.

Yakima took a pull from the whiskey bottle, chunked more wood into the belching stove, grabbed his Winchester, and sat back down in the chair near the door, resting the rifle across his thighs.

He sat listening to the stove and to the woman's breathing, the occasional wind gust making the walls creak. After a time, a spur chinged on the street. A man's low voice rose. Yakima continued to sit statue-still, listening while fingering the Winchester's hammer, until deep voices spilled up from the first story, and, finally, there rose the weary clomp of several pairs of boots on the stairs, and the faint metallic ring of room keys.

Yakima rose quietly from the chair and stood with his shoulder against the wall beside the door, holding the Winchester straight up and down in front of him. The clomping left the stairs, and footsteps muffled by the carpet runner sounded in the hall.

Whispers.

Just beyond the door, floorboards creaked. Beneath the door a shadow moved.

Yakima's heart thudded. He shifted his weight from foot to foot and squeezed the rifle in his hands, wishing he'd had Veronica crawl under the bed, after all. He closed his left hand around the cocking lever, ready to rack a shell into the breech, and pointed the barrel at the doorknob, waiting for the door to burst open and for guns to wail.

He pricked his ears, listening. His mouth was dry. Just beyond the door he could hear the faint rasp of breathing. Another floorboard creaked. The shadow under the door moved again.

"Nah," he heard a man whisper very softly about a foot from the door. "They'll keep till mornin'."

Someone else said something too faintly for Yakima to hear, and then the shadow moved away from the door. The floorboards in the hall creaked again, the sounds fading quickly, and then boots clomped on the stairs, dwindling as the newcomers headed for the third story.

They hadn't stopped at Barstow's door. They wanted Yakima out of the way first.

The half-breed stood by the door until the thudding in the ceiling had died. He set his rifle across the chair and looked out the window. If Fallon were coming, he wouldn't be far behind. The street, however, was dark, the dusting of snow and the frozen wheel ruts glowing in the starlight.

Fatigue was a yoke on Yakima's shoulders. It had been a long, cold trek out of the mountains. He looked at the bed. A few winks would do him some good.

Sitting down at the edge of the bed, he rested back against the brass headboard, stretched a leg out on the bed before him, keeping his left foot on the floor, and loosed a long sigh. Veronica rolled toward him, snaked an arm across his belly, and rested her head against his chest.

"Is everything all right?" she asked in a sleep-raspy voice.

He slid her hair back from her forehead, rested his hand on her warm shoulder. "Yep."

He closed his eyes, felt sleep rise up to meet him.

When he opened them again, he sat up with a start.

Pale light pushed through the window, illuminating the room in a cream wash. The stove hulked darkly. The room was cold. Yakima slid out from beneath Veronica, who groaned but continued sleeping. He eased her head down on the bed, and moved to the window.

The stars were faint. Birds chirped.

Yakima's heart thudded. He'd slept most of the night. It was damn near morning.

He stared out the window, planning. He'd get Veronica over to the depot to await the train. Then he'd see Barstow off on the trail to the honyonker's ranch. Once both his charges were safely on their ways, he'd let his five stalkers decide the rest of it. He pretty much knew how it would turn out, but he'd let them make the first move.

He turned to face the door, frowning, raking his hands across his face, trying to clear the sleep from his brain.

What about Fallon? If anyone had clomped up the stairs last night, Yakima would have awakened. Had the man decided to let his son's killer go free, or let the law handle it?

He crouched over Veronica, set a hand on her shoulder, and shook her gently. "Wake up," he said. "Time to go."

Chapter 26

Yakima tapped on Barstow's door. It opened immediately. The honyonker was fully dressed, wearing his coat and hat, mittens stuffed in a coat pocket. He was unshaven, hollow-cheeked, eyes anxious and wild. He hadn't slept.

He hefted his shotgun in one hand, toe sack in the other, and followed Yakima and Veronica down the dim hall, the floor of which creaked fiercely beneath their boots. Behind one of the room doors, someone snored.

Yakima paused at the top of the stairs and looked down into the dingy saloon hall. He could hear the wind nipping at the building and the faint scuttling of a mouse. Otherwise, silence.

He glanced back at Veronica and Barstow, then started slowly down the stairs, holding the Winchester in his right hand and running his left hand along the railing.

The steps creaked and groaned under his boots as well as Veronica's, who came down directly behind him, and Barstow's, who descended about three steps behind her, holding his shotgun up defensively and casting cautious glances back up the stairs.

Yakima raked his own gaze across the saloon's long, shadowy hall stretching away to his left. Chairs were turned upside down on tables. Square-hewn ceiling joists stood darkly amidst the dawn silhouettes. The storm door at the front of the room was closed, and pearl light washed through the two frosted front windows on either side of the door.

Nothing moved amongst the tables and chairs, the two hunched black stoves, and the bar directly below the stairs. The only sounds were the occasional wind gust outside and the complaining staircase.

Still, the muscles along Yakima's spine drew taut with a nettling, uncanny danger.

At the bottom of the stairs, he stopped and looked around, frowning, raking his gaze once more across the room. His heart beat insistently. His eyes tried to probe the shadows under the tables and angling away from the stoves, but they were still too dark, too murky.

Veronica drew up between him and the end of the bar as Barstow dropped down off the last step, flanking her and Yakima. "What's wrong?" she said. "There's no one—"

She stopped as one of the shadows on the right side of the room, up between the first stove and the wall, rose suddenly. A boot scuffed the floor and there was a raspy breath followed by the click of a gun hammer.

"Down!"

Yakima threw his left shoulder into the woman and glimpsed a bright flash as he dove sideways behind the bar. The rifle thundered loudly in the close quarters. The bullet shattered a bottle on a shelf above the bar, spraying whiskey.

Barstow bellowed as he dropped to his knees, crabbed quickly behind the bar, dragging his shotgun. Yakima had fallen atop Veronica's sprawled, quaking body, and now he pushed up away from her, loudly racking a shell into his Yellowboy's breech, raising the rifle but keeping his head down just below the bar.

The rifle roared three more times, the bullets smashing more bottles above the bar and sending whiskey and glass flying. Veronica screamed. Beside Yakima, Barstow jerked and crabbed farther into the four-foot gap between the bar and the wall behind it as a bullet chewed slivers near his right shoulder.

Above the rifle's blasting echo, a man shouted from somewhere at the front of the room, "Plaza, don't kill the woman, goddamnit!"

Yakima lifted his head and rifle above the bar, quickly aimed at the spot he'd seen the bushwhacker's gun flash. A blurred figure in a cream hat crouched near an inky black stove. Yakima fired two quick rounds, the Yellowboy roaring and leaping in his hands, and the two ejected shell casings careened over his shoulder to clatter on the floor around his boots, where Veronica lay belly flat, shielding her head with her arms.

Amidst the thunder of his rifle, Yakima heard an indignant grunt and saw the blurred, hatted figure near the stove jerk back against the wall.

In the corner of his left eye, more shapes moved. A deep voice shouted, "Cut loose on the half-breed sonofabitch, boys!"

Yakima pulled his head and rifle down as a barrage of gunfire hammered the bar and the wall above and behind it, above a young man's voice shouting, "We got the bastard, Pa!"

More bottles shattered in a tinny roar, and whiskey sprayed

over Yakima's head and shoulders as he ran crouching along behind the bar. Near the far end, he snaked his Winchester over the top and, bearing down on the three rifles flashing from different points throughout the room's left side, began firing and levering in earnest.

As the Yellowboy roared, one of Fallon's sons screamed shrilly while Fallon himself cursed sharply.

Through his own wafting powder smoke, Yakima watched a bulky figure near the door fall against a table, knocking two chairs onto the floor with a crash. Yakima continued firing, and, when another bullet careened over his head from the right, he slid the Yellowboy that way and fired another shot before the rifle's hammer clacked benignly onto the firing pin.

The man he took to be Plaza made a gagging, choking sound on the right side of the room, as though he'd been hit in the throat, and there was a solid thump as the man's knees hit the floor. It was followed by the clatter of a falling rifle.

Yakima set his rifle on the bar top and glanced down at Veronica and at Barstow kneeling frozen, holding his shotgun in both hands, his back against the wall down which whiskey streamed. Broken glass peppered the flat top of his billed watch cap. His brown eyes were fear-bright, his bushy brows stitched.

Yakima slipped his Colt from its holster and leaped smoothly up and over the bar, hitting the floor on both feet and extending the cocked Colt straight out before him. Crouching, he shifting the gun around at the room, aiming in the general direction Fallon and his sons had fired from. He knew Plaza, whom he'd hit twice, was likely dead. He wasn't sure about the other three.

He moved ahead quickly, tracing a meandering course

around the tables. His left foot nearly slipped out beneath him, and he looked down to see the broken-nosed boy lying prostrate in a thick blood pool, a hole just below his right eye and another in his left shoulder.

Regret clawed at the edges of his consciousness. He'd hoped Fallon would have taken the boy's broken nose as a warning, and turn around and save his sons a meaningless death. Well, he hadn't done it, and his boys had paid the price. But Fallon and Plaza had, too.

As Yakima continued forward, he found the other boy piled up over a chair, unmoving, and Fallon himself rising onto hands and knees and trying to crawl to the door, grunting loudly, hoarsely, leaving a trail of smeared blood. Yakima extended the Colt at an angle, and blew a hole through the back of the rancher's head.

Fallon collapsed and lay quivering as his life poured out of him. "There you go, you sonofabitch."

Hearing the ceiling creak with scrambling feet, and several voices pitched anxiously in the second and third stories, he holstered his six-shooter and ran back to the bar. "*Let's go!*"

He grabbed his Yellowboy off the bar and ran around to the end of the counter to find Barstow kneeling where he'd been a minute ago, and Veronica pushing herself up slowly from the floor—stiffly, eyes wide with horror. Broken glass glistened on their hats and shoulders.

Yakima picked up his saddlebags, pulled Barstow up by his collar, and shoved the man toward the front door.

"Go now!"

Casting a cautious gaze up the dim stairs, he pulled Veronica up by an arm and shoved her after Barstow, who was now striding quickly toward the front of the saloon as more louder thuds sounded in the ceiling. Yakima thumbed cartridges from his shell belt into his Winchester, backing toward the door while keeping an eye on the stairs.

Barstow had fumbled the door open and slipped outside when a face appeared at the top of the stairs, and the gradually intensifying light flashed off a gun barrel.

Yakima aimed the Yellowboy from his shoulder and fired. The boom loosed dust from the rafters, and the bullet slammed into the wall just above the wainscoting. The would-be shooter gave a yelp and pulled his gun back behind the wall at the top of the stairs.

Yakima fired once more in warning then backed outside and pulled the door closed behind him. He turned to see Barstow and Veronica standing on the stoop and staring worriedly across the street. Yakima followed their gazes to the corner outside a drugstore with a green false front, where Sheriff Noble stood partly concealed by an awning post and a rain barrel, holding a rifle in his gloved hands. His breath frosted in the lightening air around his bowler-hatted head.

He regarded Yakima and his two charges skeptically.

Yakima shoved Veronica brusquely forward and told her and Barstow to keep moving. Following them off the stoop— he wanted to get as far from the hotel as possible—he tramped westward along the street, facing the sheriff who turned his head to follow the trio with his gaze. There was no one else on the street, but Yakima glimpsed faces in several dark windows around him.

"Christ," Noble said. "Did you kill 'em all?"

"Just those tried to kill me. So, yeah, I guess you could say I killed 'em all."

He glanced at Veronica who regarded him warily, and gestured for her to quicken her pace for the depot. Noble stepped off the stoop fronting a drugstore, moving toward

Yakima, holding his rifle up high across his chest. "That was a mighty important man in these parts, mister. You laid a right hot trail for yourself."

Yakima stopped and levered his Winchester, the metallic rasp echoing loudly on the quiet dawn street. "You want some of what he got?"

Noble stopped. Yakima kept following Barstow and Veronica toward the depot. The sheriff turned his head to one side, narrowing an eye at the half-breed, and lowered his rifle to his side. "I told Fallon I'd stay out of it. I reckon that's what I'll do . . . since you're just passin' through and all."

"That'd be the right choice." Yakima glanced at Barstow. "The honyonker's gonna hitch up his wagon and head on back to his ranch."

"I don't have nothin' against Mr. Barstow."

"Good."

Noble glanced at the hotel. "Them others after you, too?"

"Yep."

Noble curled his mustached upper lip. "I hope they get you."

Yakima was walking backward now, facing the sheriff and holding his rifle across his waist. "Go on back to your office, have a cup of coffee. Since I don't know what side of the fence you might come down on, I'll kill you next time I see you."

Noble just stood there, and Yakima turned to walk forward. "Barstow, hitch up your wagon and hightail it. I'm gonna make sure Miss Berryman catches that train."

Barstow angled toward the livery barn, brows furrowed, nodding and quickening his heavy-footed stride. As he and Veronica approached the depot, which showed a light in its windows and smoke spewing from its chimney, Yakima glanced back once more. Noble was striding toward his office, head and rifle hanging.

No movement around the hotel yet.

Yakima turned and followed Veronica into the depot.

Snakehead Dawson and Luis Lavoto stood looking out separate windows of the Point Bluff Inn's blood-drenched, carnage-littered saloon.

Both men were clad in only balbriggans, socks, and hats. Lavoto held a pistol in his left hand, and he was wearing his boots. Snakehead held his revolver in his right hand, and he wasn't wearing boots. It took too long to pull a boot on his ravaged right foot, and he'd wanted to get down here fast to see what the ruckus was about.

Behind him and Lavoto, Phil Little, the Englishman Blyster, and the whore-killer, Larsen—all in similar states of undress—stood looking curiously around at the two dead men and the two dead younkers. The chubby whore, who'd spent the night with Blyster, sat on the steps in a ratty man's checked robe, night ribbons jouncing in her hair as she shook her head disapprovingly, saying, "Just wait till Karl sees this mess. He done told me that breed was gonna be trouble."

Snakehead turned from the window right of the door to look at Lavoto standing at the other window, crouched and staring out toward where the breed had disappeared with the woman.

"Now, ain't you glad we got Blyster and Larsen there?" Snakehead said with a buoyant, self-congratulatory air. He turned toward the dead men. "Look what happened to these poor fellas, and they musta had that breed dead to rights, too!"

Lavoto cursed in Spanish and, holding his injured wrist tight to his flat belly, swung around and headed for the stairs. "Shut up and get dressed."

"You know I'm right, don't you, Luis?" Snakehead swung around and, starting toward the stairs, inadvertently slammed his swollen, bloody foot against a table leg.

His scream was so shrill that the others in the room, including the whore, clamped their hands against their ears and stretched their lips back from their teeth.

Chapter 27

The stove in the depot building was fully stoked, and two old women and an old man sat near it, old cracked luggage and carpetbags piled on the benches around them. The old man smoked a corncob pipe and regarded the half-breed and the beautiful, chestnut-haired woman in the long mink coat squint-eyed.

Yakima parked her on a bench near the stove, and told her to stay put.

"When the train comes, get on it and don't look back."

She frowned up at him, grabbing his wrist as he started to turn away. "What's going to happen?"

"I reckon that's up to them."

"Why don't you ride out?"

Yakima looked at her. "Sooner or later, we'll have to settle it." He reached into his pants pocket, pulled out a wad of greenbacks, and held it out to her. "Take that. When you get to Denver, buy another ticket for home or wherever the hell you wanna go."

She took the bills, awestruck, and slowly flipped through them. Looking up at Yakima again, stitching her brows, she said, "There's six hundred dollars here."

"Thank a dead sharpie named Cisco Dervitch."

He glanced east out the windows. The sun was poking its bloody head above the mountains. The clock on the wall showed fifteen minutes remaining until the train was due. The depot master regarded Yakima skeptically from behind his ticket cage.

"No," Veronica said, slowly shaking her head and holding the bills in her open palm. "I can't take this."

"Take it." Yakima closed her fingers over the bills. "What the hell would I do with it?" He closed his hand over hers, and squeezed. "Take care of yourself."

He was halfway to the door when her voice rose behind him. "Yakima?"

He didn't look back as he opened the door but continued out onto the loading platform, facing the main street that stretched between the tall, false fronts. Coal and wood smoke hung low over the town, and several dogs were out sniffing at alley mouths while shopkeepers swept snow from their walks.

He stood in front of the door, his Winchester resting on his shoulder. He dropped his saddlebags at the base of the building behind him then leaned against an awning post. Digging his tobacco pouch from his shirt pocket, he began building a smoke as he stood staring east.

The hotel stood a hundred yards away—tall, narrow, red, and ominously silent.

Yakima watched the street and smoked.

A shopkeeper sweeping the boardwalk in front of his shop watched him warily, occasionally following Yakima's gaze back toward the hotel. Another sweeping shopkeeper on the other side of the street and east a ways followed suit. When the hotel's door opened and five men filed out, both shopkeepers stopped sweeping, looked from the hotel to Yakima then glanced at each other across the street, hustled into their shops, and slammed their doors behind them.

The thumps of the slamming doors, one after the other, echoed on the quiet street. A train whistle sounded—two shrill blows in the distance. Yakima glanced south to see the train coming along the gray rails, the big diamond-shaped stack spewing thick black smoke, the chugging of the steam engine and the clickety-clack of the iron wheels growing louder as the short combination pulled within a quarter mile of town, and closed.

He faced up the street. The five desperadoes, clad in heavy coats, some in fur boots and mufflers, all wielding rifles or revolvers, stood abreast, about five feet apart, in the street fronting the hotel. The chubby whore who'd been sitting in front of the piano the night before stood on the hotel's boardwalk, a blanket wrapped around her shoulders, ribbons in her hair, cigarette smoke dribbling from her mouth.

The five wolves stood frozen, staring up the street at Yakima, heads canted at cocky, challenging angles. They were the three Yakima had wounded in the roadhouse and two other grim-looking strangers in nondescript trail garb, one bearded and average-sized, the other tall and gawky-looking and wearing a red wood cap. These two stood to the left of the group.

Beside them stood the man Yakima had shot in the foot, the one called Snakehead, who stood with most of his weight on his good boot while the other hung lax at his side. He was the only one not wearing a hat but only a blanket drawn up over his head, which gave him the look of a middle-aged, dog-faced woman. Even from this distance of sixty yards, he looked paler than the others, and he was showing his teeth like a rabid cur.

Beside him stood the tall Mex, Lavoto, in his wolf coat

and with his arm in a sling. Beside him stood Phil Little, the rat-faced hardcase in a green-striped blanket coat, ragged fur hat with earflaps from which long, stringy, sandy hair tumbled down over his shoulders. His hands in mismatched gloves were closed around the stock of his Spencer repeater.

They had the sun behind them. It illuminated the breath jetting around their faces, glistened off their rifles.

Yakima cursed silently. Since it was five against one, he'd have liked to have the sun in his favor. But he didn't, and he couldn't very well ask them if they'd switch positions.

As the train whistled again on its final approach to the depot, the half-breed pushed off the awning post and stepped into the street. He set his Winchester on his shoulder as he walked toward the hotel and the five waiting wolves.

They glanced at each other and began moving toward him, matching their strides with his own, Snakehead having to shuffle clumsily to keep up with the others. His teeth shown in the snarl beneath his curled upper lip. Lavoto had his chin down, and his mustached lips quirked an evil, eager grin. He was the only one not holding a rifle; in his good hand he held a long-barreled, silver-chased Colt.

Yakima saw the flicker of shadowy movement in the dark windows around him. A man moving up along the side of a building and holding an axe on his shoulder, heading toward the main street, stopped suddenly when he saw the two factions moving toward each other.

Wheeling, he headed swiftly back in the direction from he'd come.

Halfway between the depot and the hotel, Yakima stopped. The five desperadoes stopped roughly twenty feet away from him. Yakima could hear the chuffing of the stopped train behind him, and to his left, on the other side of the depot, and he imagined Veronica climbing aboard, safely on her way out of here.

Had Barstow left the barn? If he had, he'd likely chosen a back route home.

The Mex held his Colt straight down by his left thigh as he tipped his head back on his shoulders, a belligerent look pinching his black eyes. "Who are you, friend?" He grinned. "Just so we know the name to tell the undertaker."

Yakima smiled. "I'm your executioner, you sonofabitch."

Lavoto's eyes flickered. He'd just started to swing his pistol up when Yakima snapped his rifle to his shoulder.

BOOM!

The Mexican flew straight back off his heels, firing his Colt into the ground in front of him, as a quarter-sized hole appeared in the middle of his forehead, and the street behind him was sprayed with blood and white brain and bone matter.

As Yakima quickly ejected the spent shell and levered a fresh one, Snakehead screamed and hardened his jaws as he raised his own Winchester. He fired at the same time that Yakima's second bullet tore a dogget of flesh from the man's neck.

The man's own bullet tore into Yakima's shoulder with the sensation of a hard smack from a smithy's hammer and the burn of a glowing andiron. Yakima twisted and stumbled backward, saving himself from a bullet that had been aimed at his head while another sliced a hot line across his left cheek.

Stumbling, he levered and fired the Yellowboy. Phil Little howled as the bullet tore through his left kneecap. His own bullet blew Yakima's hat off. Several others stitched the air around the half-breed's head and shoulders, nipping his coat and plowing into the ground behind him.

Yakima staggered, gritting his teeth and firing and levering the Winchester as quickly as he could, hastily aiming at the men now weaving and bobbing and staggering before him, triggering their own rifles behind a thickening cloud of powder smoke.

Snakehead had dropped to a knee, holding his bloody neck with one hand while, screaming and pinching his eyes down to fine slits, he raised his Winchester one-handed and fired. The bullet tore across the side of Yakima's right thigh as he drilled the tall, scar-faced gent in the throat.

As the tall gent dropped his gun and clamped both his hands to his neck, eyes nearly popping from his skull, Yakima continued levering and firing. Two shots sailed wide of the remaining, pitching and screaming shooters, while the last load in his breech painted a red line across the side of the second, bearded stranger.

The man ran stumbling toward the boardwalk on the south side of the street, while the knee-shot gent shouted, "Goddamn you, breed!" and drilled Yakima's upper left arm.

Yakima tossed away the Winchester, slipped his Colt from his holster, and aimed at the knee-shot Little who now sat on his butt in the middle of the street, throwing down his own rifle and reaching for a sidearm. Yakima's Colt roared, and the man's right eye disappeared while the plunking round exited the back of Little's head to ping into the frozen street behind him.

Little's head jerked back, then forward, long sandy hair dancing on his shoulders.

For a half-second he sat up straight as though at sudden attention, his remaining eye wide and glassy, blood dribbling down from the socket of the other one. He sagged straight back to the street with a ragged sigh, kicking and flapping his arms as though trying to take flight.

Snakehead was stumbling, grunting loudly, as he fled to the left side of the street. Holding his neck with one hand, his revolver in the other, he sort of dumped himself over a frozen stock trough. He extended the pistol over the top of the trough, but before he could snap a shot off, Yakima fired his own Colt.

The bullet tore a dogget of wood from the side of the trough. Snakehead jerked with a start as he sent a round screaming just over Yakima's head to smack the ground behind him with an angry whine. Another gun barked on the right side of the street, and Yakima turned to see the shorter of the grim-faced strangers hunkered down behind an awning post before a lady's clothing shop, extending a rifle uncertainly in his bloody hands.

Yakima aimed his Colt in that direction and squeezed the trigger. The hammer pinged, empty. The grim-faced stranger snarled as, from one knee, he aimed down his rifle's barrel.

A shout rose, and there was the thud of running horses and the hammering, wooden rattle of a fast-moving wagon. The grim-faced stranger held fire, and, frowning, turned his bloody head to peer east along the main street behind him.

Thumbing cartridges from his cartridge belt into his Colt and wincing against the pain of his multiple wounds and grazes, Yakima stared along the street before him to see two horses lunge out from behind a shop on the street's left side. The two horses pulled Barstow's buckboard into the intersection, the honyonker standing in the driver's box, whipping the reins over the backs of the two lunging horses in the traces.

Horses and wagon shot straight across the intersection, heading from left to right. Barstow bellowed and shouted, whipping the reins.

Snakehead, still hunkered behind the stock trough,

shouted, "The wagon!" He wriggled around, aiming his pistol. "Get back here, you sonofabitch!"

He fired two quick shots.

In the wagon's driver's boot, Barstow flinched just before the horses pulled him off across the intersection and out of sight behind the buildings on the main street's right side. Yakima punched a cartridge into his Colt's last empty chamber, snapped the loading gate closed, spun the cylinder, and aimed the Colt at the back of Snakehead's blanket-wrapped head sticking up behind the stock trough.

He squeezed the trigger. The Colt leaped and roared.

Yakima stared through his wafting powder smoke.

Snakehead slumped against the stock trough, blood dribbling out from the hole in the man's brown blanket, just above his right ear. The blood glistened in the soft morning sunlight.

More shots sounded in the southeast, echoing woodenly, muffled with distance.

Yakima looked around. The bearded stranger was nowhere in sight. A shout rose, more shots echoing beneath the fast-dwindling hammering of the wagon that was heading south, unseen from Yakima's vantage.

The half-breed heaved himself to his feet, grunting, wheezing, and wincing against his wounds, feeling the blood gushing out from the holes turning cold under his clothes. He ran, limping, east along the main street and turned right at the intersection where Barstow had disappeared. Ahead, the bearded stranger was following the trail as it curved around behind a barn and corral, angling southwest.

Yakima ran, gritting his teeth, and then he saw the running man before him stop and fire two quick rounds with his Winchester, aiming toward the wagon racing into the distance behind the galloping horses.

Yakima raised the Colt and fired.

The grim-faced gent dropped, clutching the back of his right thigh. Yakima ran up to him. As the man tried to swing his rifle up, snarling like a trapped wolf, Yakima finished him, and, leaving him slumped in the frozen trace, he continued jogging ahead to where the wagon sat at an odd angle on the trail's right side.

Barstow was in the box, hunkered over his daughter's coffin. The blows of a hammer rose, and the hingelike screech of nails pried from wood.

Jogging miserably, holding his gun hand over his bloody shoulder, Yakima closed the gap between himself and the wagon.

"Barstow!"

The man standing crouched in the box whipped toward Yakima. He had a pair of saddlebags draped over his shoulder. He gritted his teeth and flung an arm out toward Yakima, pointing, "You leave me be!" His shout was feeble, brittle. "I got a right to this!"

Then he scrambled over the coffin, half-leaped and half-fell over the side panel of the wagon box, and dropped from sight.

Yakima continued forward. When he reached the wagon, both right wheels of which were hanging over the side of a deep, broad ravine, he looked inside the box.

The coffin was open, the pale dead girl staring up through copper pennies tied over her eyes, her waxy hands folded primly across the belly of her cheap, conservative dress—a dress that any modest country girl might wear to church on Sunday morning. Rosie Dawn laid at an odd angle, sort of shoved to one side of the coffin, and half-turned, her hair mussed, as if something had been lifted up from beneath her.

Yakima reached toward her miserably, rested a hand at the end of the box, and stood there for a time, swallowing down the hard knot in his throat, fighting the desolation that threatened to buckle his knees.

Finally, he turned from the poor, forsaken whore, dropped down into the ravine, and stopped. Barstow was a few yards down the ravine, scrambling up the steep other side on his hands and knees, grabbing at small cedars and tufts of wiry brown grass.

He was grunting and wheezing loudly. Blood shone at the back of his blue wool coat.

He tossed the bulging saddlebags up ahead of him, one open flap spilling greenbacks. The honyonker was slowing, his grunts and groans growing louder. Finally, as he tried to throw the saddlebags once more, he stopped, twisted around onto his back, and slid on his butt back down the ravine.

He hit the sandy bottom with a groan, his chest rising and falling sharply. The saddlebags slid down the steep slope to pile up beside him, more money spilling from an open pouch.

Yakima stared down at the man grimly, holding his Colt straight down by his side. "You sonofabitch."

Barstow was pale. Blood shone on his chest. More dribbled out from a corner of his mouth.

He tried to speak, winced, tried again. "Go to hell."

He let his voice trail off. A pained look stretched across his gaunt face, and he sobbed, "Oh, Christ!" and then his head fell to his shoulder, and his body lay slack against the side of the bank.

Yakima stared down at the dead honyonker and the saddlebags. His face was hard, grim, his eyes dark in their deep sockets.

With a weary sigh, he stumbled forward, dragging his

boot toes, and reached down for the saddlebags. He tossed them across his shoulder, worked his way back out of the ravine, and started tramping heavily back toward town, his chin tipped toward his chest.

He sensed a presence and stopped. Veronica stood before him, her face flushed from the cold, her eyes worried.

"Yakima . . ." She looked at the saddlebags. "What . . . ?"

"She told the bastard where the money was hid."

Veronica looked at him. As she studied his pain-racked eyes from which a few tears began to dribble, understanding washed across her own features.

"It's all right." She moved to his side, gently lifted his right arm over her shoulder. Letting him settle his weight on her, she started walking slowly back toward town, stumbling under his sagging bulk. "It's all right, Yakima. We'll get you well, and we'll take it back."

He stumbled forward, dragging his feet and clenching his fists. "We'll have to bury the girl. The sonofabitch was just gonna leave her there."

"We'll do that, too."

"Ah, hell!"

For Western action this thrilling, this authentic,
there's only one Frank Leslie.
Read on for a special preview of

THE KILLERS OF CIMARRON

Coming from Signet in June 2010.

Colter Farrow hooked a leg over his saddle horn, nudged his floppy-brimmed, coffee brown hat back off his sunburned forehead, and raised his spyglass so that it touched the upper end of the letter "S" that had been burned into his left cheek.

He could no longer feel the brand's searing burn. The nights of agony and torment in the aftermath of the savage branding—the glowing iron pressed against his cheek until his nose had filled with the stench of his own burning flesh—had gradually diminished so that now he could touch his hand to his face, or a spyglass, and become only vaguely aware of the hard, knotted tissue that would mark him forever.

But he was never, ever only vaguely aware of the horrified looks, pitied glances, and incredulous stares that the S brand constantly won him.

Nor was he unaware that the scar would prevent him from acquiring the handsomeness that he, at vain moments in his youthful past, had expected to gain once the boyish softness of his features had been tempered by a few judicious swipes of manhood's chisel. He would never be a handsome man. And no girl would ever marry him, because—and of this he'd become certain over his year of riding branded, a disfigured young wandering man who'd ridden up to Wyoming from southern Colorado on a mountain-bred coyote dun—he not only wore the hideous scar, but the scar wore him, so that it had become him. Him, the scar.

It was the first and last thing anyone ever saw.

Colter Farrow adjusted the spyglass's focus until the three riders washed up out of the wind-buffeted brome and buffalo grass and over a low knoll, moving toward him at easy lopes, the brushy cut of Little Gooseberry Creek falling away behind them. The three riders—sunburned and ragged-looking but well-armed—rode through a stand of aspens, the leaves beginning to turn now at the bittersweet end of a short high-country summer. Several crows lighted from the crooked limbs of the gnarled trees, and winged raucously back toward the chokecherries and willows lining the stream.

One of the men, wearing a long wolf coat and a felt sombrero with a bending brim, turned his head to one side to spit chaw. He wore two cartridge belts around the outside of his coat, and the pistol-filled holsters attached to the belts were thonged on his thighs clad in checked wool.

Sitting his white-stockinged black to Colter's right, Griff Shanley said, "You recognize 'em?"

"Nope." Colter lowered the spyglass to frown across the bending wheat grass and silver-green sage at the three men loping toward him, Shanley, and their partner, Stretch Dawson.

All three rode for old Cimarron Padilla's Diamond Bar brand in the shadow of the snowcapped Cheyennes, and they were looking for herd-quitting steers and unbranded calves, mavericks that they'd missed in the fall gather of a month ago, getting ready to settle down in the Diamond Bar bunkhouse for the long, Cheyenne Mountain winter.

"But then," Colter added, handing the spyglass over to

Shanley, "I don't know anyone up here but you fellas and the few I met at the Diamond Bar headquarters."

Shanley held the spyglass to his eye for a time, his wind-blistered lips stretched back from his chipped, tobacco-stained teeth framed by a three-day growth of beard stubble, then handed the glass to Stretch Dawson, an aging, good-natured rider from Dakota.

"Nah," Dawson said, as the riders drew to within sixty yards and checked their mounts down to trots. "I never seen them rannies out here. Saddle tramps by the look of 'em. Regulators, maybe, judgin' by the hardware they're packin'. The Pool mighta hired 'em to keep rustlers out of the mountains this winter."

"I don't know," Shanley growled, keeping his voice low as the riders approached, their hoof thuds and tack squawks growing louder beneath the humming wind. "They look a might ringy to me. 'Specially if they've got a passel of Diamond Bar beef boxed up in a canyon nearby. Might reward us to sit watchful, fellers."

"Out here, you're always watchful amongst strangers, you old mossyhorn."

"Ah, shut up about that mossyhorn shit," Shanley snapped at Dawson. "I ain't all that much older than you, Stretch. The difference is, I've learned more in my time above ground, and"—he shaped a sneering grin—"had a helluva lot more women than you, my friend."

"Bull-sheeet!" scoffed Dawson.

The two men—lifelong thirty-and-found ranch hands—had partnered up so long, mostly in remote line shacks around Wyoming and Colorado, that they could hardly exchange a civil word to each other. Colter knew, though, from having known many other men of the same breed, that they'd die for each other at the drop of a hat.

Colter hoped it didn't come to that here. Judging by the old pistols each wore in soft leather holsters that were cracked and yellowed with age and weather, neither was very practiced with a shooting iron. If it came to a lead-swap here, with the three obviously gun-handy hardcases closing on them fast, they'd likely die, and Colter would be left to shoot it out alone.

The three strangers reined their sweat-lathered mounts to halts twenty yards away. Shanley's horse whinnied shrilly, and Stretch Dawson's old steel-dust mare jerked her head up with a start. The horse of the rider straight out from Colter returned the greeting. The riders merely stared, hard-eyed, over their horses' heads at Colter and the other two drovers, coolly taking the stockmen's measure.

The one on the left—a dark-haired, blue-eyed gent with a black soup-strainer mustache and a calico shirt under a black cowhide vest—said with a stern air, "What're you three doin' out here?"

Due to age more than any formally assigned hierarchy, Griff Shanley usually acted as unofficial ramrod of the line-shack crew. He cocked his head to one side and narrowed an eye. "I was about to ask you the same thing, amigo." He softened the statement with a grin that made his gray eyes flash in the crisp afternoon sunlight.

Three strangers studied him with stony faces. Keeping a tight rein on his blaze-faced coyote dun, Colter studied the strangers back. They looked harried and owly. The middle one had his hand on the big Schofield jutting from the holster on his left hip, not as though he were about to use it, but as though he were always ready to use it.

Obviously, they didn't like Shanley's question. The eldest drover flushed and glanced from Colter to Stretch Dawson as the pregnant silence grew more and more tense, the only sounds being the breeze and the raspy blows of the tired horses.

Finally, the man on the right parted his lips juicy with chaw streaming down over his red spade beard. "We're lookin' for the trail to the Lone Pine Stage Station. We was told we'd cut it just after we crossed Rattlesnake Creek, but we didn't see no trail, and here we are a good five miles beyond Rattlesnake."

He and the other two men shifted their eyes between Colter, Shanley, and Dawson. That's it, Colter thought. They're lost. And they're in a hurry. The information did nothing to quell the uneasiness he felt with these three obvious gunhands sitting twenty yards away from him, and looking ringy as coons trapped in a privy, but it explained their restless, impatient demeanors.

Stretch Dawson shook his head. "You won't find the trail to Lone Pine anywhere's near Rattlesnake Creek. From here, you'd pick it up over yonder." He canted his head toward a large, rocky-topped bluff about two miles to the southwest, off his own right shoulder. "Wagon Mound Bluff's where you'll find it. This side but before Wagon Mound Canyon. Nasty country in there. That's why they done closed the Lone Pine Station. Trail kept washed out. The new station's farther east."

"We ain't askin' about the new station, mister," said the black-haired rider, perpetually squinting his eyes. "We done rode through the new station, and that's where they told us we'd pick up the trail to the old station by Rattlesnake Creek."

"Well, that's a pity," said Shanley. As usual, Colter couldn't tell him if the old drover was merely being sarcastic. He doubted few people ever knew when Shanley was being serious and not funning around. "And what explains that bit of lousy information is the fact that the stationmaster at Rock Creek Station is new around here. Howard Rigsby. The company shipped him in from Kansas. Don't know shit from Cheyenne, and he'd probably send you to Cheyenne if you was lookin' for Laramie!"

Shanley smiled at his humor. Stretch Dawson did, as well. Colter felt his own mouth corners rise, not so much because he found Shanley humorous but because he wanted as much as his partners did to lighten the mood and keep the minds as well as the hands of these three long coulee riders off their guns.

His lopsided grin wasn't catching, however. The faces of the stranger remained as hard as the granite faces of the Cheyennes looming in the west.

"How long will it take for us to ride Lone Pine from here?" asked the dark-haired man.

"Oh," Shanley said, closing one eye and thinking about it. "The rest of today, a few hours in the mornin'."

"Say," Stretch Dawson said, pitching his tall frame forward and resting his forearms on his saddlehorn. "What you boys wanna waste your time ridin' all the way to that old, abandoned station for, anyhow? Folks say Injuns use it for a camp, now and then, and . . ."

Colter's gut had tightened as the overchatty Dawson, too curious for his own good, had leaned his head out to his right to inspect the saddle of the man sitting straight out in front of him. Whatever Dawson had seen there, apparently draped over the hindquarters of the rider's claybank stallion, wasn't what he'd expected.

Or had wanted to see.

Stretch's big V-shaped face, with its silver-brown mustache colored up like a summer sunset, and the smile he tried to fashion only gave him a frightened, constipated look.

The rider in the gray sombrero scowled. "Now why did you have to go and do that?"

"Do what?" Stretch said.

"Look at them saddlebags behind me."

"I didn't look . . ."

"Oh, don't try to hornswoggle me, you old saddletramp!" the man in the gray sombrero fairly shouted. "You ever hear the sayin', 'curiosity killed the cat'?"

Colter looked from Dawson to the three hardcases. Now, suddenly, they were all three smiling. They weren't fun or humorous smiles. They were dark smiles. The smiles of men who knew something bad was about to happen and they weren't all that unhappy about it.

Because they were used to bad things happening. More to the point, they were used to doing bad things, and even rather enjoyed it.

Colter became aware of the Remington riding in the cross-draw position in the soft leather holster angled back away from his left hip. The fingers of his right hand tingled the way they often did when he rode to high altitudes . . . or when he was about to kill a man.

The black-haired man must have noticed the movement. He switched his dark gaze to Colter. His lips shaped a sneer. "Good Lord, boy—who in the hell laid that brand on your cheek?"

The others looked at Colter, then, too, revulsion and mockery mixing in their expressions.

Colter said evenly, "Ain't you ever heard about curiosity killin' the cat, mister?"

The sneer died on the black-haired gent's lips. The others let their evil smiles grow, sliding their eyes toward the dark-haired man, wondering what he'd do about the smart retort he'd just taken from the kid.

Shanley tried to ease the tension.

"Look," the old puncher said, dipping his chin and holding up his gloved hands chest high, "Stretch didn't mean nothin' by that. He was just curious, that's all. We three . . . we don't care what the hell you boys are up to. All we care about is our herd."

He paused, stared at the three hardcases who stared back at him, their lips curled beneath their mustaches.

"Okay?" Shanley said. "Can we all live with that and just ride on out o' here real peaceful like?"

"Well, I don't know," said the middle hardcase, his hand still on his pistol grips. He had green eyes under a shelf of straight-cut corn yellow bangs, with deep smallpox scars on his cheeks. "I don't really see as how we can, old man. You see—any deputy marshal who rides through here lookin' for us and stumbles across you . . . Well, he's gonna get the full story, now, ain't he? How you seen us right where you see us now, and how we told you where we was headed . . . with twenty-six thousand dollars in stolen Army gold."

The green-eyed hombre kept his gaze on Shanley. The black-haired man looked at Colter, Shanley, and Dawson in turn from beneath his shaggy eyebrows. The man in the gray sombrero worked his cud, his eyes bright with mockery.

Colter's heart tattooed an even rhythm against his breastbone. His right hand, splayed across his right thigh, itched. He kept his gaze forward on the cutthroats, but in the corner of his right eye he could see sweat glinting on Shanley's and Dawson's chiseled, weathered cheeks.

Colter waited.

The cutthroats expected their main opposition to come from the two older gents to Colter's right, not from the young freckle-faced kid in shapeless hat, ragged trail clothes and suspenders and wearing an old, rusty Remington on his hip.

But they were wrong.

No sooner had the green-eyed hombre jerked his revolver from its holster, the other two following suit, than they were all three screaming and tumbling back off their horses' asses as the horses themselves lurched and bucked and whinnied and arched their tails at the three quick explosions.

The black-haired gent cursed loudly as his horse kicked him inadvertently as it wheeled and galloped after the others.

The man reached for the gun he'd dropped, and Colter's Remy roared once more.

The .44 slug plunked through the man's left temple, exiting the back of his head in a spray of brains, bones, and blood. The man's head jerked back and forwards and then followed his shoulders to the ground where he lay, kicking himself in a semicircle as the life fled him quickly.

The others, both shot through their briskets, were finished. They lay slumped and twisted, hats off, bloody, dusty, and rumpled from their horses' trampling hooves.

Colter held his reins tight in his right fist as his coyote dun skitter-stepped, nickering. Shanley and Dawson's mounts both did likewise as the two aging drovers looked around, lower jaws hanging, right hands clamped over the handles of the hoglegs that were still in their holsters.

They looked from the dead men to Colter and then to the smoking pistol in the kid's right hand.

Shanley glanced at Dawson, then back to Colter, and said, *"Ho-leee sheeeit!"*

From
Frank Leslie

THE GUNS OF SAPINERO

Colster Farrow was just a skinny cow-puncher when
the men came to Sapinero Valley and murdered his
best friend, whose past as a gunfighter had caught
up with him. Now, Cole must strap on his
Remington revolver, deliver some justice, and
make a reputation of his own.

THE KILLING BREED

Yakima Henry has been dealt more than his share of
trouble—even for a half-white, half-Indian in the
West. Now he's running a small Arizona horse ranch
with his longtime love, Faith, and thinks he may
have finally found his share of peace and prosperity.
But a man from both their pasts is coming—with
vengeance on his mind...

**Available wherever books are sold or at
penguin.com**